Murder at Liberty Hall

ALAN CLUTTON-BROCK

With an introduction by Curtis Evans

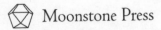 Moonstone Press

This edition published in 2020 by Moonstone Press
www.moonstonepress.co.uk

Introduction © 2020 Curtis Evans

Originally published in 1941 by The Bodley Head, London
Murder at Liberty Hall © 1941 the Estate of Alan-Clutton Brock

ISBN 978-1-899000-22-7
eISBN 978-1-899000-23-4

A CIP catalogue record for this book is available from the British Library

Text designed and typeset by Tetragon, London
Cover illustration by Jason Anscomb
Printed and bound by CPI Group (UK) Ltd, Croydon, CRO 4YY

Contents

Introduction by Curtis Evans   7

MURDER AT LIBERTY HALL   13

Introduction

In February 1926, Thomas Stearns Eliot delivered a series of lectures on English metaphysical poetry at Cambridge University, where literary critic F. L. Lucas arranged an introduction to 'half a dozen of the most intelligent undergraduates I know'. Among these Cambridge stars was twenty-one-year-old Alan Francis Clutton-Brock, whom Lucas described as 'the son of his father; nice, quite clever and much improved since he came up, when he was the silliest young man I've ever seen.'

Alan Clutton-Brock (1904–76) was the son of Arthur Clutton-Brock, an Oxford-educated art critic and journalist who took the iconoclastic T. S. Eliot to task for pronouncing Shakespeare's *Hamlet* 'an artistic failure'. After graduating from Eton and Cambridge, the younger Clutton-Brock became a popular art critic and something of an artist himself. In 1941 he published his only detective novel, *Murder at Liberty Hall*.

The product of a British intellectual with a youthful sense of whimsy, *Murder at Liberty Hall* was well-received by reviewers, particularly in the United States, where the *Saturday Review* praised the novel's 'sly humor and good puzzle', while the *New York Times Book Review* gave it what may be fairly termed a rave notice: 'This is one of those gleeful cerebral thrillers ... full of quips and cranks and wanton wiles ... The effect is always amusing ... And, oh yes, there's a perfectly good mystery.'

The story is attractively set at a progressive, co-educational school, which the author views with humorous scepticism. During the

1930s, so-called 'progressive education' attracted increasing interest and education reformers began to call for curricula which were not tied to subjects but rather related more closely, as one study put it, 'to the natural movement of the children's minds'. Traditionalists scoffed at such revolutionary notions and British detective fiction—in many ways a politically conservative branch of literature in the interwar period—tended to go along with this criticism, with mystery writers lampooning progressive education, right along with other seemingly queer and comical innovations of the era such as vegetarianism, nudism, abstract art and Freudian psychology.

Murder at Liberty Hall takes place in May 1939, shortly before the outbreak of the Second World War, as German refugees are streaming into England to escape the horrors of Hitler's regime. The narrator is James Hardwicke, scientist and authority on human genetics, who to his expressed mortification has acquired a 'Fleet Street reputation' as an expert on criminal tendencies. As the novel opens, Mrs. Rachel Eakins, a wealthy philanthropist, has invited James to Scrope House School, to identify an apparent pyromaniac running loose among the student body. As Mrs. Eakins attempts to explain in her rambling letter, 'we try to think of the unfortunate boy or girl as a patient, and we do need someone who will view the whole problem of crime in the light of really modern science'. James is inclined to ignore this odd invitation but is pressed into accepting by a persuasive lady friend, Caroline Fisher, who hopes to get a position there.

So off James goes with Caroline—his woman Watson, if you will—to investigate this case of arson, but soon enough James's investigation at Scrope House expands to include murder too. Readers will find a good murder plot at the heart of *Murder at Liberty Hall*, although, there are quite a few digressions. However, these very digressions make up some of the most interesting parts, and humorous commentary runs through it like a taunting red ribbon. On a food faddist faculty member: 'I can't imagine why she stays on ...

It's quite obvious that her nonsense doesn't suit the nonsense of the rest of the people here.' Or on teaching the schoolchildren at Scrope House the birds and the bees: 'The farm is some way from the school ... but the children often go there when they feel like it. There's some idea that it's good for them ... I think the idea is that they should learn the facts of life from watching the farm animals.'

Aside from humour, there are certain passages in the novel which so resemble sentiments expressed by Alan's old Eton schoolmate, George Orwell, that Orwell Society member L. J. Hurst was moved to publicly query, 'how much input did Orwell have into Clutton-Brock's only mystery?' Certainly Clutton-Brock uses the novel to both defend cricket and critique Communism in terms rather close to Orwell's. When a Jewish refugee teacher speculates that he might have been denounced as a Nazi spy as punishment for leaving the Communist Party, the naive English liberal James protests. The teacher quickly schools James in the brutal facts of that era's remorseless totalitarian realpolitik. His view of life is positively Orwellian: 'My dear Hardwicke ... Once you get the idea that any action is justifiable if it's for the good of the party anything can happen. The ordinary rules mean nothing at all; it's quite incredible, until you see it happen, how quickly a charming, perhaps rather silly enthusiast, as you put it, will develop into a ruthless Machiavellian.'

Furthermore, a passage in *Murder at Liberty Hall*, and one in Orwell's *War-time Diary*—dated 20 June 1940 but not made public until 1968—are almost identical: 'Why is it, by the way, that although England normally has one of the smallest armies in the world it has the largest number of retired Colonels?' (*Murder at Liberty Hall*) and 'A thought that occurred to me yesterday: how is it that England, with one of the smallest armies in the world, has so many retired colonels?' (*War-time Diary*)

So just how much did George Orwell and Alan Clutton-Brock stay in touch after leaving Eton? Orwell mentions in a letter that the two saw quite a bit of each other in 1928, when they were young men in their mid-twenties. They were also in proximity for a time, after Alan had married Sheelah Mabel Stoney Archer and was living with her and their two young children in Greenwich. Drs Laurence and Gwen O'Shaughnessy lived nearby with Laurence's sister Eileen, whom Orwell married in 1936, and his diaries document time spent there.

In his 2003 biography *Orwell: The Life*, author D. J. Taylor notes that Orwell wrote to the Air Ministry in March 1941 about obtaining a position with the Public Relations Department, a 'popular berth for literary men in war-time' that then was being administered by no other than Alan Clutton-Brock. Taylor quotes a contemporary who recalled that Alan, 'looking resplendent in his blue squadron leader's uniform', informally interviewed Orwell at his digs about the position; and he reproduces this amusing scrap of the conversation which supposedly took place there between the two men:

> ACB: I can't say anything about the work, of course, but I assure you it's tedious beyond belief. And the dreadful people you meet!
>
> GO: I wouldn't want a commission, you understand. I'd be quite happy in the ranks.
>
> ACB: And you have to do six weeks of foot training first—insufferable! In fact, until it occurred to me to think of the whole thing as a kind of ballet, I didn't think I'd survive it!
>
> GO: But I like drills. I know the Manual by heart. I need the discipline.

I cannot promise that this conversation—so reminiscent of the comment attributed to the great camp English actor Ernest Thesiger about his service during the First World War ('Oh, my dear! The noise! And the people!')—really took place, but would it not be ever so lovely if it had? For his part, Taylor declares that this 'bizarre dialogue ... seems wholly authentic'.

In January 1936 Alan's wife Sheelah was killed in a car accident along with a former neighbour, Dr Norman Dyer Ball. Norman and his wife Doris Bell Collier Ball had been the previous owners of the O'Shaughnessy residence but had moved out of London in 1935. Left with four young children to raise, widow Doris wrote mysteries to supplement her income as a doctor and under the name Josephine Bell published forty-five detective novels, beginning with *Murder in Hospital*, which introduced her charming and handsome amateur sleuth, Dr. David Wintringham.

Sheelah's young children, Juliet and Francis, went to live in Rhodesia (now Zimbabwe) with her sister, where Francis died from polio in 1945. (The late Juliet Clutton-Brock later became a prominent English archaeozoologist.) In December 1936, widower Alan married Barbara Foy Mitchell and they had a daughter, Eleanor, in 1946. From 1955, Alan and Barbara resided at Chastleton House (now a National Trust property), the superb Jacobean country manor that he had inherited from a distant cousin. Alan became Slade Professor of Fine Art at Cambridge (1955–58) and served as art critic at *The Times* for ten years. In his 1976 obituary, the paper lauded him as 'a man of high intelligence and charm' whose 'wit, wide reading and store of historical knowledge were instinct in all that he wrote'. These winning qualities encompass Alan Clutton-Brock's *Murder at Liberty Hall*, now happily back in print after eight decades.

CURTIS EVANS, *September 2020*

Scrope House School is not drawn from life, and I had no actual school or any real persons in mind when I was describing it. I am not aware, and indeed it is most unlikely, that any of the events I have related ever occurred in any school of any kind. All the characters as well as the opinions expressed in this novel are equally imaginary.

—ALAN CLUTTON-BROCK

Chapter One

My post that morning contained a proposal of marriage from a woman who described herself as my spiritual twin, an invitation to give a series of unpaid lectures on religion and modern psychology, and an offer from an American Negro to provide the facts for and share the profits of his biography if I could be sure of finishing it within three months. It also contained my first communication from Scrope House School, a letter which I found very difficult to understand. It began thus:—

We have heard so much about your wonderful work and though, of course, there is no reason to think that the patient is necessarily a twin, nevertheless we try to think of the unfortunate boy or girl as a patient, and we do need someone who will view the whole problem of crime in the light of really modern science. Naturally we have a practising psycho-analyst on the staff, Dr. Hickman, whose name will no doubt be familiar to you, but he says that he can do nothing until he knows who it is that he should treat. And perhaps, he says, he can do nothing even then, since many criminals—it is sad to have to use the word—will not *co-operate*. I mentioned your name and Dr. Hickman said it was much more in your line than his; he has not specialized in criminals at all, and, for a school psychologist, that would never have done...

But there is no profit in quoting the rest of the letter. What it seemed to amount to was that a crime had been committed, apparently by schoolchildren—one cryptic phrase suggested that the crime might be arson—and I was to come at once. The signature was Rachel Eakins, the notepaper extremely opulent. Obviously, I thought, as I laid the letter on one side, this was only another instance of that extraordinary delusion, the delusion that I am an expert on crime, from which so many people suffer who merely knew me by name.

I am afraid that you also will almost certainly know me by name, and, unless you are very simple indeed, this will make you suspect that I am not serious about my own work, that I am not a genuine scientific worker, but only one of those people who tell you about the expanding universe, or the effect of glands on the destiny of the human race. But this is not really my fault; I can honestly assure the reader that when I first began to work on the life-histories of identical twins it never even occurred to me that I might thereby gain a Fleet Street reputation or be frequently subjected to the temptation of writing a brisk article at fifty guineas a time. Fortunately or unfortunately—it depends on what view may be taken about the advantages of being able to earn money in this fashion—I had taken up with two out of the very limited number of things that can attract the attention of those who think they know what is news and what is not. For to cultivate an intuitive sense of news values, as I have heard it described, is to find oneself gradually restricted to a very few subjects which are either tedious in themselves or have become so as a result of being dragged in on all possible occasions. And to this class of subject, as everyone will recognize, even if they should have only the most rudimentary sense of news values, both crime and twins belong. The conjunction of the two is irresistible, and that is why I am so widely known as James, 'identical twin', Hardwicke.

What, you may ask, is the connection between twins and crime? I am tired of saying that there is none. Only a few days ago I read an article which followed one that I myself had lately written in the same paper; it was by a journalist who had received one of the handsomest rewards that are open to his profession—I refer to a Deanery—and in it he protested that he had known many virtuous twins, men of sterling character, eminent scholars, distinguished soldiers, or upright men of affairs. He was sure, he continued, that when the stock was good there was no tendency for twins to become criminals, though no doubt there might be such a tendency among the proletariat who in any case produced far too many twins and triplets, to say nothing of ordinary single births. It is no use trying to clear up such misunderstandings, and I have given up trying to do so in the public press. But here I may perhaps indulge in the luxury of correcting a popular delusion for which many of my friends hold me directly responsible.

The particular piece of research which won me so much notoriety is as follows: I have made it my business to inspect the life histories of as many identical twins as I could find. Identical twins are, of course, twins deriving from the same ovum which has split into two, not twins from two ova fertilized at the same time, and they are always very much alike. My object was to judge the effect of environment as opposed to that of heredity, and for this purpose I obtained the histories of twins who had been separated at birth. Such cases are usually to be found in institutions, since twins are not usually separated in ordinary families though they sometimes may be. I have also consulted the records of criminals and lunatics who were identical twins and in this way I have definitely established the fact that if one identical twin has become, let us say, a criminal, then there is a considerable probability that the other twin is also, or will become, a criminal. And this probability is much greater than the probability that two non-identical twins, or, of course, two ordinary brothers or sisters, similarly separated at birth, will go the same way in after life. You see the idea? It is merely an accident that I have had to concern myself so often with criminal twins, and if there had been any statistics about twins who married red-haired women or took to agriculture it would have done just as well and a Dean would be writing, though without so much heat, to say that many twins of his acquaintance had not married red-haired women or taken to agriculture.

A friend of mine, a psychologist, often tells me that in his opinion my notoriety has not come by chance. Character, he says, is destiny, whatever that may mean, and if I had not been the kind of exhibitionist who inevitably gets known in Fleet Street, I should never have hit on so exquisitely felicitous a combination of subjects. I must, he thinks, have instinctively wished to satisfy the mysterious tropisms of journalists and with such a talent, he once added, I might even have done well as a sculptor. Naturally this is not my opinion, but there it is, and I have given this perhaps too lengthy explanation partly as a relief for my feelings and partly to show how it was possible for me to be consulted about a crime, how I came to be invited to Scrope House School, and why I spent some time there posing as a detective.

I should naturally have ignored Miss, or Mrs. Eakins's letter, like all the other mad letters which are of no use except to amuse me in the morning, if I had not had lunch a day later with Caroline Fisher, with whom at that time I suppose I was more or less in love. It must have been because I was in love with her that I am now unable to say what she was like; I remember, of course, some details of her outward appearance, as that she had a good figure, and that I did not at that time like the way she did her hair. But for the most part she must appear simply as a girl, like the girls who sometimes turn up with one's friends, an exasperating interference with rational discourse, impossible to neglect, but equally impossible to bring easily into the conversation.

At that time Caroline was excited about Scrope House, where she had recently spent a week-end; it was the proper thing then, and for all I know still may be, to spend a week-end there and to come back with a batch of amusing stories about the place. Caroline was enthusiastic about the merits of this school, and began talking about it at luncheon.

'I wish I could get a job at Scrope House,' she said.

'Why?' I asked.

'Well, if you knew what the girls' school I went to was like, you wouldn't ask.'

'I daresay,' I said, 'that it's a better school than yours was, but do you want to be a schoolmistress?'

'I really think I might,' Caroline answered. 'At Scrope House, at any rate.'

At this point I thought of the letter I had received the day before, and remembered that it had been addressed from somewhere 'near Scropeham'.

'Is Scropeham anything to do with Scrope House?' I asked.

'It's a town a few miles away,' Caroline said.

'Well, has a certain Rachel Eakins anything to do with the school?'

'Oh, Mrs. Eakins,' Caroline said. 'Why, she *is* Scrope House; at least, it's her money that keeps the place going. Have you heard from her, or something?'

I was suddenly carried away by a weak desire to please, and an equally weak desire to enjoy as much of Caroline's society as possible. In such matters I am, of course, like everyone else, unstable as water.

'I've been asked to work at Scrope House myself,' I said. 'I've no doubt I could take you with me as some kind of assistant or what-not.'

Caroline was enchanted, and I soon saw that it would be impossible to take back my offer.

'But you wouldn't exactly be a schoolmistress,' I said, 'not if you went as my assistant.'

'All the better,' said Caroline. 'I suppose it's the same identical twin business. I expect the Scrope House people would be a great help to you in that; it's just the kind of thing they'd be interested in. After all, it's essential for them to know whether education can make any difference at all, or whether everything depends on heredity.'

'They'd be rather in a hole,' I said, 'If I told them that education was no use at all, wouldn't they? However, that isn't really why they asked me down. I really don't quite know why they have asked me; I had an extremely obscure letter from your Mrs. Eakins.'

'Yes, she is rather vague at times,' said Caroline. 'Have you got the letter here?'

I had left the letter in my rooms, and so I asked Caroline to come back with me after we had finished lunch.

'But it's perfectly obvious,' Caroline said, when she had read the letter. 'I suppose it's your training that makes it impossible for you to understand anything.'

'Good gracious, no,' I protested, 'it isn't as though I was a philosopher.'

'Philosophers and scientists are often much the same,' said Caroline.

'I doubt it,' I said, 'but anyway, what is the letter about?'

'As I said, it's perfectly obvious,' Caroline answered. 'There's been an outbreak of pyromania in the school—I'm told it's common enough with adolescents—and they're getting frightened. They've got to find out who is setting alight to things.'

'Oh, is that it?' I asked. 'And you really are sure that that's what Mrs. Eakins means?'

'I'm certain,' said Caroline. 'Besides, I heard all about it last week-end.'

'Well, that's hardly fair then,' I said. 'You knew all along. But why should they want me?' I asked. 'What do they think I can do?'

'Oh, well,' said Caroline, 'that doesn't matter. You're going, anyway. It won't matter to you if you can't do anything, and I dare say they'll be quite satisfied if they get you to the school and you tell them all the latest information about heredity.'

'Perhaps they may be,' I said. 'But supposing I'm burnt in my bed?'

'Goodness,' said Caroline. 'It's not that kind of fire. Nothing but a few shavings on a staircase, and that kind of thing. Some books were burnt one day, I believe.'

'And I suppose,' I asked, 'that the fire couldn't spread?'

'Not possibly, I should think,' Caroline answered. 'After all, it's only some unfortunate schoolboy.'

I forebore to point out that arson is a crime within the capacity of anyone, and that the extent of the fire does not depend on the age of the person who lights it.

'What they seem to want,' I said, 'is some sort of detective.'

'Exactly,' said Caroline, 'and I don't see why you shouldn't do.'

'Oh, well,' I said, 'if you really think they want for a detective a man who has had such a cloistered existence as I have, why, then, I suppose I'd better go. But mind, it's only to please you.'

'Thank you, James,' said Caroline. 'And how are you going to get me in?'

'Secretary, do you think?' I suggested.

'I won't spend my time writing your letters,' Caroline answered, 'and besides, it seems rather tame. What about colleague? Anyway, they'll only think I'm your mistress whatever you say, and that'll be enough to please them—a sort of guarantee that you're an *esprit fort*.'

'All right,' I replied, 'I'll say colleague. I'll say you worked with me on the strange case of the vanishing pawnbroker, if you like, and that since then I've never cared to work without you.'

'Anything you like,' said Caroline, 'anything... What does it matter?'

'You don't seem to realize,' I said, 'that I've got an essentially academic mind.'

'Well, and now you're going to a school,' said Caroline. 'What more do you want?'

In the end Caroline almost forced me to Scrope House, in spite of a number of attempts that I made to back out. She procured a car from a friend of hers; we could only have it for this one journey because the friend was to pick it up at Scrope House in two days' time, when he was beginning a tour of the North of England. She stood over me while I wrote to Mrs. Eakins, she did my packing for me, and she offered me ceaseless encouragement which did not have the effect on my spirits that she intended. But when we were actually on our way she seemed, I think, a little subdued and nervous now that this absurd adventure, for which she was so largely responsible, had really begun. And for myself, in spite of the fact that Caroline's company was now firmly assured to me for at least several weeks, I felt profoundly miserable.

'I really cannot be expected to do any detecting,' I said.

'There's no reason why you shouldn't help as much as you can,' said Caroline. 'I think they really are in a difficulty, and it is a very good school. And then there are all the refugees they've got there. I think we ought to do what we can.'

'Yes,' I said, 'but there's nothing I can do. I'm too shy. When I'm in the country I'd willingly walk a mile out of my way to avoid a small boy who might say good morning to me.'

'You want psycho-analysing,' Caroline said.

'I might take the opportunity while I'm at Scrope House,' I suggested.

We drove on in silence, and when we were within a mile or two of our destination, as it seemed from the map, we had to stop because there was a large parcel, positively a crate, in the middle of the road. I got out to look at this object; it was about three feet high, and had an address, which I read aloud to Caroline, very firmly printed in large capitals…

'THE MOST REV. HIS GRACE THE LORD ARCHBISHOP
   OF YORK,

      YORK,

         YORKSHIRE.'

'I suppose,' I said, 'that we're in Yorkshire, but it's impossible to believe that the Archbishop dropped this.'

'Why?' asked Caroline.

'Oh, I don't know,' I said. 'Intuition.'

'Well then, you're detecting already,' she answered. 'What had we better do with it?' I asked.

'We'd better take it along,' said Caroline, 'and see that it reaches its destination when we reach the school.'

'I should be more inclined,' I said, 'to leave it at the side of the road. Then we can pass by on the other side. You may be a born Samaritan, but I am a born Levite.'

'Oh, we can't do that,' said Caroline.

I made an effort and picked up the parcel. As I lifted it, it tilted to one side and a flood of water escaped through the brown paper which formed the outer wrapping of the crate; it soaked my legs to the skin. When I had recovered from the shock and had reproached Caroline for the sadistic habit of laughing at other people's misfortunes—'I suppose you'd laugh,' I said, 'if I fell into a dangerous whirlpool'—she asked me what I thought the parcel was for.

'How should I know?' I asked in return, and then she got out of the car and began to unwrap the parcel. Inside were three large jars with no lids on them; they had evidently been filled with water and when the parcel tilted the water would inevitably come pouring out.

'It's very simple,' said Caroline.

'Very,' I said. 'But is there a simple mind behind this device?'

'Yes,' said Caroline. 'A schoolboy, I should think.'

It may seem very odd, but I had not thought of that.

'I wonder what Mrs. Eakins would think of this?' I asked.

'Oh, you mustn't tell her,' said Caroline. 'It would be most unfair.'

'Sneaking, I suppose,' I said. 'My dear Caroline, I'd do and I have done a great deal for you, but even so, I won't become a private schoolboy again... not that I ever was one, in mind at any rate.'

'You mustn't say anything about it,' said Caroline. 'You'll want to win the boys' confidence, and you won't do that if you begin by getting someone into trouble.'

'But I thought there were no punishments or discipline at Scrope House,' I said, 'and so Mrs. Eakins couldn't do anything even if I did tell her.'

'It doesn't do to be too ingenious,' said Caroline.

Mrs. Eakins's house, where we had been invited to stay, was nearly two miles from the main part of the school. It had been the Tudor dower house of the mansion, originally Tudor as well but entirely rebuilt in the eighteenth century, which now formed the principal building of the school. But the Dower House was now a great deal more Tudor than it had ever been before; when Mrs. Eakins first took it, it had degenerated into a ruinous farmhouse and she had probably been attracted by its fragmentary condition. She shared that curious passion of the very rich for making over old houses, and this hobby can hardly be indulged with a house that obstinately remains in good condition. If you touch a well-preserved house, it's Vandalism, and the only thing to do is to hope for a fire which will burn the beastly thing down. But as it was the Dower House had been sufficiently ruinous for Mrs. Eakins and her architect to have a glorious time importing oak beams from the farm buildings and old wood from decrepit fowl-houses, uncovering large open fireplaces in awkward and unlikely places, stripping the plaster from beams which the original builder of the house had mistakenly covered, and revealing mysterious cavities which would just do for bathrooms. To go round the house with its owner was like being asked to understand a jig-saw puzzle in three dimensions; everything had been adapted, stripped, moved, or transfigured. At first sight, of course, the house merely looked bogus, and so it seemed to us on the day of our arrival; it was only afterwards that we understood the loving and extremely expensive care with which antiquity had been respected. But the gardens, even at first sight, were very beautiful, extensive, and immaculate; we could see at a glance that we were about to share the smooth comforts of the rich.

The butler told us that Mrs. Eakins was resting, but Miss Stanhope, her secretary, would be down before dinner to see if there was anything we needed. When she appeared, Miss Stanhope told us that Mrs. Eakins would be in the Italian garden while the sun lasted; she was sure we would understand, and, if we wanted a walk in the garden ourselves—the long border was looking extremely well now and, indeed, the whole garden was going to be thrown open for the Queen's Institute in a week's time—we would not go through the wrought-iron gates at the end of the silver-leaved border. We went for a walk in the garden and Caroline wanted to have a peep at the Italian garden through a hole in the yew hedge, but I wouldn't let her. 'We're not here to detect Mrs. Eakins,' I said, and insisted on keeping as far from her hiding-place as possible. I was feeling acutely embarrassed, and wanted to hide myself; I felt coarse and intrusive amongst all this hushed luxury, and we had to make an elaborate detour to avoid a chauffeur—how beautifully clean and soft was his dark blue uniform—carrying rugs and books.

'I wonder what that shrub is called?' Caroline said, speaking quite loud before we were out of earshot.

'For God's sake don't make so much noise,' I implored her.

We were alone at dinner, and at first we couldn't think what to talk about in front of someone else's butler and footman. The remedy was to drink as much as possible, and after a while I was almost at my ease. Afterwards in the drawing-room, where no one came to disturb us and there was a tray of whisky and other drinks, we were as cosy as possible, so long as we did not move about and run the risk of breaking anything. Caroline was a little tiresome, wanting to look at everything, and disturbing books and papers in a way that made me feel nervous again, but we soon settled down to our own affairs, almost as comfortably cloistered, for the moment at any rate, as Mrs. Eakins herself.

Chapter Two

Next morning we learnt that Mrs. Eakins would make a special effort and have lunch with us. She appeared at half-past twelve in the morning room, dressed, as it seemed, entirely in coffee-coloured lace, hung in loops and festoons which yet, by some miracle of her dressmaker's art, were held together in the semblance of a well-cut dress. Her hair was white and marvellously fine and clean, her face soft, delicately pink, and preserved, as one would imagine, from collapsing altogether not by any bony structure beneath the flesh but by much the same art as that which had been employed on her dress. She addressed us with the brilliant affection of the accomplished hostess, as though for the first time in her life she had met people whom she really wanted to see, yet at the same time subtly indicating that this extreme of pleasure was only for the moment and must not be presumed upon. Her first remark, after some usual greetings, was uttered as if it was meant to be the most lavish of compliments, yet somehow it failed to give me pleasure.

'You don't *look* like a detective,' she said.

'Naturally I don't...' I was beginning to expostulate, when Caroline interrupted.

'It wouldn't do for a detective to look like one, would it?' she said.

'Oh, no, of course not,' said Mrs. Eakins. 'I suppose it's some kind of disguise then. But do let me thank you again for coming; you can't *think* what a relief it was when I got your letter. Poor Mr. Edgeworth is really at his wits' end, and he feels it so much.'

Mr. Edgeworth, I had already learnt, was the head master of Scrope House.

In spite of her vagueness, and her evident need for protection from all the rough surfaces of life, I soon discovered that Mrs. Eakins was a determined woman; she arranged everything in advance and was well accustomed to having her own way. She was not going to tell me anything about what had happened at Scrope House or why I had been called in; Edgeworth, I gathered, had been asked to call at the Dower House at five-thirty, and then we could have a nice little talk; Mrs. Eakins had arranged to leave us alone, we could have the study to ourselves. This luncheon, which she had undertaken as a duty, and as a reward to me for accepting her invitation, was to be a social occasion, and she resolutely made it so. As we knew few of her friends, and could hardly be expected to do so, she talked to us as if we were children, but very benevolently and at the same time with a good deal of quite agreeable, though by no means well-informed, flattery about my work. She really did it very well, but then people like that—she was the widow of a rather unimportant cabinet minister—always do such things very well; it is their business.

After lunch Mrs. Eakins soon retired again into one of her impenetrable cocoons, and I made some shift to read a book which I had brought down with me on the neurotic disorders of adolescence, in order to prepare myself for my promised interview with the head master. But very soon the influence of the Dower House overcame me, and I retired to my bedroom to take a nice nap. It seemed to be the proper thing to do, and Noakes—the butler was called Noakes—was very sympathetic when he woke me at five, suggesting, with a bedside manner which ought to have brought him a large income if only he had chosen a more suitable profession, that I might like a little tea before Mr. Edgeworth came at half-past five. I don't know what Caroline did in the afternoon, but I suspect that she went over to the school to collect advance and inside information.

Edgeworth was very red in the face and energetic in his move-ments. I felt as if he might at any moment break something valuable, and he shouted as though he didn't know that Mrs. Eakins was asleep. To Caroline, who had, of course, insisted on being present at the interview, he was extremely cordial and man-to-man; to me he was, I suppose I might say, boy-to-boy, with occasional and disconcerting lapses into sentiment. But I rather liked him; with school masters it is usually necessary to make liberal allowances for the unnatural and assumed affability which their trade demands of them.

'Jolly good of you to come down,' he began. 'I hope we're not taking you away from your work; much more important to human-ity, I dare say it is, than anything we're doing here, but we school masters live in a little world of our own, and we're all very worried, as I expect Mrs. Eakins told you.'

I said that I would be glad to help him if I possibly could, and asked him what exactly was the matter.

'Well, it's these fires,' he said. 'There seems to be no doubt they can't all have been accidents, and, as of course you know, it's quite a common trouble at schools. Boys—and girls, too, I believe—occasionally have a phase of stealing, or destroying, or setting fire to things. But we've never had more than a trace of these particular diseases of adolescence and we rather counted upon not having them. I expect you've heard all sorts of extravagant claims for our system, and I don't want you to think we subscribe to them, but there did seem to be some reason for thinking that if children were given a chance and not subjected to the usual idiotic discipline, then there wouldn't be all the usual troubles. But, of course,—and this is really one of the chief difficulties of the situation—we've got a lot of refugee children in the school, and goodness knows it's natural enough if one of them should have broken down under the strain. And if so, it's doubly unfortunate, because it might give a handle to all those ridiculous people who want to stop refugees coming into the country. They're mostly Jewish children, but we've got several children of intellectuals or left-wing politicians who managed to get away in time. Friedrich Schmidt's boy, for example—he's the most perfectly Nordic creature I've ever seen...'

'Then it's probably him,' I said. 'Perfectly Nordic people, without any Jewish blood to keep them sane, are often hopelessly unbalanced.'

'Do you really think so?' asked Edgeworth. 'That's most interesting. Do you mean that's an established fact?'

'Good heavens, no,' I exclaimed, feeling very remorseful when I saw how seriously he had taken my rash statement. 'Why it would take ten years of work on the statistics, which we certainly couldn't obtain at the moment, to establish any connection between mental stability and physical characteristics in Germany. Good Lord, no, I was only expressing a prejudice which seemed in harmony with my views about the nature of the universe... But do go on.'

'I rather gather,' Caroline interjected, 'that you've had some trouble among your refugees before. I was told that some of the refugees on your staff had received threatening letters, and so on— the usual thing.'

I myself had heard nothing of this, but asked no questions at the moment. Later I asked Caroline what she was referring to, and she told me that she had only heard some vague gossip, a suggestion that Nazi agents might have been trying to make trouble for some of the refugee school masters who were working at Scrope House. Edgeworth himself paid very little attention to Caroline's suggestion.

'Well, yes,' he said, 'I believe there has been something of the sort, but I don't know that we need go into that now. The real point is that we don't want these fires, supposing they continue, to give anyone an opportunity for making trouble. If we could only find out who started the fires, I believe everything would be all right. And, of course, there's the danger from the fires themselves, and the fact that there's an unstable boy or girl in the school who certainly ought to be having treatment. It may not be a refugee at all.'

'Yes, I see,' I replied. 'Well, we'd better go into the exact circumstances of these fires. By the way,' I added, 'are you quite sure they couldn't be practical jokes? Has there, by any chance, been an epidemic of practical jokes in the school—imitation blobs of ink on the desk, exploding cigarettes, anything of that kind?'

Edgeworth was evidently surprised. 'No, not particularly,' he answered. 'Is there any reason to expect that kind of thing? Is there, I mean, any connection between pyromania and practical joking?'

'Not that I know of,' I said. 'But one could imagine practical jokes becoming dangerous, don't you think?'

'Yes, I suppose so,' Edgeworth answered.

'But perhaps,' I said, 'there wasn't anything about these fires to suggest a practical joke?'

The most alarming of the fires, I learned, had happened at the beginning of this month—we were now in the last days of May, 1939. This had started in a cupboard under the stairs leading to a laboratory. The cupboard had contained some crates filled with straw, in which bottles and retorts had been packed. Obviously, it seemed, these could not have caught alight unless it had been done deliberately. The fire was discovered by a laboratory assistant before it could get very far, and in any event it could not have done very much harm as the building was of concrete, but there was a great deal of smoke coming through the stairs and children working in the laboratory were frightened. Then there had been a pile of books found smouldering in the grate in one of the recreation rooms. On another occasion a pile of unwound lavatory paper had been burnt in one of the water-closets, and this had scorched the woodwork. In a near-by farm a haystack and some farm buildings had been burnt down, but this might have been an accident, and would have passed as such if the other fires at the school had not subsequently occurred. There was always the possibility of a haystack burning by spontaneous combustion, but there was also the point that children from Scrope House often went up to the farm, and some of them actually worked there for a week or so at a time, as pupils of the farmer.

When I had been given this information, together with some more details with which the reader need not now be burdened, I really did not know what to say, but while I was trying to invent an intelligent question, Caroline helped me out; she asked how many people knew about these fires, and how many knew that they must have been intentional. We learnt that Edgeworth had freely discussed the fires with his staff; it was clear that some of the children must know that the books had been intentionally placed in the grate, though whether they would conclude that the other fires were equally deliberate Edgeworth did not know.

'There seems very little to go on at the moment,' I said.

'Yes, I know,' said Edgeworth. 'We don't expect any miracles from you, you know. We're very glad to have you at the school, quite apart from this business, and if you could tell us about your work, we should all be most grateful. Do you think you could give a general lecture to the school?'

I said that I should be pleased to give a lecture, and meanwhile I would poke about and get to know as many people as possible; that seemed to be the best method of beginning.

'I expect,' said Caroline, 'that a good many people on your staff will have some suspicion about who could have started the fires.'

'Well, possibly,' Edgeworth answered. 'I think you might profitably talk to Hickman, our psychologist, you know. And you'd be glad to know Richard and Susan Dawes; perhaps you've read his book on the Caroline poets, or you may have come across some of his more general essays? And then there's his poetry, of course, though I don't know...'

He paused, and I politely claimed more familiarity with the writings of Richard Dawes than I actually possessed.

'Oh yes,' said Caroline, 'I've read several of his books.'

'Susan Dawes wrote a couple of novels,' Edgeworth continued. 'But she's very left-wing now, and that gives her no time for writing. Then you'd like to meet some of the science people, no doubt. Rosenberg is measuring all the boys' and girls' feet at the moment; he did tell me why, but I couldn't quite understand it. No doubt he'll tell you, and then you could explain it to me. Miss Symonds, one of the matrons, might be useful; she often notices things about the children that the rest of us don't see. I'll tell you what I'll do... if you'll dine with me the day after to-morrow, I'll ask several people to meet you, and meanwhile do go about the school as much as you want; you'll find everybody thoroughly used to inquisitive visitors and only too glad to answer questions.'

'Was anybody seen behaving suspiciously at the time when the fires were lit?' asked Caroline. I thought she was rather overdoing the part of the earnest detective.

'Nobody,' Edgeworth answered. 'They were mostly lit at a time when any of the children could have been on the spot, and we found it impossible to narrow the field at all. You know our system allows the children to move about much more freely than at most schools; it's a variant, really, of the Dalton system, and there's no time in the day when the whole school is definitely in the classrooms or anywhere else, though they are pretty regular about meal times. Somebody might have been seen piling up the books in the grate—that must have taken a few minutes to do—but as to putting a match to the boxes and straw under the laboratory stairs, that could be done in ten seconds and without any risk of being seen. I'll make more inquiries if you like, but I think I've already done everything possible in that line, without causing more of a disturbance than I wanted and thoroughly upsetting any children who might be nervous. Naturally, we've taken every possible precaution for the future, but goodness knows what will happen next, and it may be a really serious fire next time; it's a thing you can't stop, unless the pyromaniac gives himself away.'

'They usually do give themselves away,' I said, and then Edgeworth had to leave. He was not, I am afraid, much comforted by anything we had said.

We spent another restful and luxurious evening alone, but the next day Caroline insisted on a tour of inspection of the school, although I thought it was just the morning for a quiet time in the garden, codifying, as I suggested, all the known facts.

'You could do that in two minutes,' Caroline objected, and with some justice.

As we walked down from Mrs. Eakins's house we had a good view of the school, which consisted of the very large Palladian mansion, the original Scrope House, surrounded by an extremely miscellaneous collection of other and smaller houses, outhouses, wooden huts, open-air shelters, and several concrete buildings which seemed to have been designed for a film about the future.

'We'll call on John Dupuy first,' said Caroline. 'He's the man I know best here.'

'All right,' I said, and imagined that we should find him by himself, but before I could protest I found myself on a platform with twenty children staring at me and a young man at my side talking earnestly about the pragmatic sanction.

'Do you know,' said Caroline, altogether too brightly, 'my whole memory of history as it was taught at my school is of hundreds of hours being told about the pragmatic sanction, and yet to this day I don't know what it is. The word merely suggests interminable hours at inky desks. But then this is a very different school, isn't it?'

It seemed to be the custom for visitors to interrupt the lessons in this blatant fashion; Dupuy, at any rate, was not in the least disconcerted.

'I hope so,' he said. 'But won't you introduce me?'

'This is James Hardwicke,' said Caroline.

'Oh yes, of course,' said Dupuy. 'Well, I suppose the pragmatic sanction isn't really in your line. But, I say, do you think you could tell us about the Overbury mystery? I expect you've got several theories about that. It's better than the Crippen case, I always think.'

At this point three boys and one girl got up and left the room, without saying a word and without a word from Dupuy.

'What have they gone for?' asked Caroline.

'The Overbury mystery isn't in their schedule,' said a girl in the front row. 'It isn't in mine either, but I wouldn't mind hearing about it.'

'Unfortunately I don't know anything about it,' I said.

'Oh, I'm sorry,' said Dupuy. He turned to his class. 'Mr. Hardwicke,' he said, 'has done a lot of work on criminals and heredity and so on. I expect we shall have an opportunity of hearing about his work from him later. We mustn't bother him now, though I wish we could bring him into this history lesson.'

'Let's get on with the pragmatic sanction,' said a gruff voice from the back of the room.

'Right you are,' said Dupuy. 'If we can't persuade Mr. Hardwicke to talk to us now, perhaps he'd like to stay and see how we are getting on. I'm sorry,' he added, turning to Caroline,' 'but they won't let me get up a diversion.'

'We shall meet later, I expect,' I said.

'Oh rather,' said Dupuy, and then at last I succeeded in getting Caroline out of the room.

'I absolutely refuse,' I said, 'to go into any more classrooms. I wouldn't do that again for a hundred pounds.'

'Don't be silly,' said Caroline. 'It won't be so bad next time.'

'There isn't going to be any next time,' I said.

'But if you like,' Caroline continued, 'we might go and look at the laboratories. There won't be a class there, everyone will be working by themselves.'

At last I consented, and we approached one of the concrete buildings which looked as if it had been designed to travel at one hundred miles an hour. I wondered if this was where the fire had taken place and, sure enough, there was a cupboard under the stairs, quite empty now, but with some signs of scorching.

George Rimmle, who was taking a class in chemistry in a large room upstairs, seemed to be almost as much annoyed by our interruption as by the presence of his class, whose questions, I gathered, sometimes distracted him from his own research. But it was a very small class of six adolescents, who answered our questions politely, technically, and briefly. Only one child was inclined to be talkative, a girl about sixteen years old who was holding up to the light a jar in which could be seen some very pretty golden scales fluttering down in the liquid in which they were immersed.

'How lovely!' exclaimed Caroline, having at last found something in which she could take an interest.

'Yes,' said the girl. 'I made some beautiful crystals yesterday. Exactly like emeralds. Would you like to see them?'

Caroline said they were exactly like emeralds.

'I believe you can make very beautiful flames,' I said, 'if you use the right chemicals, strontium or something.'

'That's potty,' said the girl. 'I don't care for flames.'

I retired baffled from my first examination of my first suspect, but I must confess that I was appalled by the thought of the frightful and destructive conflagrations that lurk in the powders and liquids of any laboratory. If by any chance the pyromaniac was a chemist, anything might happen, but then presumably he was not a chemist, or it would have happened already; a mere box of matches would not appeal to anyone who had the use of this admirable laboratory. The field of suspicion was already limited, though I did take the trouble to get Rimmle aside and ask him if any of his pupils had shown too much interest in combustibles or explosives. And were there, I asked, any chemicals missing, by any chance?

'How should I know?' Rimmle asked.

'Oh well, you might have noticed,' I said.

'Rosenberg hasn't been getting on to you about that atropine, has he?' Rimmle asked. 'He's not still bothering about that?'

'Oh, no,' I protested. 'I haven't met Rosenberg yet. But what's this about atropine?'

Rimmle told me that some time ago, it must have been at the beginning of the winter term, he had lent Rosenberg a bottle of atropine in powder form which he had had by him for some time. Rosenberg wanted it for some experiments on the nervous system of mice, and was going to make up a solution. He returned the atropine not long after, and Rimmle put it away again in his poison cupboard. But then Rosenberg wanted a little more and, when he had got it, found that there was something wrong with it. Eventually it was discovered that it had been mixed with boracic powder. Rimmle thought this must have been done while Rosenberg still had it, but Rosenberg thought it must have been done in Rimmle's laboratory, and pointed out that there were always some children in Rimmle's laboratory, but that the room in which he did his own experiments on mice and other animals was not used by schoolchildren. They both got quite heated about it, and accused each other of carelessness; Rimmle still seemed resentful.

'In the ordinary way,' he said, 'it wouldn't matter, but in a place like this with children all over the place...' He seemed to dislike the presence of children, and though he was probably a conscientious chemist, it seemed doubtful whether he could be described as a born teacher. I concluded that it was quite possible that some thermite or other material conducive to fire could have been manufactured in his laboratory without his knowing anything about it.

That seemed to be enough detection for the day. I considered, but did not consider for long, the possibility of going back to Dupuy's classroom and delivering a lecture on the great fire of London, with a view to observing his pupils' reactions; it seemed better to go back to the rich amenities of the Dower House. I was getting quite used to the place by now and no longer tip-toed about the corridors or whispered in the sitting-rooms. In fact, I put my feet up. It is wonderful how soon one becomes acclimatized to luxury, and I soon began to wonder whether I should ever again be content with my old rooms in London. As to Caroline, she positively sprawled on the velvet cushions. We were very lazy, no doubt, but there was nothing in the atmosphere of the Dower House to spur or encourage the detective and perhaps it may be remembered, as some excuse for my apparent lethargy, that I was all the while conducting a complicated and not particularly successful love affair.

Chapter Three

Edgeworth's dinner party was not very amusing. I did not take very kindly to Richard Dawes, the poet and essayist, nor was I much impressed by his wife. Of all the staff of Scrope House, Dawes had perhaps the greatest pretensions to a more than local reputation, that is, if you exclude the scientists, and a scientific reputation seems to need some added support if it is to receive general recognition at the dinner table. It was therefore natural that Dawes should be received with, and expect, a good deal of deference. He was in charge of the teaching of English literature at Scrope House, but he soon let us know that his heart was rather in his own writing. Yet he seemed to be by nature a grub and a pedant, a plodding collector of classical scholarships, and this, as I afterwards gathered, he had actually been in earlier life. But then, by some accident of an academic career, he had edited a collection of amatory poems of the seventeenth century; the effect on his own mind had been electrifying and thenceforward there poured, there positively guttered, from his pen innumerable essays disclaiming scholarship, disclaiming even literature, as a poor substitute for life. Unfortunate authors whose lives of laborious toil had left them little time for anything more than comfortable marriages or convenient love affairs were held up to derision; to die early, worn out by the pangs of tragic love, that was the only thing to live for. There followed a novel, set in the late seventeenth century, in which the hero, who might have been considered excessively sentimental by any lady novelist, was put forward as a bitterly disillusioned

observer of the life of this period. For it was Dawe's odd illusion
that he himself was strikingly disillusioned; it was because he saw the
hollowness of everything else, so his argument seemed to run, that he
set so much store by love. Finally there came poems, many but roses,
in each of which he uttered, with the wry smile of the heartbroken,
yet another reflection on the shortness of life, the fading of flowers,
the impermanence of youth, and the misery of the universe in which
positively the only consolation was love. And now, I gathered, he was
trying out the wry smile on politics and the miseries of 1939; how, he
asked us, should a sensitive and civilized human being live in these
days of terror, and then he gave us his prescription, the mixture as
before, disillusionment and love. A. E. Housman, as Mr. Auden tells
us, 'kept tears like dirty postcards in a drawer,' but Dawes plastered
them, obscene posters, on every hoarding.

It may have been gratifying to Susan Dawes to be publicly
recognized as the wife of one who so much appreciated love. If she
occupied all the attention of such an Anthony, of one who so loudly
and persistently counted the world well lost for love, her friends might
argue that she must herself be some kind of Cleopatra. But they might
also argue, especially as Dawes seemed to expect all real love to be
tragic, that she did not in fact occupy all his attention. She did not, at
any rate, seem altogether pleased by his attitude, at this present dinner
party, to international politics. She herself was a theoretician of the
left, full of abstract terms and party labels, attributing everything
that happened to movements and to historical necessity rather than
to the actions of individuals. Her husband's persistent concern with
the proper reaction to crises of the sensitive and civilized individual
must have seemed to her intensely improper, and she certainly showed
her disapproval. But he accepted her corrections without demur, as
from the expert on this subject, and he seemed genuinely anxious to
adjust himself to a new way of thinking, a new outlook on politics as
having some connection with life. It must certainly have been even

more exasperating for Susan Dawes in the past, when Dawes was presumably entirely concerned with the proper relation between literature and life and took no interest in politics at all.

Miss Symonds, the matron, took little part in the conversation, and had to be provided with vegetarian dishes. She was, as I afterwards learned, a theosophist, and had got to Scrope House by mistake, supposing that a progressive school would be favourable to the kind of delusion which is sometimes known as 'new thought'. Edgeworth may have been right in thinking that she showed some intuition in her dealings with children—he would not otherwise have kept her on to corrupt the school by putting forward such beliefs as that tigers have learnt flesh-eating from the example of wicked men—but nothing that she said on this occasion suggested that she could help me. Dr. Hickman was also silent, and I wondered whether he felt depressed by his failure to keep the school free from neurotic disorders. Caroline and Susan Dawes eventually took charge of the conversation and kept it rigidly to politics, while Edgeworth was content to show an occasional and knowledgeable interest in this subject, though he found it difficult at this moment to bring his hearty optimism to bear upon it. From time to time Dawes would interject some sidelong and civilized comment from Parnassus. Or was it from Cythera? It was, at any rate, from some very superior station.

As we were leaving Edgeworth's house and I was looking forward to my well-earned bed, Susan Dawes managed to get me alone outside the front door.

'I should like to consult you, Mr. Hardwicke,' she said, with the air of a conspirator.

'What about?' I asked, fearing that some more detection was to be asked of me.

'I'd rather not tell you here,' she answered. 'It's not about these fires, or at least only incidentally. Will you come to tea to-morrow? Our cottage is not very far from the Dower House.'

I had, of course, to accept her invitation, though I wondered whether I was going to be asked to solve all the problems of all the staff and be employed for ever in the school as a kind of universal aunt.

I arrived punctually at the bleak cottage in which Mr. and Mrs. Dawes lived; it was at the top of a hill and exposed to all the winds.

'We're a long way from the school here,' Mrs. Dawes said, 'and that's a great advantage, I can tell you. Richard and I can work here without any fear of being disturbed, and we aren't expected to be always at the school.'

Was Richard, I wondered, meditating an erotic poem in some chilly study at the back of the house at this very moment?

'Well now,' began Mrs. Dawes, 'I've a lot to tell you. I do think something ought to be done about it, and it had much better be by an outsider. Have you any influence with the Foreign Office?'

'None whatever,' I said.

Mrs. Dawes seemed to be disappointed. 'But I expect you could do something,' she said. 'You must know people.'

'Nobody at all,' I said.

'Oh, well,' she said, 'it's really your advice I want. I'm pretty sure there's a Nazi spy, either in the school or connected with it in some way. I can't give you the source of my information, but I received a very serious warning. I know this sounds melodramatic but after all it's the sort of thing that happens, isn't it?'

'I knew a man once,' I said, 'who couldn't read any novels except those of Oppenheim. He said he was the only modern novelist who described the sort of thing that really happens.'

'Exactly,' said Mrs. Dawes.

'But what makes you suspect a Nazi spy?' I asked.

'That's what I can't tell you,' Mrs. Dawes said. 'Oh, it's not that I can't trust you completely, but I don't want to give other people away, and I was told in the strictest confidence. But I feel pretty sure, from one or two things I've heard, that some of the refugees on our staff have had threatening letters. I'll give you an instance of the kind of thing that's been happening. You know I work for a political monthly, the *Popular Front*, and I arranged for Rosenberg to contribute three consecutive articles. He sent in the first two and they were just what we wanted, a complete exposure of the weakness of the Axis and a reasoned appeal for an alliance with Russia. But he wouldn't let me have the third, and wouldn't give me a reason. He didn't sign his name to the articles, of course, and we kept the secret of their authorship very carefully; in fact, we took what might be thought almost absurd precautions, though no doubt they were really very necessary. But one explanation of his failure to send the third article may be that he was threatened, and I shouldn't be surprised if one of the refugees here—it might even be one of the older boys or girls—were being forced to send information abroad by threats about their relations who haven't got away. And there's one further point; supposing it's a boy or girl who's being forced to do the spying, you might expect him or her to find it a terrible strain. It would be an unspeakable position for a child at school, and the fires might be a symptom. I should think that's just the kind of thing that would drive you to pyromania.'

'I suppose it might,' I answered.

'And then there's a further possibility,' Mrs. Dawes continued. 'Somebody might actually have been sent by the Nazis to pose as a refugee but really to work for them as a spy.'

'Would it be worth their while,' I asked, 'to send someone here?'

'You never can tell,' said Mrs. Dawes. 'This place is pretty well known. The difficulty is that I don't know, and only an expert could know, how cunning spies really are. Would it, for example, be possible for a spy to appear as genuine as Rosenberg? Could he keep it up? Could he write articles which really were good anti-Nazi propaganda?'

'That would seem to be going rather far,' I said.

'You think so?' asked Mrs. Dawes. 'Now that's just the sort of thing I wanted to know.'

She had raised an interesting question, I thought, and I should certainly have liked to be in a position to let her know exactly how cunning spies can be.

'Well,' I said, 'I'll think about it, but we mustn't be in too much of a hurry.'

'Oh, no,' she agreed, 'and I'm quite content to put it into your hands.'

'You've no other reason for suspecting Rosenberg except that he didn't send in the third article?' I asked.

'No, not really,' she replied, 'and it's only one of two possible explanations; he may have been threatened himself if he went on with the work. My information didn't go beyond a general warning. Not as yet, that is…'

But she was interrupted at this point when the servant announced a Mr. Sinclair.

'Oh, hullo, Mark,' Mrs. Dawes said, and introduced me. He was a young man with a shy manner, and I afterwards learnt that he was the art master at Scrope House.

'We've been talking about these fires,' said Mrs. Dawes.

'And about your Nazi spy, I take it,' Sinclair answered.

'Who told you about that?' asked Susan.

'I'm sorry,' Sinclair said, 'I didn't know you didn't want it talked about. But in any case you can't keep anything to yourself here.'

'No, perhaps not,' Mrs. Dawes said. 'Well, as you seem to know all about it, what do you think?'

'I haven't really thought about it,' Sinclair answered. 'It all seems very unlikely but perhaps such things can happen. Only, what would a spy want with Scrope House?'

'Well, we must have thirty or forty refugees here,' said Mrs. Dawes, 'and then there's the *Popular Front.*

Sinclair did not seem interested in the *Popular Front*, and I had the impression that he thought Mrs. Dawes was looking for a mystery where none existed. There was a pause in the conversation which Mrs. Dawes ended by asking Sinclair if he was going to the party next Wednesday.

'What party?' he asked, in an absent-minded way.

'Why, Dr. Hickman's, of course. It's a bottle party,' she continued, turning to me. 'We always give bottle parties here; it's quite a good plan for people as poor as we all are. I don't mind telling you that I rather look forward to them, though there's usually nobody there but people from the school. Would you like to go to this one, Mr. Hardwicke?'

'Very much,' I answered, 'if you think I should be wanted.'

'Oh, of course,' Mrs. Dawes said. 'I'll remind Dr. Hickman to send you an invitation. You're going, aren't you, Mark?'

'I expect so,' Sinclair answered. 'But what time is it?'

'Just gone six,' Mrs. Dawes replied. 'Richard'll be back in a minute.'

'Good Lord,' Sinclair said, 'I didn't know it was as late as that. I must rush off.'

I wondered whether I should also take the opportunity of making my escape; in this way I might avoid any uncomfortable exposure of my incapacity for counterespionage, but, on the other hand, it might be a bore to have to walk a good part of my way with Sinclair, who did not seem a very easy person to get on with. I decided to stay for another two minutes.

'You haven't met Mark Sinclair before?' Mrs. Dawes asked, when he had gone.

'He's a curious character,' she continued, 'as I dare say you noticed. I've often thought that he's disappointed because he has to teach instead of getting on with his own work. He has a habit of calling unexpectedly and then saying nothing. I think he comes for company, and then doesn't like it when he gets it. He's a lonely man; he's never got over the death of his wife.'

'Did that happen recently?' I asked.

'Not very,' Mrs. Dawes answered. 'Let me see, I think it was about six months before I married Richard and came here, and that was almost exactly two years ago. But, all the same, I think that's what's the matter with Mark.'

I got away without any more conversation about spies, but I wondered if I should be running any risk of overtaking Sinclair on the road. However, I saw no sign of him, though there was a long straight road before me, and in the distance I could see a bicyclist approaching. When he got closer I saw that it was Richard Dawes; he got off his machine when he reached me and wished me good afternoon.

'Mrs. Dawes has been giving me tea,' I said.

'Oh, yes,' he answered, 'I hope it was a good tea. I'm sorry I wasn't there, but I dare say'—he gave his usual wry smile—'that you got on very well without me.'

'Not at all,' I answered, 'I mean…'

'I know what you mean,' Dawes said. 'I shall tell Susan she didn't manage to amuse you.'

This was getting intolerable, so I myself attempted a vague smile and hastily changed the subject.

'Is there a short cut to the school?' I asked.

'There's a path across the fields,' Dawes answered. 'But it's a longer way round, like all footpaths.'

'Well, good-bye,' I said, 'I must get some work done before dinner.'

I rather wished I had taken the footpath, as Sinclair must have done, even though it was the longer way. It seemed obvious that when Mrs. Dawes had a visitor by herself, Dawes instantly assumed, though in an arch and forgiving manner, that she was beginning an intrigue.

I felt that it would be worth walking a very long way round in order to avoid giving Dawes an opportunity of being broad-minded about an offence which one had not committed.

Nothing of much importance happened before the day of Dr. Hickman's party. Mrs. Eakins, it is true, made another appearance, and this time she did refer to the fires and to the reason for my invitation to Scrope House. She asked me whether I had discovered anything.

'We've learnt a good many miscellaneous facts,' said Caroline, no doubt imagining that she could make a more impressive show of our achievements than I could. 'But, at the moment,' she added, 'there's nothing conclusive.'

'I hope there won't be a really serious fire before Mr. Hardwicke has made up his mind,' Mrs. Eakins said, with some impatience, as though wondering whether she was getting her money's worth. I hastily turned the conversation to the lecture I was giving that very evening to the school. It was, if I may say so, a great success, in that it was very well attended and I contrived to disappoint, as thoroughly as I had intended, an audience which had assembled in the hope of hearing all about the underworld. I gave them a great many statistics. I also took the opportunity of talking to and observing a number of the schoolchildren.

The next day was the day of Hickman's party, and in the morning I received a note from Mrs. Dawes. She had received, she now told me, some rather more definite evidence on the subject we had discussed at her house, and wanted to consult me again. We should meet at Hickman's party, but it might be difficult for us to have a proper talk about it then, and she hoped I would come and see her, either before or after the party. It was an obscure note—did it refer to more evidence about the fires, about the Nazi spy, or about both?—and I decided that after the party would certainly do. Perhaps, after all, I could get her to tell me what she had learnt at the party, and that would save trouble and possibly also save me from the embarrassing forgiveness of Richard Dawes, if he found that I was once again closeted with his wife.

I brought a bottle of sherry from Mrs. Eakins's excellent cellar to the party; I asked the butler where he thought I could buy a bottle of something, and he at once suggested this admirable expedient. Mrs. Eakins did not, of course, attend the party, but her bottle, a very singular wine from Greece—it was said to have honey from Hybla mixed in it—was sent round with some ceremony and an elaborate excuse for the donor's absence. Hickman, who now seemed much happier than when we had met before, stood by a table which served as a bar and on which the guests put their bottles. He showed an elaborate lack of interest in what his guests were bringing; according to Caroline the generosity or meanness which the guests might show at these bottle parties, which occurred at fairly regular intervals, was a fruitful subject of conversation between the staff. Edgeworth always brought a bottle of champagne, both because it was expected of him as head master and because this was another means of showing that he was a man as well as an usher. Dawes brought a bottle of inky claret which I gathered was well known. Sinclair brought a bottle of liqueur whisky which, with pardonable vanity, he recommended to a good many people, including myself. Rimmle brought a bottle of what he called vodka, though it had really been made from absolute alcohol in his laboratory, and seemed to have been flavoured with pear-drops. The guests wandered about a good deal, either in the two sitting-rooms or on the verandah, and in the garden at the back of the house.

I was interested to see Rosenberg, the possible spy, and I talked to him for some time. I plied him with Rimmle's vodka, a drink which produced as effectively as real vodka an immediate and violent heat in the pit of the stomach; I hoped that this might induce him to speak of his sorrows, if he had been threatened by Nazi agents, or to express his real opinions, if he were a professional spy. But either he was on his guard or there was nothing for him to reveal, for nothing emerged, but instead he talked very intelligently about my work, with which he was entirely familiar. He was a biologist by profession, and I had already heard something of his work, so that we got on very well. After a while he said that he would take no more of Rimmle's vodka. 'I am afraid,' he apologized, 'that I can't drink your native English spirit.' He went to talk to someone else, and I felt ashamed of my low and unsuccessful expedient, but I comforted myself by reflecting that if he were a spy he deserved to suffer next morning; if he were not it was I who deserved to suffer, and I certainly would.

Edgeworth's face grew redder and shone with a benevolent glow, a Christmas fire which seemed inappropriate on a summer evening; I have never seen anyone unbend so vigorously. He thanked me profusely for my lecture, for my awfully jolly little talk, and then apologized for talking shop. Caroline was conversing earnestly with her friend John Dupuy, and I watched her rather anxiously as she became more and more friendly with him; I knew that she was not altogether to be trusted at parties, and I did not know how respectable these parties were supposed to be or how much laxity of conduct would be condoned. One had the impression of an almost compulsive, ritual and too deliberate relaxation, as if all these school masters and school mistresses—there must have been about forty people at the party—were earnestly protesting their common humanity and, above all, their kinship with the great metropolitan world. Perhaps, I thought, it was not so much for reasons of economy that the parties were always arranged in this way, but because the words 'bottle party' have so alluringly vicious, so plainly unacademic a flavour.

The noise and heat were becoming greater, gestures more emphatic, the atmosphere thicker with smoke, when I noticed that Hickman was standing on a chair and making an effort to attract the attention of his guests. I edged my way through the crowd until I could hear what he was saying, though even then, so loud was the conversation all round me, I could only catch a few of his words. He was pointing to two girls and two boys, who must have been introduced into the party just before, for I had not previously noticed them. These children, I gathered, were going to sing, and when Hickman had attracted the attention of those in his immediate neighbourhood, though the noise from the other end of the room was still very loud, they began their performance. At first one could distinctly hear a few notes, but after a while the forlorn quartet could only be seen, their mouths moving grotesquely, while no note of music succeeded in penetrating the discordant clatter around them. Hickman was very much annoyed, and I saw Edgeworth leading him sympathetically away, while Sinclair said a few words to the singers. Edgeworth then came up to offer the children some lemonade, which had evidently been kept specially for them, and Sinclair took the opportunity to say good-bye to his host and leave the party. But nobody else left, and this was evidently not intended to be the end of the evening's amusement.

There were now so many people in the room, and it was growing so hot indoors that I decided to go outside. There were a number of people on the verandah, standing up or sitting at little tables, but few in the garden, which I found very pleasant in the cool of the evening. I amused myself by listening to the very strange noise that a party makes when it is heard from a distance. From the garden the noise did not seem so chaotic as from within, and it was as if I had been sitting amongst an orchestra, where it was impossible to distinguish any plan in the composition that was being played, but as soon as I moved away the proportions and purpose of the sound became clear. The conversation made a wavering obbligato accompaniment, now in the bass and now in the treble, to choral passages of laughter into which by an effort of the imagination I could read a broken and disturbing rhythm. I listened for a minute or two, selecting and arranging the sounds in a presumably subjective pattern, when I noticed that the obliggato of conversation was beginning to lose its volume, until the composition almost resolved itself into a duet of male and female laughter. Suddenly the bass voices stopped, and there continued alone a shrill, wild, and continuous cachinnation. The effect was prodigiously dramatic, and for a moment I listened without moving, as to the finale of a concert, before I recollected myself and moved towards the house behind several other people who were pushing indoors from the garden and the verandah. When I managed to make my way through the crowd I saw Susan Dawes gesticulating at the other end of the room and shrieking with hysterical laughter, while everyone stared or stood in silent discomfort and her husband was vainly trying to persuade her to be quiet. When he saw that she would not or could not stop, he tried to get her out of the room, but she suddenly collapsed and Edgeworth and Dawes were able to carry her away.

'It must have been that awful vodka,' said Caroline, who had made her way towards me, but Mrs. Dawes's delirium had been so wild and alarming that it was not easy to accept her behaviour as a mere accident of intoxication. The party was altogether subdued and before long we all went home, though Dupuy tried to detain Caroline and was evidently very drunk. I saw Hickman trying to persuade him to go home, but he soon gave this up and began to put him to bed on a sofa.

Chapter Four

I t seemed to me that I had scarcely fallen asleep—it was actually
about three hours later—when Noakes woke me up and told
me that I was urgently wanted on the telephone. Edgeworth was
at the other end of the line, and he told me that Susan Dawes was
dead, that the doctor had refused to give a death certificate, and that
he wanted me to come at once to Dawes's house. I did not wake
Caroline, but walked as fast as I could to the place, feeling rather ill,
but quite clear in the head. When I arrived I found Edgeworth and
the school doctor—not Hickman but the ordinary doctor, a Doctor
Frawley—arguing in the sitting-room.

'This is a terrible thing to have happened,' Edgeworth said.
'Dr. Frawley says that poor Susan must certainly have taken some
poison.'

'There's no doubt about it, I'm afraid,' Frawley said. 'The idea
of a heart attack after too much to drink is quite out of the question.
The dilated pupils, the paralysis of the nerves, and so on—it's quite
unmistakable. And apparently there was delirium to begin with.'

'Good Lord,' I exclaimed, 'I've just thought of something. Can
I use the telephone?'

Edgeworth looked at me in some surprise. 'You're not going to
ring up the police, are you?' he asked. 'That's what we were just
talking about before you came.'

'No,' I answered. 'We can do that later. I want to get on to
Hickman now.'

It took some time to rouse Hickman, but when eventually he answered the telephone I asked him at once how Dupuy was looking.

'He's asleep, I suppose,' said Hickman. 'What on earth…?'

'He's still at your house, then?' I asked.

'Why the devil shouldn't he be?' Hickman said.

'Perhaps you wouldn't mind going at once and seeing if he's all right,' I said. 'I'll explain later.'

Hickman left the telephone and came back a minute or so later. 'There does seem to be something rather odd about him,' he said. 'He's not asleep; he's in a queer state.'

'He's alive then?' I asked.

'Good Lord, yes,' Hickman exclaimed. 'What the devil do you mean?'

'Are his pupils dilated?' I asked.

'Yes, as a matter of fact they are,' said Hickman. 'I noticed that at once. But why…?'

I thought it was time to explain.

'Mrs. Dawes has been poisoned,' I said. 'She's dead. I rather wondered if Dupuy could have taken the same stuff; he was behaving oddly when I last saw him.'

Hickman showed unmistakable and, I should suppose—but how can one tell?—genuine surprise.

'I'd better send for Frawley,' he said, and I told him that Frawley was with me at the moment.

'I'll go at once,' said Frawley, and I was left alone with Edgeworth.

As I had noticed before, the appearance of the Dawes's living-room was depressing at the best of times; in the middle of the night it looked appallingly cheerless. The effect was partly produced by the striking incongruity of the various objects which Dawes and his wife had contributed to its furnishing. Without hesitation I ascribed the view of the Parthenon and the photograph of the Hermes of Praxiteles to Dawes; no doubt they were a relic of his early days of classical scholarship, as were the many bound books that must have been school or university prizes. With these rich but oppressive volumes Mrs. Dawes's collection of the publications of the Left Book Club, in their orange paper covers, contrasted as oddly as her inevitable reproduction of Van Gogh's sunflowers with the Hermes. One could perceive as clearly where all Mrs. Dawes's attempts to brighten her husband's room, with striped curtains, mirror, or sofa, came to an end and where the original drab character of the room still asserted itself. A reproduction of a Boucher illustrated yet another contrast, between the new and the old Dawes. It seemed almost as suitable a place as a doctor's waiting-room in which to receive such news as I had just heard.

'If Dupuy has been poisoned too,' Edgeworth said, 'it can't be suicide.'

'Did you think it might have been?' I asked.

'I don't know, how could I know anything about it?' Edgeworth said. He was evidently distraught, and I thought it best to ask no more questions at the moment.

After a pause, he began speaking again. 'Dawes is upstairs,' he said. 'He's taking it very hardly, of course. I thought I'd better leave him alone. I suppose it is the best thing to do, isn't it?'

'Oh yes,' I said, 'I should think so.'

'I imagine it means the police,' Edgeworth continued. 'Of course it does. Had I better wait till Frawley gets back?'

'We ought to tell them as soon as possible,' I said. 'By the way, how did you get here?'

'Frawley rang me up,' Edgeworth answered, 'he wanted someone to be with Dawes, and I imagine he thought, as head master, I'd better take on the responsibility at once. Oh well... I'd better get on to the police.'

I thought this was Edgeworth's job, though he evidently wanted me to do it. I felt they would pay more attention to him than to a stranger.

It seemed to be a most difficult task to explain anything to the man at Scropeham police station, but eventually Edgeworth made himself understood.

'They're sending Sergeant Willis,' he said, when he had rung off. 'But I don't see that they can do anything to-night. And they're sending someone to Hickman's house. They don't want anything touched here, as Susan probably took the poison during the party.'

'Did Frawley say what kind of poison it was?' I asked.

'He couldn't be quite sure,' said Edgeworth, 'but he thought it might be atropine or deadly nightshade berries, or something of the kind.'

'Did he think it could have been an accident?' I asked.

'He didn't say,' Edgeworth answered. 'What do you think?'

'It might have been,' I said, 'though it's difficult to see how. Children sometimes eat deadly nightshade berries, I believe, but surely Mrs. Dawes wouldn't have done so. No doubt it will all be cleared up in time.'

When Frawley came back he told us that Dupuy would probably be all right.

'Hickman thinks he can manage for the time being,' Frawley said. 'I didn't think there was any need to move him. He can't have taken a very heavy dose. There's a lot of difference between a toxic and a lethal dose, of course. Have you got on to the police?'

Edgeworth told him we had.

'Yes, that's best,' Frawley said. 'I advised Hickman to leave everything as it was in his house… not to clean up after the party, I mean, though there's rather a mess in the drawing-room.'

'You weren't at the party yourself?' I asked Frawley.

'No,' he said. 'I never go to that sort of thing. Very few doctors like late hours. But I wish I had, I might have done something, though you can never be sure with atropine, if it was atropine. It's absorbed into the system very quickly.'

We waited for about a quarter of an hour for the police to come, and during that time Edgeworth explained that he had sent for me because, as he put it, he wanted me to take a 'watching brief' on behalf of the school.

'I've no idea,' he added, 'whether the police are likely to be intelligent about this kind of thing, and it can certainly be no harm to have someone intelligent standing by, to see how things go. Of course this is going to be a bad thing for the school, but the sooner we know what has really happened the better; a persistent mystery would be worse than anything.' He then told me that he knew the chief constable, a Colonel Redder, and that Mrs. Eakins knew him too. He thought something could be arranged and no doubt, with my reputation, the police would be only too glad to give me all the information I might want. But it would be best to say nothing to Sergeant Willis until everything was arranged with his superiors. I certainly had no desire to claim any kind of status, whether as amateur or professional detective, now or in the future, and I decided that I would leave it to Edgeworth and Mrs. Eakins between them to determine what I should do, if anything.

Sergeant Willis seemed to have no character at all, which was a great relief. On the few occasions when I have had any contact with the law I have always noticed and admired the remote, unemotional, detached manner of the law's officers in their relations with the public. I know, or at least my friends have often told me, how excited and violent the police are supposed to become during political meetings or processions and how partisan their conduct is usually supposed to be. But in their attendance on the disturbances and tragedies of private lives their unimaginative and quiet demeanour seems to me wholly admirable and has a wonderfully sobering effect on even the most distracted minds. A coroner's inquest, as I afterwards learnt, is conducted in a deliberately low key; it would be almost impossible, so powerful is the effect of suggestion, for a witness to raise his voice, and those who are any distance from the coroner can barely hear what is being said. Whether as a result of deliberate training, or as a natural protection against the violent events and emotions with which they are continually brought in contact, the police seem to have learned the same grey and subdued manner of conversation, and Sergeant Willis had hardly been in the room for a minute before we felt that we were engaged in a necessary but exceedingly dull committee meeting. He only showed a flicker of individual feeling when some explanation that Edgeworth was giving became rather involved; he recapitulated and added to some information which he had already given; this made it difficult for Willis to get the statement clear, and he could not help showing that in his opinion Edgeworth was making unnecessary work. Nothing new emerged in this slow interrogation, unless perhaps when Sergeant Willis saw Frawley privately in another room, and eventually I wondered if I could go to bed.

'Much the best thing you can do, sir,' said Willis, and I went away as the dawn was breaking.

Caroline, when I told her during breakfast of the death of Susan Dawes, was at first excited and then sobered; she asked me quite humbly what I proposed to do about it, and seemed to have no ideas of her own. I said that I supposed that someone ought to ask Dupuy a few questions; no doubt he had taken the poison at the same time and from the same source as Mrs. Dawes, and when he was well again he ought to be able to remember something about it. I asked Noakes if Mrs. Eakins had heard the news, fully expecting that if it had already been broken to her she would be even more prostrated than usual, but to my surprise I heard that she was up and even at that moment telephoning to the chief constable. The excitement must have acted, most unexpectedly, as a tonic. This decided me to leave the Dower House as soon as possible, so that I might avoid a solemn interview with Mrs. Eakins and at the same time give the impression of being very active in the pursuit of my duties. Caroline, docile for the moment, promised to stay and make a good impression on Mrs. Eakins.

Hickman, when I got to his house, said that Dupuy was much better and that it might even do him good for me to have a talk with him. I found him in bed upstairs, still rather shaky, but quite willing to talk about what had happened. He seemed distressed by Susan's death, but, as it appeared, pleasantly stimulated by the thought of his own escape; to come near to death and to evade it appears to be agreeable to everyone's vanity. He said that he couldn't imagine that anyone would wish to poison either himself or Mrs. Dawes, and that it was quite incredible, in his opinion, that they should have shared a common enemy. Most probably, he thought, it was all an accident; there were far too many chemists at Scrope House, and some of them were intolerably careless. I asked him what he had drunk, and he said that he didn't want to think about it.

'It might be as well to try and think' I said. 'The police will be round very soon and, if they've got any sense, that's the first question they'll ask.'

'I had a good deal of whisky,' he answered. 'I may have drunk something else, but I can't be sure of anything.'

'Perhaps the poison has produced a retrospective amnesia,' I suggested.

'That's a very charitable suggestion,' Dupuy answered. 'But I've no doubt I should have suffered from amnesia in any case, even without the poison, and a very good thing too. But perhaps I shall remember a little more as time goes on; one does sometimes.'

'Do you remember anything about Susan Dawes becoming delirious?' I asked.

'Oh, yes,' he answered, 'I certainly remember that, and now that I come to think of it, I remember feeling pretty queer myself, thirsty, you know, and my mouth very dry.'

At this moment Hickman came into the room and asked me if I knew that there was a policeman in the house.

'He's sitting among the ruins of the party, poor devil,' he said.

'Poor devil,' said Dupuy. 'I wonder if he's finishing off the drinks?'

'Oughtn't someone to tell him there may be poison in them?' I suggested.

'Good heavens,' Hickman exclaimed. 'Do you think…?'

'I should think he'd know better than to destroy evidence,' I said. 'But look here,' I continued, 'I think I'd better be going. Has the policeman asked any questions?'

'No,' said Hickman. 'He doesn't seem to want to know anything at all, I should think he's waiting for his superiors to do all the talking. No doubt there's a very strict military discipline in the police force.'

Hickman took me to the front door and I asked him what he thought about Dupuy's state of mind. He became very professional at once, and seemed to be repeating a set-piece.

'You're much mistaken,' he said, 'if you imagine that I have only to look at somebody with my X-ray eyes in order to fathom all the secrets of his soul. People always seem to think that because I'm a psycho-analyst I've only to give one glance at my victims…'

Evidently the school authorities had often expected a lightning diagnosis.

'No, no, of course not,' I said, as soothingly as I could manage. 'But I thought you might have noticed, just as an ordinary intelligent person, you know…'

'Well, but what are you trying to find out about Dupuy anyway?' he asked. 'He's probably had a shock but it doesn't seem to have done him much harm. He's suffering from guilt, of course.'

'Oh, is he?' I said. 'That's interesting.'

'Not particularly,' he answered. 'Most people suffer from guilt when they have a hangover. Partly physical, I expect.'

Here, it would seem, Hickman was being deliberately broad-minded and going against his own school of thought, and so to please him I put his own case for him.

'Or else,' I said, 'it's the natural reaction after too many inhibitions have been released by the action of alcohol. The hangover itself may be psychogenic, the result of feelings of guilt.'

'There's that, of course,' he answered. 'But what else,' he continued, 'would Dupuy have to be guilty about?'

'That's your province rather than mine, isn't it?' I said, evading his question. I certainly did not want to go about arousing suspicion against anybody in either Hickman's or anybody else's mind.

I wondered what I had better do next. I could report to headquarters and find out from the head master or from Mrs. Eakins whether it had been arranged for me to meet the chief constable and give the police the benefit of my wide experience of the life-histories of identical twins. Or else I could continue asking questions by myself. On reflection, I thought that I had better acquire a little information by myself since I should then be able to make a better impression on the police. The obvious person to talk to seemed to be Sinclair; he had appeared to know what Mrs. Dawes was talking about when she was dropping hints about Nazi spies.

It took me some time to find Sinclair; he was not in the studio where it was his duty to instruct his pupils not to bother about the rudiments of drawing. But several children were there, profoundly intent on their work, and eventually I persuaded one little boy—he was working away with his tongue between his lips covering a large sheet of paper with a many-coloured pattern. Very briefly, and with evident annoyance, he told me that Sinclair had gone for a walk to the village; I tiptoed out of the studio feeling like a most philistine intruder. I walked towards the post-office and eventually met Sinclair returning from his errand.

'I've just been to your studio,' I said. 'I never saw such a hive of industry. I shouldn't imagine you have much to do there yourself; the children look as though they'd bite your head off if you so much as addressed a word to them.'

Sinclair looked pleased. 'Yes, they're wonderful, aren't they?' he replied. 'Of course, the children you saw are a chosen few, the ones who really want to paint the whole time, if it were possible, but almost any of the younger children, if you give them time and encouragement at the start, will eventually begin painting as though their lives depended on it. And the talent they have... it's frankly incredible. You know those patterns they do; perhaps you noticed what astonishingly difficult and subtle colours they use, and apparently with unerring precision. I saw a little girl once who'd made a pattern of purples and browns, rather dull I thought it, and told her so. She looked at me quite patiently, though a little reproachfully, and then showed me that she had only to change, very slightly, almost imperceptibly, the background of white paper by covering it with white paint; the whole colour scheme then became instantly and unmistakably right. It was really quite beyond me; I felt as though I were a student watching Matisse at work. But perhaps an even greater mystery is why they inevitably lose all their talent as they grow up. Something to do with puberty, perhaps? But that's in your line rather than mine.'

'Not at all,' I said. 'I don't know anything about it, but it's most interesting. Are you writing about your experiences?'

'Oh no, no...' Sinclair said, 'I don't know anything about it. You want a psychologist, I take it, but then psychologists never know anything about painting, do they? I'm sorry,' he added, 'I didn't mean to suggest that you...'

'Not at all,' I answered, 'I'm not really a psychologist, and I don't know anything about painting, not in the sense that you mean. But what I wanted to ask you,' I added, returning to duty, 'was about Susan Dawes and those spies of hers. You've heard that she died, of course?'

'Oh yes, I was very sorry to hear...' Sinclair seemed to find it difficult to withdraw his mind from the subject of children's paintings.

'Well, when we first met,' I continued, 'you seemed to know what she was talking about when she got on to the subject of Nazi spies. As a matter of fact, she'd just been talking to me on the same subject, and she'd suggested that the fires they've been having at the school might have been connected, in a roundabout way, with the presence of a spy in the place. That's what interests me, of course; the fires are my business not the spy. But then she wrote me a letter, on the day before she died, in which she suggested that she had found out something more. I never learnt what it was that she'd discovered, but it occurred to me that she might just possibly have told you, or you might have heard from an independent source.'

'No,' said Sinclair, 'she certainly never told me anything about it. I'd heard her speak about the possibility of a spy some time ago, but that was all.'

'But,' I said, 'when you talked about this possibility at her house, when I was there at the same time, she seemed surprised that you knew about it. That's partly why I came to you; I thought you might have heard about the spy from some other source.'

'Oh, no,' said Sinclair. 'I only heard about it from her. I expect she was surprised to hear me talking about it because it was in front of you and she had asked me to be discreet. It was her way of reproaching me; she probably thought that if I talked like that in front of you, though actually, of course, it didn't matter, since she herself had been talking about it to you, then I might talk as freely in front of other people. I'm afraid she rather liked an atmosphere of secrecy and mystery.'

'Then you don't think she really knew anything definite?' I asked. 'Because, of course,' I added, 'there's just the bare possibility that she was murdered to prevent her passing on her information.'

'Was she murdered?' asked Sinclair.

'I'm sure I don't know,' I said. 'But it's obviously a possibility.'

'I suppose so,' he replied.

'When she talked to you before, did she seem to have any definite information?' I asked.

'On the contrary,' Sinclair said. 'It was extremely indefinite. She only told me, as I expect she told you, that she had heard from some mysterious source of information that some of the refugees were being threatened and that these threats might have come from a Nazi agent actually working in the school. But she may, as you suggest, have learnt something more by the time that she wrote to you. By the way,' he added, 'no doubt the police will be asking a lot of questions; are you going to tell them about the note Susan wrote to you?'

'I'm not sure,' I said. 'Perhaps I'd better, but the last thing I want is to make mischief for the school by suggesting that it's a hotbed of Nazi espionage.'

'I suppose they'll have to be told everything,' Sinclair said.

'Probably they'll hear about it from Dawes,' I said. 'They're sure to ask him a lot of questions. Do you know how Dawes is taking the whole thing?'

'No, no, I've no idea,' Sinclair said. 'Why do you ask? No doubt he's terribly upset.'

'Yes, of course,' I said. 'They were devoted to each other, then?'

'Oh, yes,' Sinclair replied. 'I should have thought they were obviously devoted to each other. Rather too obviously, perhaps.'

I meditated, and then asked him what he meant.

'Why, only that Dawes is rather a demonstrative person, isn't he?' Sinclair said.

'You didn't mean,' I asked, 'that he pretended to be more fond of his wife than he actually was?'

'No, no,' Sinclair replied with some indignation. 'No, he was very fond of her. I'm sure of that. Why are you asking all this?'

'Well,' I replied, 'I was sent for to find about the origin of those fires and the whole inquiry's widened now, but I've been told not to give it up, and if I'm going to find out anything I must ask some apparently heartless questions. And if a woman's been murdered it's obviously necessary to ask whether there's any possible reason to suspect her husband. There's no harm in suggesting such a thing, because it's likely to suggest itself to everybody else.'

'Yes, I see,' said Sinclair. 'No doubt it's different for an outsider, and every possibility has got to be considered. But do you really think that Dawes might have killed his wife? I should have thought...'

'I haven't any reason for thinking so, or for not thinking so,' I said.

'Quite so,' he replied.

'Then as we're on the subject, there's the obvious question: were either Dawes or his wife unfaithful to each other?'

'I've no idea,' Sinclair replied.

'I should have thought that in a place like this,' I said, 'you, like everyone else, would have heard all the gossip there is.'

'I'm afraid,' he said, 'that I'm not much of a hand at gossip.'

He did not seem to be in a communicative mood, so I made to leave him, and suggested that if he ever heard anything that might be useful to me he might let me know. He agreed, and said good-bye amiably enough, but I felt that he would be glad to get back to his studio and to its atmosphere of disinterested concentration. We had been walking rather slowly, and by this time had almost reached the studio: Sinclair quickened his pace after he left me and was soon at his door. I decided that I had better hurry back to the Dower House since I might be wanted for a conference with the police. I must confess that I was growing much more interested in my inquiry now that something definite had happened.

Chapter Five

On my way to the Dower House I tried to arrange my mind on the subject of murderers and to prepare my mind for the possibility of meeting one. Hitherto they had been no more than units in my statistical tables, and even when any of them were more than usually interesting, like the Dusseldorf twins who had killed precisely eight women each, my imagination was still incapable of seeing them as individuals or of endowing them with plausible characters of their own. If I imagined the Dusseldorf twins at all, it was as obviously shifty and menacing creatures, as transparently up to no good as the card-sharpers, whose bluff pretence of good fellowship, when I once met them in a train, seemed to me so ridiculously inadequate. But experts, so I understand, always say that murderers are just like anyone else, whatever that may mean. No doubt this is true, though one cannot help feeling that only his presumably imbecile victims could have failed to see that there was something wrong with Joseph Smith. It was certainly best to assume that the murderer of Mrs. Dawes might be any of a number of apparently harmless people, though it still seemed to me a strangely academic speculation to wonder whether Dupuy had himself taken, in order to disarm suspicion, a small dose of the poison which he had given to Mrs. Dawes, or to wonder whether Hickman, since Mrs. Dawes was poisoned in his house, had not had a better opportunity to murder her than anyone else. It was a more familiar type of speculation to wonder whether Mrs. Dawes had had a lover, but equally farfetched, so I felt, to wonder whether this gave Dawes a motive for murdering her. And I was reluctant to consider the possibility that the extremely intelligent Rosenberg might have killed Mrs. Dawes in order to prevent her denouncing him.

The chief constable, a Colonel Redder, a Superintendent Julian, Edgeworth, and Mrs. Eakins were all sitting together when I returned to the Dower House. I could not imagine how they had succeeded in excluding Caroline from their council, but no doubt Mrs. Eakins had managed it. The old girl seemed to have been given a new lease of life, and was now pulling strings for all she was worth. Every word she uttered seemed designed for an admiring audience of whose presence she appeared to be acutely aware; this, she seemed to be saying, is how England is governed, by a quiet word here, a tactful silence there, with nothing formal, nothing underlined, and everything a question of *timing*. It was like a meeting of the Souls, if one can venture to imagine so esoteric a gathering, and I could see that neither Colonel Redder nor the superintendent were at all comfortable, though for the moment completely under the old lady's thumb. If she went on much longer, I felt that they would inevitably burst out and perhaps arrest the head master or declare that the whole school must be suppressed as a disorderly house. But when I came in, though I could see that Mrs. Eakins was not at all pleased with me and probably thought I had done wrong in going off by myself at a time like this, she managed to achieve, when she had finished what she was saying, a perfectly genuine example of tact and timing. She left us to ourselves, explaining that she was sure Colonel Redder and I would be glad of a confidential talk. Edgeworth was to stay, in case there was any information about the school that he could give. Mrs. Eakins walked impressively to the door and turned as she reached it. 'You know,' she said, 'that I'm only speaking on behalf of the whole school when I say that we're all of us only too anxious to do anything we can.'

Colonel Redder was about sixty years of age, very active and upright in figure, with a moustache and a single eyeglass, in every way so typical that I had blinked when I first saw him, as if he had been too overt a caricature of his type. His manner of talking, on this explicitly informal occasion, seemed to be a deliberate attempt to moderate the bark of the parade ground; he was studiously at ease, confidential, speaking in an aside so that the troops should not overhear what had been decided, as between men of the world, among the officers. And now that Mrs. Eakins had left the room he relaxed yet further, as at a dinner party when the women have just gone up to the drawing-room.

'I take it,' he said, 'there's some sort of love affair at the bottom of all this trouble... there always is. Very unpleasant, of course,' here he turned to Edgeworth—'but it's not always necessary for everything to come out, you know. All we want is enough to hang our man.'

'Yes, I suppose so,' said Edgeworth, in a quiet and rather miserable voice. His own *savoir-faire*, as conspicuous as that of Colonel Redder when I had talked with him before Susan's death, now seemed to have been disintegrated by the calamity, and he made little attempt to hold his own. Colonel Redder seemed to think he needed cheering up.

'We'll see what we can do,' he said, in a tone of hearty encouragement. 'I understand your position, and you understand ours. You can trust me to see what's relevant and what isn't.'

Here I thought I had better come out with my information about Susan's spies. I told Colonel Redder about her theories, and I explained that I had received a note, not long before her death, in which she claimed to have made another discovery.

'Naturally,' I said, 'I very much regret that I didn't ask her at once what it was she knew, but as it is her death prevented her from telling me anything about her new discovery, if it was one.'

Colonel Redder turned to Superintendent Julian. 'You'd better get in touch with the special branch about that,' he said. 'It's their line rather than ours, and they'll probably know if Mrs. Dawes could have been on the right track. Until we hear it'd be a waste of time for us to consider it, and, anyway, if it's that sort of case they'll have to do most of the work.'

'I can't believe it,' Edgeworth interrupted. 'I'm afraid Mrs. Dawes was what might be called an imaginative sort of person.'

'Oh, that sort, was she?' said Colonel Redder. 'Well, no doubt you're right, but we'd better be on the safe side and just make the proper inquiries.'

'Yes, sir,' said Julian.

'Well,' said Edgeworth, 'if there's nothing more I can do...'

'No, that's all right,' said Colonel Redder. 'Want to get back to your Latin, I expect?'

'I'll leave you, then,' said Edgeworth. 'I told you that Hardwicke had very kindly consented to come down to help us, about the fires, you know?'

'Yes, yes,' said Colonel Redder, and Edgeworth left the room.

'Funny sort of case,' said Colonel Redder, turning to me. 'These fires, I mean, though I've heard of that kind of thing happening at several schools. Did you get anything about them?'

'Not much, I'm afraid,' I said.

'No, very difficult for you,' the Colonel said, quite sympathetically.

'And now I suppose you want to know whether this present business has anything to do with your side of the case. Edgeworth had an idea you might be able to help us as well. Of course, they're a queer lot of blighters in this school, all right in their own way, I dare say, though I never cared much for school masters myself. Beastly job, rather like a parson's. If you think you know how to talk to them, you might be able to help us, I suppose. We might get you to ask some questions... here and there... and you might get better answers than we should... I should like to make things easy for Mrs. Eakins and if that's what she wants, I see no great harm in it.'

Colonel Redder's invitation was stiff with concealed reservations, but I decided to accept it, and not in the spirit in which it was offered.

'It's all a lot of rot,' he continued, 'if you ask me. Wasting all our time because a hysterical woman has gone to a better world. They say there's a surplus of two million women as it is.'

'Perhaps,' I answered, 'the murderer will turn out to be a woman. Poison is supposed to be mostly used by women, isn't it? And then you'll be reducing the surplus still more.'

'Something in that,' said Colonel Redder. 'Well now,' he added, turning briskly towards Julian, 'what about the scene of crime?'

'Briggs was sent round to Dr. Hickman's house last night, sir,' answered Julian.

'Yes, of course,' Colonel Redder answered. 'We'll be getting along then.' He seemed to be wondering what to do with me.

'I was at the party myself,' I said. 'Perhaps I could help you if you're going along to Hickman's house now. I could tell you where people were, and what they did, and so on.'

'Well, perhaps you could,' said the Colonel, and so we drove in his car to Hickman's house.

'Mrs. Eakins,' he said, as we were driving, 'seems to know a devil of a lot of people, a devil of a lot of politicians, too.'

'Oh, does she?' I asked, innocently enough and without, I hope, allowing the Colonel to see that I understood why he had allowed me such unusual privileges. I also took this opportunity to tell him that according to Rimmle some atropine had been mixed with boracic either in his own or in Rosenberg's laboratory. He seemed pleased with this information, though he didn't quite understand it, and directed Julian to interview both Rimmle and Rosenberg as soon as convenient.

Hickman was waiting for us, and at Colonel Redder's request began to explain what had happened the night before and how a bottle party worked. Julian took notes.

'Let's have a look at it,' said the Colonel, and we walked into the largest of the downstair rooms.

'God, what a mess,' he exclaimed. 'I haven't seen anything like this for a long time. I suppose,' he added turning to Hickman, 'you've got a frightful head this morning?'

'Not particularly,' said Hickman, but if he was attempting to wither the colonel's joviality by a stiff and distant manner he certainly failed.

'I'll bet you have,' Colonel Redder said. The spectacle of the disordered room seemed to have given him a new respect for school masters.

'Well, which is the poisoned bottle?' he asked.

'I don't know at all,' Hickman answered.

'What I don't see,' Colonel Redder said, 'is why everyone wasn't poisoned. There aren't any bottles here that have been left nearly full, or we might think that Mrs. Dawes had the first glass out of the bottle and no one else had touched the stuff.'

'But even so,' I suggested, 'the murderer couldn't have known that no one else would take a drink from the same bottle as she. He can't have meant to take the risk of poisoning a whole room full of people on the chance of getting the right one. At least, I hope not.'

'No, that's right,' said the Colonel.

'If you'll excuse me, sir,' said Julian, 'I don't think it can have been done that way. The poison must have been put straight into Mrs. Dawes's glass, I should think.'

'What do you think about that?' Colonel Redder asked me.

'I don't know,' I said. 'Naturally I didn't keep my eye on Mrs. Dawes the whole time, and I wasn't in the room for some time before she was taken ill.'

'Oh, weren't you?' Colonel Redder said. No doubt he felt that I was not going to be as useful as I had pretended. 'What about you?' he continued, addressing Hickman.

'I suppose it's quite possible,' answered Hickman. 'It's all a question of how much people would notice, isn't it?'

'People don't notice much,' said Julian. 'My experience is that witnesses never have seen as much as they pretend; that's one of our chief difficulties.'

'Well, which was her glass then?' Colonel Redder asked.

'I've no idea,' said Hickman.

'I suppose you can find out from fingerprints,' I suggested.

'We might,' said Julian, 'but very likely there'll be too many fingerprints over everything for that to be much good. Some of the glasses have got a little drink left in them,' he added. 'We'll have to find out if the poison had much taste; if it had, it's more than likely that Mrs. Dawes would not finish her glass, if it tasted at all queer.'

'Yes, that's all very well,' I said, 'but how about Dupuy?'

'You mean he must have drunk the same stuff, sir?' said Julian. For the first time he seemed to take some faint interest in anything I said.

'Yes,' I said, 'and that seems to make it rather more likely that the poison came out of a bottle instead of being put straight into Mrs. Dawes's glass. It looks as if he and Mrs. Dawes had taken or been given a drink from the same bottle. But it's not conclusive, of course.'

'Well, we must certainly have what's left in all the bottles analysed as well,' said Julian. 'That's a matter of course. It's not much use speculating until we've got some more facts to go on. I suppose these are all the bottles there are?' he added, turning to Hickman and indicating the many bottles on the table that had served as a bar.

'There's one over there,' Hickman said, pointing to a bottle that stood on a chest of drawers at the other end of the room.

'There's another in the hall,' Constable Briggs said, speaking for the first time. He seemed nervous in the presence of his superior officers, and anxious to make a good impression. 'And there's a bottle and a lot of glasses on the verandah,' he added.

'We'll have to have the whole house searched,' said Colonel Redder, and he suggested that Briggs might begin at once.

'I'll look round later myself,' Julian said to Briggs. 'You'd better not move anything.'

'No, sir,' said Briggs. 'I'll just take notes of what I find.'

'Particularly bottles,' said Colonel Redder.

'Where were you,' Julian asked me, 'when you weren't in this room? Not long before Mrs. Dawes was taken ill, I think you said it was.'

'I was out in the garden,' I answered.

'Oh, the garden,' Julian said. 'Did you see anyone else there?'

'There were a few other people there,' I answered, 'but it was rather dark, and I didn't recognize anyone particularly. I went out because it was hot and stuffy indoors.'

'The garden had better be searched, too,' said the Colonel.

'Of course, sir,' said Julian.

'There'll be a devil of a lot of work in all this,' said the Colonel. 'God knows how many bottles to be analysed and God knows how many glasses, fingerprints to be looked for everywhere, all the people at the party to be interviewed, hundreds of statements to be checked. And you'll have to make a list of all the bottles that were brought to the party and who brought them.'

'Yes, sir,' answered Julian. He appeared not in the least distressed by this prospect.

'My God, I'm glad it's your job and not mine,' Colonel Redder said.

'We'll get things straight in the end, I expect,' Julian said.

'I wish you'd get this room straight,' Hickman said, 'or let me get it tidied. All this mess is very depressing, and it means I have to live in my consulting room. I kept that locked up last night.'

'We'll make our examination as soon as possible,' Julian answered. 'By the way,' he continued, 'I suppose you don't remember anybody in particular handing a drink to Mrs. Dawes, or anything of that kind?'

'Well now, let me see,' Hickman said. 'I think sherry was her drink. Of course it was my business to look after the drinks, up to a point, but people helped themselves a good deal as well and I didn't stand by the bar the whole time. But I seem to remember Dawes getting his wife a drink. Now why do I remember that?'

Julian waited patiently.

'Oh yes,' Hickman continued. 'I remember that I asked him if he wanted a clean glass, because he held out a glass which wasn't quite empty. Now, did he take a clean glass or not? I'm afraid I can't be sure of that.'

'You seem to have a pretty good memory,' said Colonel Redder.

'Oh well, a psycho-analyst has to train his memory for details,' said Hickman.

'But you don't remember anyone else getting Mrs. Dawes a drink?' asked Julian.

'Well, let me try and think,' Hickman answered. 'Oh yes, Sinclair, I think it was, got her a drink. I remember that, because he opened a new bottle of sherry. I thought of pointing out to him that there was another bottle half-full, but then I thought he might imagine I was trying to keep a bottle unopened so that I could collar it for myself at the end of the party. It used to be a joke that some people did that when they gave bottle parties and, in fact, used them as an opportunity to replenish their cellars, but I don't suppose it ever happened really.'

'And did anyone else have any more sherry out of that bottle, either then or later?' Julian asked.

'Oh yes,' Hickman answered. 'I remember taking the bottle from Sinclair and pouring out three or four drinks for various people.'

'Did Mrs. Dawes have any more sherry after that?' Julian asked.

'I think she helped herself to a glass or two,' Hickman answered. 'I don't remember how many, but I think more than one. That must have been when she was in this room, of course. Part of the time she was probably in the verandah or the garden and that's why she must have sent people in to fill up her glass. I expect she came in when it got colder. Of course, a lot of people poured out drinks without my knowing who they were for.'

'Yes,' said Julian, 'and no doubt the murderer would be particularly careful not to attract your attention.'

'That seems reasonable,' said Hickman. 'I dare say you've noticed,' he continued, 'that when people are getting a drink for somebody else, they are always rather careful to say so. A kind of defence mechanism, perhaps, as if they were always ashamed of getting a drink for themselves and correspondingly glad to put the blame on somebody else. But, of course, the murderer would be hardly likely to give himself away like that.'

'Can you give me any idea about the order in which these drinks were poured out?' Julian asked.

'That's much more difficult,' said Hickman, 'I think Susan poured out a drink for herself—or did I pour it out for her?—rather early in the evening, and then I remember she had one rather late, not long before she was taken ill. The atropine might have made her thirsty, you know. The rest of the drinks must have come in between, but I'm afraid I can't get it clearer than that. You've got to remember that heaps of other people were getting drinks all the while, and I wasn't standing by the bar the whole time. For example, I was arranging for my unfortunate quartet—some children I'd asked to come and sing to the party. It might have been while I was with the quartet that Mrs. Dawes was given the poison.'

'More than likely,' agreed Julian, and closed the book in which he had been taking some notes.

'Mrs. Dawes seems to have helped herself pretty freely to the sherry,' said Colonel Redder.

'Oh, I don't know,' said Hickman. 'She was fond of sherry, no doubt, and she may have taken half a dozen glasses. Enough to make her reasonably merry without being drunk. She used to drink more than her husband, and I have a vague idea that he rather disapproved, though he wouldn't be likely to say so for fear of being thought puritanical.'

Colonel Redder seemed to be bored by these details and perhaps his tidy mind was beginning to be revolted by the squalor of the room and the dilapidated remains of the party.

'How would it be,' he suddenly said, 'if I had a word with this Dupuy? He hasn't left the house yet, has he?'

'No,' said Hickman.

'Well, I've got ten minutes or so to spare,' Colonel Redder said. 'I'll just have a word with him and then leave you to it, Julian.'

I didn't suppose that Dupuy would be able to tell the Colonel any more than he had told me, so I made no effort to go upstairs with him. Moreover, I wanted to see how Julian was going to tackle the shocking muddle downstairs.

'I don't see how you'll ever manage it,' I said. 'Would it be a good idea to have the whole thing photographed, and then you could see where every bottle and glass was?'

'Well, we might do that,' he answered, 'but I think it would be better to make a kind of plan and label each bottle and glass to correspond with its position on the map. I'll set that in train this afternoon, and then we'll cart the lot away for the analyst to get to work on. Where did you say Mrs. Dawes was,' he asked Hickman, 'when she was taken ill?'

Hickman pointed to a corner by a window; there was a book case near by with several small tumblers on the top.

'Then perhaps one of those glasses will be hers,' said Julian. 'There doesn't seem to be much left in any of them, though. But there may be just enough for the analyst.'

Colonel Redder soon returned and reported that Dupuy had been no damn use to him. He advised the superintendent to get a formal statement from him later, and then he went about his business. I walked out into the garden, which I had not yet seen by daylight. There I found Constable Briggs poking about under some trees.

'I don't know what you expect to find there,' I said.

'Nothing particular, sir,' he answered. 'This is just routine.'

'I don't know why you don't sift those leaves,' I said, pointing to a large heap of leaf-mould by the potting shed. 'That would be just the place to hide something.' I was amused by Briggs's thoroughness and the solemn manner in which he was making his conscientious search, and I suppose I thought I might as well go one better. I walked over to the heap and there, sure enough, was the top of a bottle, with a cork in it, just protruding above the leaves. It was very inadequately hidden, but some leaves might have blown away and revealed it. I pointed it out to Constable Briggs.

'Ah, there it is, no doubt,' he said, with some excitement in his voice. 'Or it may be nothing, of course,' he added.

I was just about to reach down and pick up the bottle when he stopped me.

'I'd better ask the superintendent to come and see this,' he said.

'Ah,' I said, impressively, 'nothing must be touched, must it?'

Constable Briggs fetched the Superintendent while I stood guard over the bottle. Julian stared at it and did not seem impressed.

'It may have been there for years,' he said, 'but you'd better pick it up with a handkerchief and bring it indoors. I suppose I'd better get it labelled and put with the others.'

As Briggs lifted it carefully from amongst the leaves, I saw that it was labelled 'Genuine Fino Sherry', a label which I had noticed on other bottles within the house, and that there seemed to be some liquid still remaining at the bottom of the bottle. That seemed to be all for the moment, and it hardly seemed worth waiting to see the police packing and counting and labelling and measuring all the afternoon.

Chapter Six

A t luncheon, when Caroline and I were again left alone, I discovered why she had been absent when I first met Colonel
Redder and Superintendent Julian. Mrs. Eakins had asked her to
go and have a talk with Miss Symonds, the matron, who, according
to Mrs. Eakins, had been greatly distressed by the death of Susan
Dawes. 'But when I got there,' Caroline said, 'she seemed very
surprised to see me, and not in the least disturbed, as far as I could
see, by Susan's death.'

'We are all in the hands of Mrs. Eakins,' I said.

'I had the impression,' said Caroline, 'that Miss Symonds thought
murder much less distressing than what she calls flesh-eating.'

'I don't believe,' I said, 'that vegetarians really mind even animals
being killed; what they can't bear is the idea of eating them. They
never seem to object to wearing leather shoes. But why should Miss
Symonds be upset about the death of Susan, anyway? Was she at
the party?'

'I didn't notice her at the time,' Caroline said. 'But she told me
that she'd looked in for a short while, though she left before Susan
was taken ill. She said that she went to the party because she was
afraid that people might think that she disapproved if she didn't go,
from which I inferred that in fact she did disapprove.'

'Why should she?' I asked.

'She said she didn't like the idea of drinking fruit-juice after it
had gone bad,' Caroline told me.

'I can't imagine why she stays on here,' I said. 'It's quite obvious that her nonsense doesn't suit the nonsense of the rest of the people here. Do you think she murdered Susan because Susan didn't believe in the transmigration of souls and Miss Symonds wanted her to see that it was true? That would be a good motive.'

'She's not a bad sort really,' Caroline said. 'She was upset because those children—the ones who sang in the quartet—were at the party, but of course they'd left before Susan was taken ill. I cheered her up by pointing this out, but she still thought they oughtn't to have gone to a party like that.'

'Perhaps they oughtn't,' I said. 'But after all they were all about sixteen or so, weren't they, and I don't know that anything very awful happened while they were there. Nobody was at all intoxicated then, at any rate.'

'I've no doubt they thoroughly enjoyed it, and all the more because Susan was poisoned there,' Caroline said. 'That's really what seems to have upset Miss Symonds. She'd been seeing one of the girls who sang in Hickman's quartet; I don't know what she expects, she seems to have a wholly idealized view of the nature of children. But what exactly,' she continued, 'are you going to do now? Are you really going to try to find out who poisoned poor Susan?'

'I'm not at all sure,' I said. 'But I do think I ought to do something more about those fires.'

'Why?' asked Caroline. 'I should have thought they'd matter much less now that something worse has happened.'

'Well, there is that,' I said, 'but then I feel that I ought to find out if possible whether there's any connection between the fires and the murder. I should be within my rights if I went on with that particular side of the investigation and I must confess I'm really getting very curious about the whole matter.'

'I thought that might happen,' said Caroline.

I suggested that she might see Edgeworth and get from him a really complete and dated list of the fires, and then perhaps we might examine in turn all the places where the fires had broken out. I thought that Caroline might for once condescend to act as secretary. Rather to my surprise she agreed to do this, and later we went over the list together. The fires, arranged in chronological order, ran as follows:—

May 3rd, 1939		Walton's farm (two haystacks and some farm buildings burnt down).
May 8th,	"	Fire under the laboratory stairs.
May 15th,	"	Large pile of books found on fire in the grate in a recreation room.
May 20th,	"	Paper set on fire in lavatories.
May 23rd,	"	Small shed, used for storing garden tools, etc., burnt down.

There had been no fire after this last date, but possibly this was the result of the constant vigilance of the staff and of the school's voluntary fire brigade. I remembered that in Edgeworth's opinion there was no real reason to think that the fire at Walton's farm was the work of the Scrope House pyromaniac, but Caroline seemed to think that this was very uncertain.

'The farm is some way from the school,' she said, 'but the children often go there when they feel like it. There's some idea that it's good for them and they're encouraged to pay visits there, even if they don't actually go to work there, as some of them do. I think the idea is that they should learn the facts of life from watching the farm animals. There's an arrangement with Walton to let them come and hang around when they want to, and the school buys a lot of milk and butter so that he would want to oblige them. But I should think it must be rather a nuisance for him.'

'There's no real reason,' I pointed out, 'to suppose that any of the fires are connected. It always seems to me mere superstition to believe that similar effects must have similar causes. There's Ockham's razor, of course, but I've always wondered whether we didn't take it too seriously. I shouldn't be a bit surprised if the universe wasn't entirely chaotic and our desire to find some connection between its events a mere unjustifiable attempt to make it seem more cosy. That's what I like about statistics; you write them down and leave it to others, if they want to, to find evidence in them of cause and effect.'

'That's hardly what a detective is expected to do,' said Caroline.

Perhaps not,' I said, 'but even so it might be as well, not for philosophical reasons but merely in order to obey the ordinary rules of scientific inquiry, to consider the possibility that there was no connection between any of these fires.'

'It's obviously too much of a coincidence,' said Caroline. 'After all, we're not here to indulge our vanity by illustrating our capacity for an academic suspension of disbelief. Isn't there something in Newton's Principia about assigning the same cause to the fall of different bodies in different parts of the earth? We might as well stick to Newton for purposes of detection.'

I agreed that the detective could not afford to be too scrupulous and that his was not really an exact science. I suggested that we might go along at once and pay a call on Walton to try to find out whether any of the schoolchildren were about the farm on May the third. It was a beautiful evening and the walk would do us good.

We were fortunate enough to meet Walton riding back to his farm on a tractor. He stopped the machine outside some sheds and a few words about the wonders of modern machinery—Caroline seemed to think that her acquaintance with Russian films had made her an expert on tractors—were amiably received by him. No doubt he had recognized that we came from Scrope House and, since the school was one of his best customers, was anxious to be as polite as his nature would allow. We could see where some sheds had been burned down, and so were able to bring up the subject of the fires.

'I wouldn't send my children to Scrope House,' the farmer confided in us, 'even if I could afford it. I've got no quarrel with the school authorities, but all the same, a place where the children are allowed to run wild and play with fire without anyone stopping them... What else can you expect but trouble?'

'I can't quite see why they should go setting fire to your buildings,' said Caroline, 'just because the school doesn't make too many rules.'

'I'm not saying they did,' said Walton, 'but all the same they're about the place the whole time, and then you know what they've been doing down at the school itself. I shouldn't feel safe in my bed if I were there. And there's been this murder; it's all over the papers. I shouldn't think that would do the school too much good.'

'Why, you don't think,' Caroline asked, 'that that has anything to do with the fires, do you?'

'I never said it had,' Walton answered. 'Don't see how it could.'

'Some people think it might,' said Caroline, most injudiciously, as I thought.

'Some people will think anything,' Walton said. 'But it's no wonder there's a lot of gossip.'

I thought we had better get back to the subject of the fire at Walton's farm and asked if it had been very serious.

'Serious enough,' Walton answered.

'But you can't be sure it was any of the Scrope House children?' Caroline asked.

'I've got my own ideas,' said Walton. 'And with all the other fires too... it stands to reason.'

'Oh well, I suppose the insurance has put you right,' said Caroline.

'Insurance isn't always what it's cracked up to be,' Walton answered, 'and as it happens the fire didn't catch one of the sheds I'd have been specially glad to be rid of.'

'It's always the way,' said Caroline brightly.

'But were there any children about on the day the fire started?' I asked.

'That's what I've been asked a hundred times,' Walton answered. His voice was rather sulky but I thought I could understand his annoyance. 'They're always here, as I'm telling you,' he continued. 'There's two of them coming along now.' He pointed to two boys coming up the track towards us about a hundred yards away.

We took our leave and when we were out of Walton's hearing I asked Caroline what she thought of this conversation.

'Impossible to say,' she answered. 'We didn't get much out of Walton, did we? I expect he's what they call a warm man, close, secretive, and intensely acquisitive. Farmers always are.'

'In literature, perhaps,' I conceded.

'Did you notice that he didn't seem to like the idea that there was any connection between the fires and the murder?' Caroline asked me. 'He got quite excited about it. I wonder why.'

'I don't see much in that,' I answered.

'There may be something in it,' Caroline said.

'There may be, but what?' I asked.

'Well, perhaps he doesn't want anyone to establish the smallest connection between the fires and the murder, and thus between himself and the murder,' Caroline suggested.

'Do you mean, because he's the murderer himself, or somehow responsible for it?' I asked. 'Really, Caroline, if you go on like that we shall never come to an end. You remind me of Madame Tabouis explaining what's in Hitler's mind.'

We were passing a group of cottages collected round a pub, which Caroline suggested we might visit.

'We can get all the drinks anyone could possibly want at the Dower House,' I said.

'A visit to a pub's a social occasion,' said Caroline. 'You don't go there just to drink.'

I saw it was no use protesting any longer and resigned myself to the misery of intruding on the peaceful entertainment of the rustics, who would obviously think me, and still more Caroline, very much in the way. I remembered an occasion when I had gone into a village pub, and on that occasion only with a man and not with a woman; in a very short while four or five young men had finished their drinks, which they normally took half an hour to get through, and had left the pub, not with any black looks but still in a sufficiently marked fashion to make me feel most uncomfortable. The landlord explained that any strangers upset them; he thought it silly, but there it was, and it wasn't good for trade. It has always seemed to me that a village inn ought to be treated as a club, and just because its customers cannot afford to isolate their club from strangers and women as efficiently as the members of the Athenæum, that is certainly not a good reason for annoying them. But Caroline seemed actually to imagine that she was welcome and ordered her bitter in a very knowing way, starting a conversation with the landlord about its qualities. After some desultory talk about the weather and whether many strangers came that way, Caroline told the landlord, and anyone else among his half-dozen or so customers who might be listening, that we had been past Walton's farm and had noticed that there had been a fire there.

'How did it start?' she asked. 'Was it a haystack that caught alight on its own?'

'Some say it couldn't have been,' said the landlord. 'Not the right time of year. Some put it down to the schoolchildren.'

'I suppose schoolchildren might have been careless,' Caroline said. 'You don't mean anyone thinks they did it deliberately?'

'Ah, that's more than I can say,' answered the landlord. 'But that's what Mr. Walton and some others think, and then, of course, there's been other fires, too.'

'Still,' I said, 'you can't be sure they were all started by the same person.'

'That's right,' agreed a man standing by the bar, a farm labourer as he appeared to be. 'You never know with fires,' he continued, 'and there's some say it was the insurance. There were two good stacks went, as well as the buildings.'

'What's a stack worth in these parts?' asked Caroline, in her role as agricultural expert.

'Well, it varies,' said the landlord.

'Did they get the police in?' I asked.

'Talking of police,' said the farm labourer who had spoken before, 'that's a queer thing happened down at the school. I dare say you read about it in the paper. You don't happen to come from the school yourself, do you?'

'Well, in a sense I do,' I replied. 'I'm just staying with friends there.'

'Were you there when it happened?' asked the landlord.

'Yes I was, I'm afraid,' I said.

The whole company began to pay attention and were obviously waiting for me to give them full and gripping details of this melo-dramatic event, but I did not feel that this was a good idea and so I remained uncommunicative, saying that I really knew no more than I had read in the papers. After a short while Caroline and I left the pub and we almost immediately fell into the hands of even more persistently curious inquirers. As we got out into the road we saw two boys from Scrope House, probably, as I thought, the two boys whom we had previously seen walking towards Walton's farm. They were now with another lad, a little older-looking than they and of more bucolic appearance, who wore a school cap which had nothing to do with Scrope House, where any such badge or mark was carefully avoided as likely to encourage the team-spirit and *esprit de corps*. When the two boys from Scrope House saw us they at once deserted their companion and came over to us. I recognized them as the two boys who had sung in the quartet at Hickman's party and I suppose they must have recognized me and have hoped for a special and thrilling interview with a private detective about the murder which they had themselves all but witnessed. Their first questions were all directed towards extracting some inside information, but as I discouraged their inquiries they saw eventually that it was no good and walked along beside us in silence. Then the older of the two boys abruptly changed the subject and asked me what school I had been at. I told him and he then asked me whether there had been prefects or monitors or anything of that kind there.

'Not exactly,' I said, 'but each house had a ruling oligarchy, not elected by democratic vote, you understand, but co-opted each year by those who already belonged to it. Then there was a supreme oligarchy, chosen from amongst the whole school. They were allowed to wear coloured waistcoats and a flower in their buttonholes, to turn their coat collars down, to roll up their umbrellas, to walk arm in arm, and to put sealing-wax on their hats.'

'Sealing wax?' exclaimed the boy.

'Yes, sealing wax,' I answered, 'and I think they could put it on their books and on the handles of their umbrellas, too.'

These details seemed to be of absorbing interest to the two boys and for a moment or two they were silent while they digested them. Then the older boy began again.

'Ted Walton,' he said, 'that's the chap we were talking to just now, says that at the grammar school they're not allowed to wear coloured socks until they've been at the school for three years. He'll be wearing coloured socks next term.'

'Oh yes,' I said, 'but you can wear coloured socks when you like, can't you?'

'Yes, of course,' he answered, 'but it's not the same thing. Anyone can wear anything here.'

'And why not?' I asked.

'It's not the same thing,' he persisted. 'Ted Walton says that in their first year at his school the chaps have to keep all the buttons on their coat buttoned up, then they're allowed to unbutton one button for each year they've been there. That's why they always have three buttons on their coats.'

'And what happens when they've been there four years?' I asked.

'Oh, then they become bloods,' he answered. 'But, I say, what did they do to the new boys at your school?'

'Oh, nothing much,' I answered, 'but there was the usual system of greater hardships and fewer privileges at the beginning of one's sentence.'

'Was there any fagging?' I was asked.

'Oh Lord, yes,' I answered, 'any amount of forced labour. And while we're on the subject,' I continued, 'would you like to know how often you can receive letters in your first year at Pentonville?'

At first both boys merely blinked at me, and then the younger asked, in accents of awe: 'Have you been in prison as well?'

'No, not as well,' I answered, 'once is quite enough.'

'Don't be so tiresome,' Caroline interposed. 'Can't you tell them what they want to know without making so much fuss?'

Encouraged by this the older boy pursued his investigation.

'Didn't the new boys,' he said, 'have to do something to show that they really belonged to the school, if you see what I mean? A boy I knew in the holidays…'

'In the hols,' interrupted the younger boy, gently correcting him.

'In the hols then…' the older boy went on. 'A boy I knew told me that at his school the new boys have to eat porridge with ashes all over it.'

'It wasn't as bad as that at my school,' I answered. 'But in college, that's the house where all the scholars lived together, the new boys had to sing a song in front of everyone else.'

'And I suppose,' my inquisitor went on, 'that if they couldn't sing they were beaten or something?'

'Well, no, I can't say they were,' I answered. 'In fact, however badly you sang I think the audience was very patient and always applauded.'

The boys seemed disappointed at these marks of over-civilized weakness, so to cheer them up I went on.

'But in Australia,' I said, 'the initiation ceremonies go on for years and years, and at one point the younger boys stand in a row and their elders throw pieces of raw liver at their mouths and they have to catch and swallow the pieces. If they touch the liver with their hands they die, and if they can't keep it down or even if they attempt to bite it up, however big a piece it may be, they die. They aren't killed or anything like that; they just die on their own, because they've failed.'

'Cool!' exclaimed the older boy, expressing both amazement and satisfaction.

'Is that a school in Australia?' the younger boy asked.

'No, not a school exactly,' I answered. 'I was talking about the Australian natives. It's a custom...'

'A custom more honoured in the breach than in the observance,' the younger boy said, intoning the words and striking a dramatic attitude.

'I should think so,' said Caroline. 'You're not thinking of throwing liver at the new boys at Scrope House, are you?'

'Oh no,' the older boy answered. 'It wouldn't be any good. At Scrope House they wouldn't feel they'd got to catch it or anything; they just wouldn't pay much attention, I expect.'

'I expect so,' I said.

'Besides,' he continued, 'there are all the girls, and they've got no idea how to behave.'

'In Australia,' I said, 'no woman is allowed to come within a mile of an initiation ceremony.'

'It wouldn't be like that at Scrope,' said the boy. 'But we'll tell Ted Walton about it.'

'You think he might try it at his school?' I asked with some anxiety. 'Really, I wouldn't advise... I never thought...'

'Oh no,' the boy reassured me. 'They wouldn't try anything new there. They've got all their own customs there and wouldn't think of changing anything.'

'Ted Walton's the farmer's son, I suppose?' Caroline asked.

The younger boy told us that he was and that he went to his school every day by bus, but by now it was time for us to turn off for the Dower House, if we were not to be very late for dinner, and so we parted with our new acquaintances.

'What do you make of that?' Caroline asked, when the boys had gone their way. 'It doesn't make sense, does it?'

'I'm not sure,' I said. 'I think it's rather interesting.'

'Do you think they are mass-observers or something,' she asked, 'and have been told to study the customs of different schools? It wouldn't be a bad idea for the mass-observers.'

'No, I don't think so,' I said.

After dinner I rang up Hickman and asked him who were the two boys who had sung in the quartet at his house; he told me that Robert Crossley was the older and John Mandeville the younger. I asked Hickman if he knew them at all well.

'I haven't treated them, or anything like that,' he said, 'if that's what you mean.'

I told him that they both appeared to be strangely interested in the more bizarre features of the English public school system. It had seemed to me very puzzling, not altogether agreeable, and my curiosity had been aroused.

'What sort of features of the public school system?' Hickman asked.

'Oh rituals of clothing, initiation ceremonies, licensed bullying, and that kind of thing,' I said.

Hickman seemed to be interested. 'I've always thought that might happen,' he said. 'After all, there's every reason to suppose that the adolescent mind reverts quite normally to the primitive. They're only recapitulating the history of their race. But it would be particularly good if that happened here, where there's absolutely no encouragement. It would be a blow for the diffusionists, wouldn't it, if we could find the boys inventing the whole public school system, absolutely on their own?'

I knew that pyschoanalysts waged perpetual war with the diffusionists, who, of course, believe that the customs of every race originally derive from one country. I therefore did not point out that it was quite impossible, in this instance, to cut out the possibility of outside influence. Even the Scrope House children must talk with boys from other schools, and no doubt even they occasionally read school stories.

'How are you getting on with the police?' I asked him.

'They've taken everything they want away,' Hickman told me. 'It was a tremendous business, everything numbered and labelled and packed into crates, photographs taken, and so on. It would have made a splendid scene in a film. I wish I'd had a film camera.'

'Did they all keep their hats on?' I asked.

'Well, no, I can't say they did,' Hickman answered, 'but they were very professional, for all that. It's a great relief to have got the room tidy again.'

I asked him how Dupuy was, and was told that he was much better. He was leaving Hickman's house next day and would soon be about again.

Chapter Seven

The next day Edgeworth paid a call on me; he said that he wanted to know whether I had any theories, either about the fires or about Susan's murder, but actually, I should think, he wanted to get away from his responsibilities as headmaster and to talk to someone who would not require from him an authoritatively cheerful demeanour. With me he could show how worried he was.

'I've no idea what the police are doing,' he said. 'They're keeping me altogether in the dark.'

'I expect they're in the dark themselves,' I said. 'After all, they've got any number of samples of different drinks to analyse, the dregs from all those bottles and glasses. And then they're looking for fingerprints, which ought to be an interminable job. And then they've got to question everybody who went to the party, to ask them what bottle they brought and whether they saw anything out of the way. They can't possibly have got very far as yet.'

'Yes, they asked me what I brought to the party,' Edgeworth said, 'and whether I saw anything unusual. What would a policeman think unusual? I really can't stand this suspense,' he added. 'It's getting on everybody's nerves. Are you going to see the Chief Constable to-day? I rather wish you would.'

'Do you think he'd want to see me?' I asked.

'I think I could arrange it,' he said. 'By the way, they've been asking poor Dawes a lot of questions.'

'I suppose that's inevitable,' I said. 'You don't happen to know what sort of questions?'

'No,' Edgeworth said, 'but you can find out from the Chief Constable if you want to. You won't want to bother Dawes again yourself, will you?'

'Oh no,' I said. 'But I should like to know more about him. He doesn't seem to be popular with everybody.'

'I think,' Edgeworth said, 'that he's a man whom you either like or dislike a great deal. Personally, I've always liked him, and, of course, he's just the sort of man we want to teach English here. He gets away from the purely academic point of view and that's all the more remarkable because he could be as academic as the best of them if he wanted.'

'Life instead of Literature, you mean?' I said.

'Well, yes, that's more or less what I mean,' he answered.

'Yes, that's what he's always talking about in his books,' I said. 'The only thing is, I've never been able to understand these distinctions between literature and life. It's rather like the distinction between natural and unnatural; I should have thought that anything whatever that happens is natural, unless you care to introduce miracles. And I suppose you're alive when you're reading Shakespeare just as much as when you're climbing up Juliet's balcony.'

'Oh yes,' Edgeworth said, 'but you can see what Dawes means.'

'He probably means that he prefers climbing up Juliet's balcony,' I said. 'The question is: does he often get an opportunity to indulge this preference? I've read some of the things he's written and I've heard him talk, and Caroline has told me what she's heard about him, but I don't really know much about his life. I seem to remember Mrs. Dawes telling me that she married him almost exactly two years ago?'

'I should think it would be about that,' Edgeworth answered.

'And before that?' I asked.

'He wasn't married before, if that's what you mean,' he replied.

'No, no,' I said, 'but had he what is usually known as a past? His poems and even the rest of his writings suggest that he spent most of his time on the tiles, but was it, as I should be inclined to suspect, all a pretty fancy on his part?'

'I really don't know,' said Edgeworth, and his expression suggested that he very much disliked these questions. 'Is it relevant?' he asked.

'Perhaps not,' I said. 'Perhaps the real point is whether Mrs. Dawes had her adventures. But if you look at it from the point of view of the police they're sure to ask, even more crudely than I, whether Dawes murdered his wife because he wanted to get rid of her, or again because she was unfaithful to him.'

'But I'm sure he didn't murder her at all,' said Edgeworth. 'The idea is ridiculous.'

'Yes, but the police are bound to consider it,' I said. 'After all, somebody must have murdered her and whoever it is you would almost certainly find it ridiculous to think of him as a murderer. Is there anyone in the school whom you would care to consider as a possible murderer?'

'There certainly is not,' Edgeworth answered.

'We'd better face the possibility, then,' I said, 'and especially now when we can do so without putting ideas into the heads of the police. If you know that either Dawes or his wife were unfaithful to the other it might be as well to tell me, and then we shall know what we have to face and what to conceal, if we think we could or should do so. For instance—do you know whether Mrs. Dawes had a lover? It might be Sinclair, perhaps; he seems to have gone round pretty often to see her at her house, though I'm bound to say that when I saw them together I saw no signs of any such relationship. Or it might, perhaps, be Dupuy; he seems to be a personable young man and inclined to make up to young women. I must admit that at Hickman's party he spent most of his time hovering round Caroline, but you never know.'

'I suppose we've got to think about all these possibilities,' said Edgeworth. 'But, to tell you the truth, I've always made it my business not to know anything about any love affairs between the staff. It's the only way I could manage without getting myself into a very awkward dilemma. I couldn't object, as the headmaster of an ordinary school would object, to anything but the strictest monogamy—after all, this school exists to produce unconventional people and polygamy is often a symptom of unconventional behaviour in other respects. But equally I might have had to object if any love affair had become too open and obvious. You can imagine that I wouldn't want a lot of idiots going about and saying that the headmaster of Scrope House positively taught free love.'

'Yes, but after all,' I continued remorselessly, 'you must sometimes have had to know exactly what was going on in order to be able to turn a really efficiently blind eye to it.'

'Well, perhaps that has occasionally happened,' Edgeworth reluctantly allowed. 'But really, in this instance, I don't know anything. Oh dear...' he sighed heavily.

'Yes?' I prompted him.

'It was on the tip of my tongue to say that poor Susan would know,' he said.

I must have showed the astonishment I felt. 'Obviously,' I said, 'or did you mean that she would certainly have known if Dawes had had a mistress?'

'No, I'm sorry,' Edgeworth said. 'I only meant that she always seemed to know every piece of gossip that was going about, and if she were alive she would be the obvious person to go to.'

'Well,' I said, 'is there anyone else in the school with the same capacity for collecting gossip?'

'I don't know that there is,' said Edgeworth, 'I only know that I haven't got that capacity. To tell you the truth I'm afraid poor Susan's information was not always entirely reliable.'

It seemed to be no use asking Edgeworth any more questions about Mrs. Dawes or her husband, and I reflected that Caroline would probably be a better hand than I at collecting gossip, if it should prove necessary. Unfortunately it seemed quite likely that the whole staff of Scrope House would band together to suppress all information, for fear that the police should get a misleading impression. That, I imagined, would be a natural instinct at a time like this; probably most of them had very different standards of what was respectable and what was not from those they would attribute to the police. I pointed this out to Edgeworth and expressed a hope that I, at any rate, should be told any awkward facts or even gossip that might come up.

'After all,' I said, 'I'm more likely than the police to understand what's relevant and what isn't. The police must inevitably think in terms of the *faits divers* in the *News of the World*, but I think I can safely say that I understand the sort of people you've got here. In essentials they're my sort of person.'

Edgeworth agreed. 'I wonder,' he said, 'what the police actually are thinking now. I must confess I should like to know where we are. You might be able to find out and, that reminds me, I was going to get on to the chief constable and arrange for him to see you.'

'If you think it's a good idea...' I said.

He remained silent and seemed to be thinking, and I was also silent in the hope that he was thinking over what I had said and perhaps deciding whether to tell me something. This proved to be exactly what he was doing. 'I've just remembered...' he began, though no doubt this was untrue and he had been wondering all along whether he should or should not divulge this particular piece of information.

'I've just remembered something,' he said, 'but I don't think it could have anything to do with the murder. About three years ago and, mind you, this was before Dawes got married or even knew

Susan, there was a good deal of talk which even I couldn't help hearing about Dawes and some woman in London. I don't quite know why there should have been so much talk about it, because, after all, it wasn't anything so very wonderful, even if he did go up to London occasionally to visit some woman. His visits were mostly in the holidays, of course.'

'Do you mean that there was rather more than the usual mild curiosity?' I asked.

'I think there must have been,' said Edgeworth. 'I don't believe I should have heard of it otherwise.'

'Perhaps Dawes himself was responsible for most of the gossip,' I suggested.

'How do you mean?' Edgeworth asked.

'Well, he might have talked in the same way as he writes,' I said. 'There is something rather exhibitionist—don't you think?—in all those love poems, and then look at the way he drags in love even when he's reviewing an anthology of eighteenth century sermons. Possibly Dawes wanted to attract attention to his adventure. Possibly he wanted people to think he was having an adventure when he wasn't having one.'

'Well, now that you mention it,' Edgeworth answered, 'I do remember that someone suggested, rather maliciously, that it was all eyewash and that Dawes only went up to the British Museum reading room. But in any case I don't see that this can have anything to do with Susan's murder.'

'It doesn't look like it,' I said, 'unless, of course, it was a serious affair that's still continuing and Susan was murdered because she got in the way.'

'That seems very unlikely,' Edgeworth answered. 'After all, why should he have married Susan in that case?'

'Why, indeed?' I said. 'But he might have married her and then seen his mistake and gone back to the previous woman.'

'I suppose it's just possible,' said Edgeworth, 'but very unlikely. Anyway, it's certainly not worth telling the police.'

After Edgeworth had gone I discussed what he had told me with Caroline. I wanted her to know in what direction she might most profitably listen to the gossip of the school.

'I think we can certainly conclude,' I said, 'that if Dawes had been unfaithful to Susan, then someone would know something about it. With that temperament, he couldn't have helped giving at least a hint to someone. He wouldn't have enjoyed having a secret unless he let a good many people know that it was there. It would be rather like the way Colonel Lawrence published his books...'

'What's Colonel Lawrence got to do with it?' Caroline asked.

'Well, he published his books so privately that no one could read them and yet so publicly that everyone heard about them; the advance publicity would have made any publisher's mouth water. And, indeed, his whole life was rather like that; consider what happened when he became a retired colonel. If there's one thing you can say about England it is that it provides for the retirement of colonels; there are whole towns which are positively made for them. Why is it, by the way, that although England normally has one of the smallest armies in the world it has the largest number of retired Colonels? Anyway, no retired Colonel need fear that his presence, in any number of agreeable districts, will attract unwelcome publicity. But this sort of seclusion, in the pleasant glades of Cheltenham, was by no means sufficient for Colonel Lawrence; he had to hide himself, under another name, as an aircraftman in the R.A.F. The result, of course, was to arouse a stupendous curiosity and to let innumerable people know of his whereabouts who would not otherwise have troubled to ask. Similarly with Dawes and his secret love affairs; you may be sure that if he had been in the place of Romeo he would somehow have roused the whole Montague and the whole Capulet family to watch him climb the balcony, and no doubt the balcony itself would have been flood-lit.'

'Well, I expect you're exaggerating,' said Caroline. 'But if you're right about Dawes, and if he has been unfaithful to Susan, we ought to have heard about it already.'

'Yes, that's true,' I admitted. 'So perhaps you'd better concentrate on the possibility that Susan was unfaithful, though I can't really think this a very good motive for murder. But the more you find out the better, in any case.'

'If Susan had been unfaithful to him,' Caroline asked, 'wouldn't he have advertised equally well the fact that he'd been deceived? After all, he specializes in the display of a bleeding heart, at any rate in his poems.'

'There's something in that,' I said, 'though he might have only just discovered it and have killed his wife immediately after. And, in spite of the fact that he always puts himself forward as a perpetual victim of women, if he really were victimized it would probably be an extremely severe shock to his vanity.'

Soon afterwards the Chief Constable rang me up and asked me to tea the same day; Edgeworth had evidently been at work. Colonel Redder lived about five miles away, so I went over in Mrs. Eakin's superlative motorcar, and was driven by her suave and alarming chauffeur. First we had tea with Mrs. Redder, and made polite conversation, with many anecdotes about the war of 1914–1918 from the Colonel. Whenever in the course of these anecdotes he had to mention the latrines, or perhaps some indelicate part of the body in which someone had been wounded, he would lean towards me and lower his voice to what, by comparison with the rest of his conversation, might conceivably be regarded as a whisper. Mrs. Redder seemed to have trained herself, like any actress in the old days when stage asides existed, to assume a calm and abstracted expression, as though she did not hear any of these ferocious sibilants. After tea we went out into the garden to see the Colonel's guinea-pigs, an animal which I have always thought rather dull and lethargic in disposition, though undoubtedly of great value in the laboratory from its readiness to undergo cheerfully almost any conceivable disease. But the Colonel was as proud of his guinea-pigs as though they had been his own children; they were housed in a very elaborate cage which was intended to resemble a rustic summer-house, surrounded by creepers, rocks, and rock-plants. In front there was a more elaborate rock-garden than at the sides; this was intersected by paths covered with tunnels of wire-netting down which the guinea-pigs could run when they wanted an outing. In the middle of the rock-garden was a very small lily pool with a miniature rustic bridge over it; this also had its covering of wire-netting. As we approached, Colonel Redder uttered a piercing whistle.

'Did you hear that?' he asked.

'Yes,' I answered.

'Now do you see that?' he asked, and pointed to the rock-garden where the guinea-pigs were all running along the covered paths as fast as they could scamper, until they were all collected in a kind of meeting place, covered in with a dome of netting, on our side of the lily pool.

'Wonderful,' I said, and the Colonel seemed very pleased.

'Always come when I whistle,' he said and took some bran from a bag in his pocket with which he fed the expectant animals.

'Do you see that big black and white one in the middle of them?' he asked, attempting another of his clamorous asides with a rather stagy glance at Mrs. Redder, who was standing immediately beside us. 'That's the oldest of the males,' the Colonel continued. 'He's always after the females. That little brown bitch over there—pretty little thing—always runs away from him. Gets under a rock when she hears him coming, but he always manages to rout her out.'

'Wonderful,' I said. 'Didn't know guinea-pigs were so intelligent.' I seemed to be catching the Colonel's habit of using clipped phrases.

'Oh, they're very intelligent, very intelligent indeed,' he answered.

After this it was Mrs. Redder's turn to show me the rest of the garden and to explain what exactly was wrong with the soil in each of the beds, but the Colonel rather hurried us along and soon suggested that we'd better get back to business.

'Saw a bit about you in last week's Sunday paper,' he began. 'My wife showed it to me. Now where did I put that cutting? Ah, yes. It says here that Mr. James Hardwicke, the expert on criminal twins, is now on a visit to Scrope House where he is studying new methods in education. No doubt the boys and girls in this famous co-educational school, run on unconventional lines, will have to watch their step, especially if there are any twins amongst them. I don't know,' the Colonel continued, 'what it means about twins; I don't see what twins have to do with crime.'

I was delighted by his perspicacity; I had evidently run the risk of underestimating his intelligence as much as that of his guinea-pigs. The newspaper, I gathered, had also made him revise his opinion of me.

'I'd rather not call in Scotland Yard about this Dawes case unless it's absolutely necessary,' he said. 'I'd like my own men to get the credit and it doesn't seem too difficult for them, just a matter of hard work and organization. And perhaps if you'll give us a hand from time to time, supposing we get out of our depth with some of this scientific stuff, that'll do as well.'

I said that I would be very pleased. 'But,' I asked, 'haven't you already decided to consult Scotland Yard about the possibility of there being a Nazi agent in the school?'

'Oh yes, I wrote to them about that,' he answered, 'but that's not the same as putting the case into their hands. As a matter of fact, I've just heard from them. They say they haven't any information at the moment about any agent in this part of the world, but they'll let me know if they hear anything. I haven't much hope of learning anything more and I don't think they have either; they said they'd got every pro-Nazi in the country pretty well taped. I can't think what they mean by pro-Nazi; I think myself there's a good deal to be said for some of the things the Nazis have done.'

I was not going to be drawn into an argument about this and so I asked instead whether anything had been learnt from the analysis of the dregs in the bottles and glasses taken from Hickman's house.

'It's a long job,' Colonel Redder said, 'and the analyst isn't through yet; he's always rather slow. But there was atropine in the bottle you found in the garden—Julian told me about your finding it.'

'Oh there was, was there?' I said. 'Did the analyst say how much?'

'I've got it written down somewhere,' Colonel Redder answered, 'but it doesn't matter for the moment. It wasn't quite a lethal dose, I remember. However, there was only about a quarter of a wine glass left in the bottle so you wouldn't expect to find a lethal dose in it, not unless the whole bottle had contained an altogether unnecessary amount of poison. Though it's true murderers mostly use a great deal too much poison, I believe.'

'But presumably a full glass of the drink would have contained a lethal dose of poison?' I asked. 'Otherwise I don't see how the murderer managed. He couldn't be sure that his victim would mop up the whole bottle.'

'No, that's right,' Colonel Redder answered. 'Julian pointed that out and the analyst told him that a fair-sized wine glass of the stuff would certainly kill you.'

'And how about Dupuy?' I asked. 'I suppose he must have poured himself out about half a glass, or the murderer must have poured it out for him, out of the same bottle. He seems to have had a very lucky escape.'

'From what the analyst said,' Colonel Redder told me, 'it looks as if even half a glass, if it was a fairly sizable glass, might kill you.'

'Then Dupuy must have taken even less,' I said. 'I must say I can't quite understand how it happened, because I gathered that

Dupuy had drunk a great deal in the course of the evening and one can hardly imagine him pouring out a few sips for himself. It isn't the way people behave when they've had too much to drink. And it's even odder that the murderer should have poured him out a non-poisonous dose, just enough, in fact to make him ill for a day or two. I suppose it's just possible that he had a full glass of poisoned sherry and then spilt most of it. It might be worth looking to see if any considerable amount of sherry had been spilt anywhere in the house or perhaps on the verandah.'

'All that isn't half so odd,' said Colonel Redder, 'as the fact that no one else in the party was poisoned. It looks as if the murderer must have just poured out a glass for Mrs. Dawes and then perhaps a quarter of a glass for Dupuy, and then chucked the rest away somewhere before he hid the bottle in the garden.'

'It seems an extraordinary waste of perfectly good poison,' I said. 'And then there's the risk of being seen while he poured the rest of the sherry away. If you saw someone emptying a bottle of sherry over the garden you'd be sure to wonder what on earth was happening.'

'But it was dark in the garden, wasn't it?' asked the Colonel.

'Yes, that's true,' I said, 'but he'd got to get to the garden. It was certainly taking a risk and one can't see why he should have had to take it. He might have emptied the bottle in Hickman's bathroom but, then, wasn't there the risk that someone would notice him taking a bottle of sherry into the bathroom? It would look almost as odd, and surely the murderer would have been particularly anxious not to attract attention by any eccentricities at this time. On the other hand he might have arrived at the party with a bottle of poisoned sherry only a quarter full, but this again might have attracted attention.'

'I can't understand it myself,' said Colonel Redder, 'but it's no good thinking too much about it yet. Perhaps it will all come out when we get the rest of the analyst's report.'

'By the way,' I asked, 'was it sherry in the bottle from the garden?'

'Oh, it was sherry all right,' said Colonel Redder. 'The label was on the bottle, anyway. It's a reasonable and quite cheap sherry that Crompton keeps—that's the wine merchant at Scropeham. As a matter of fact I've bought some of that sherry myself at times and I think a good many other people in this part of the world must have bought it as well. There were three or four empty bottles of the same kind left in Hickman's house. It's called Genuine Fino, or some such rot.'

'That'll make it more difficult to trace the bottle, won't it?' I asked.

'Yes, there's that,' said Colonel Redder, 'but I expect we'll get on to it in the end and it's just a question of hard work and routine. What kind of drink did you bring to the party?' he asked. 'I may as well have it to make the list complete.'

'Well, I am afraid it was sherry,' I said. 'Mrs. Eakins's butler gave me a bottle to take along; it was very kind of him, or perhaps I might say of Mrs. Eakins, and it saved me the trouble of trying to get a bottle of wine in a strange place. I think it was some kind of Amontillado, but you'll find the bottle when you're looking through the rest of them. It wasn't this Genuine Fino stuff, as far as I can remember.'

'That reminds me,' Colonel Redder said, 'I've still got a bottle or two of the same kind left. We might try a glass now and see what it's like; all in the interests of detection, of course.'

He rang the bell and asked the maid to bring up a bottle of 'Genuine Fino', and when it came it seemed a reasonable wine, with a taste which, as I should imagine, would conceal any poison that did not taste too strong.

'What does atropine taste like?' I asked.

'I've never tasted it,' Colonel Redder answered. 'But the analyst said you could certainly conceal it in any sherry that wasn't too watery.'

'How about Rimmle's curious story about someone mixing boracic powder with his powdered atropine,' I asked. 'Did that have anything to do with the murder?'

'It must have done,' he answered. 'But it's not much good to us. What seems to have happened is that someone took away quite a lot of the atropine, and then filled the bottle up with boracic. It was a clever idea, because the theft wasn't noticed until it was too late for anyone to be at all clear how it happened. Julian seems to think it might have been taken from Rosenberg's laboratory, not long before he returned the bottle to Rimmle, or else it might have been taken from Rimmle's poison cupboard some time before Rosenberg came to borrow some more atropine and found there was something wrong with it. The lock on Rimmle's poison cupboard doesn't amount to anything, though I daresay it served its purpose of preventing the children from going casually to the cupboard, and Rosenberg can't be sure that he didn't sometimes leave the bottle of atropine on his bench and the door of the room he works in unlocked. He says the children didn't ever work in the room where he made his private experiments and he had no reason to be specially careful. In fact the stuff might have been taken at any time during a month or more, and as it all happened some time ago, at the beginning of last winter, it's no good expecting either Rimmle or Rosenberg to remember too clearly what they did with the bottle every day. At any rate, they say they don't remember anything suspicious, and Julian can't get any more out of them.'

I stood up to say good-bye and then remembered another question I wanted to ask.

'Do you know anything about that farmer, Walton,' I said, 'whose buildings were burnt down on May the third?'

'I know the man you mean,' Colonel Redder answered. 'What about him?'

'There seems to be a rumour going about that he burnt the place down himself, to get the insurance,' I said.

'I believe I did hear something about it,' he answered, 'but there was nothing definite. You'd better ask Julian; I expect he had some inquiries made, but they obviously must have come to nothing or I should have heard more about it.'

'Well, I wonder,' I said, as politely and apologetically as I could contrive. 'Do you think it would be possible for one of your men to ask Walton a few more questions? It doesn't matter what he asks, but I have a vague idea that something might come out if the police started bothering Walton again. I don't mean that I've any reason to suspect him definitely, but there's just a chance that this fire was intentional and if so whoever was responsible, whether it was Walton or someone else, might conceivably get rattled and give us something to work on. I don't know anything about police work, of course, but I believe you sometimes try that game yourself, don't you?'

'Yes, of course,' he answered. 'But it doesn't always work.'

'No, I realize that,' I said. 'It's only a chance and I'm sure all your men are very busy just now, but if you could spare half an hour of a village constable's time, I think it might be worth trying.'

'I don't mind trying,' Colonel Redder said, 'if you think it would help at all.' He made a note in his pocket-book with so business-like an air that I suspected he would immediately forget all about it.

Chapter Eight

To my surprise I was told next morning, soon after breakfast, that Superintendent Julian wanted to speak to me on the telephone.

'Colonel Redder,' he said, 'thought you might be glad to hear about one or two more details the analyst has sent us. He asked me to ring you up. If you're free this morning perhaps we could arrange to meet. As it happens, I was going to call on Mr. Dawes, and I don't know whether you'd care to come along with me... It's Colonel Redder's own suggestion. We could meet somewhere, or I could pick you up in my car at the Dower House, if that suited you better.'

I said that it would suit me very well if he picked me up in his car, and immediately he had rung off I regretted, with half at least of my mind, that I had accepted his invitation. I could hardly imagine anything more awkward than an interview with Dawes in the presence of Superintendent Julian. The police may be able to work miracles in the way of sobering agitated or hysterical people, but I felt very doubtful whether Dawes would not be too much for them. I did not know anything about his state of mind at the moment, but it seemed very unlikely that it would be calm. And there was the further point, that if Dawes associated me with the police and saw that I was acting with them he would hardly be likely to give me his confidence at any time in the future. Nevertheless I saw no way of backing out of the invitation I had so rashly accepted, especially as I very much wanted to keep in with Julian, to get to know him and to hear what he had to tell me. He arrived about twenty minutes after his telephone call and we set out for Dawes's house in his car.

'It seems funny to be telling anything to an outsider,' the Superintendent began as we were driving along. 'But Colonel Redder thinks you might be able to help us and this is certainly a tricky case for us. In the ordinary way we can rely on hearing a lot of talk, but these people won't be talking so that we can hear them. There are servants, of course, and we may get something from them. I'm hoping for something from Mr. Dawes's daily woman, a Mrs. Butcher. Or we might get an anonymous letter, but we haven't had anything yet except a letter from a lunatic who says that Mrs. Dawes was killed by the freemasons to prevent her from exposing their secrets. I don't mind telling you that I'm a freemason myself.'

'Are you now?' I said.

'Yes,' Julian answered. 'I find it comes a bit expensive at times, but it helps.'

'What were the details you were going to give me?' I asked. 'About the analysis, I mean.'

'Oh well,' Julian said, 'it was only that the analyst has found some atropine in the remains of a drink in one of the glasses that were in the verandah. If we can trace the bottle of sherry that you found, we might be able to get somewhere, and that's partly why I want to talk to Dawes to-day. I want to see if there are any bottles of the same kind of sherry in the house. And we'll see if he's more willing to talk than before—your being there might perhaps make him open up a little. It's a good thing to go on asking the same questions at frequent intervals.'

I was interested to hear that Julian had not found Dawes willing to talk and I asked him whether he thought this silence was at all suspicious.

'He's just very quiet,' Julian said. 'I suppose it's very natural really, but it doesn't get us anywhere. Now, if he was the kind that tried to explain everything, I don't doubt he'd soon give us a line.'

Evidently, I reflected, Dawes kept a different manner for the police from that which he showed to his friends; ordinarily accustomed to unpack his heart, there were occasions when he could be reserved. I went back to the analyst's report.

'I suppose,' I said, 'that the analyst can tell from the dregs he found in the glass in the verandah whether a full glass would have contained enough poison to kill someone?'

'Oh yes,' Julian answered, 'he said that when the glass was full there must have been quite enough poison to kill anybody. It was one of those little tumblers, about half the size of an ordinary half-pint tumbler. Apart from a few of the ordinary sized tumblers, this was the only kind of glass that Hickman provided. Whatever drinks people had, they used the same kind of glass, unless they were having beer or lemonade.'

'Whose glass do you suppose the glass on the verandah was?' I asked. 'Had Dupuy or Mrs. Dawes drunk out of it?'

'There was some lip-stick on the rim,' Julian said, 'and I found out that Mrs. Dawes had been wearing rather a lot of lip-stick that night; she usually did put on a good deal.'

'Any finger-prints?' I asked.

'Too many to be any use in tracing the murderer,' Julian answered. 'You see, by Hickman's account a good many people handled Mrs. Dawes's glass that evening when they were getting her drinks and so on. And no doubt there were others he didn't notice. Anyway they mostly put their finger-prints one on top of each other and the smudges are very little use. But there's quite a clear print of Mrs. Dawes's middle finger on the glass.'

'I think Hickman said that he saw both Dawes himself and Sinclair fetch Mrs. Dawes a drink and that he himself gave her one. Didn't you find any of their prints?' I asked.

'I haven't got their prints to compare with the ones on the glass,' Julian said. 'Of course, I could get Dawes's prints to-day, but what would be the use? We've already got Hickman's statement that he saw Dawes handling the glass, and in itself that doesn't prove anything.'

'Were there any prints on the bottle?' I asked.

'Wiped off,' Julian replied. 'At least, I think they must have been, though all those damp leaves round the bottle might have washed the prints off.'

'And I take it there was sherry in the glass from the verandah?' I said.

'Yes, it was sherry all right,' he replied.

'The same kind of sherry that was in the bottle?' I asked.

'Oh yes, as far as one could tell,' Julian answered.

'It's rather odd,' I said, 'that only one glass with poison in it was found. There must at least have been Dupuy's glass as well. But perhaps he drank all his sherry up. Do you suppose that if he drained his glass clean the analyst could still detect atropine in the very minute amount that remained?'

'That seems to be more in your line than mine,' Julian said.

'I'm not a chemist,' I said. 'But wait a bit. Isn't it possible that some of the glasses were washed during the party? Perhaps there weren't enough to go round, or something?'

'Oh, we asked about that, of course,' said Julian. 'Dr. Hickman had about half a dozen glasses sent out into the kitchen to be washed up while the party was going on.'

'What time did that happen?' I asked. 'How long was it before Mrs. Dawes and Dupuy were taken ill?'

'Mrs. Dawes had to leave the party at about a quarter to twelve,' Julian told me, 'and the servants say that they washed the glasses round about ten-fifteen or a little after.'

'Then Dupuy's glass might well have been amongst those that were washed up, that is, if they weren't washed too long before the time when the symptoms of poisoning would be seriously felt.'

'According to what the police surgeon and the analyst told me,' Julian said, 'an hour and a half to an hour and three-quarters would be rather a long interval between taking the poison and feeling ill. But it would be quite possible; the interval depends on how much has been eaten and so on, and is always apt to vary.'

'Then as things stand at the present,' I said, 'it rather looks as if Dupuy had taken his dose of poison before Mrs. Dawes took hers.'

'How do you get that?' Julian asked.

'Why,' I said, 'if an hour and three-quarters is an abnormally long interval between taking the atropine and feeling ill, then its much less likely that there was such an interval in two cases than in one. But Dupuy and Mrs. Dawes seem to have been taken ill at about the same time; Dupuy says he remembers Mrs. Dawes becoming delirious and also remembers feeling thirsty—that's one of the first symptoms of atropine poisoning—not long before this happened. He himself began to behave rather wildly at about the same time as Mrs. Dawes. I think we ought to assume that Dupuy's glass was one of those that were washed up soon after ten o'clock; if he had drunk from one of the other glasses I think the analyst would have found at any rate some faint trace of the poison in it. Therefore it's probable, though not, of course, certain, that Mrs. Dawes drank the poison some time after Dupuy, because otherwise there would have been yet another abnormally long interval between taking the poison and showing symptoms of distress.'

Julian sighed. 'Have you ever been an expert witness?' he asked.

'No,' I said. 'What makes you ask?'

'I thought perhaps you might have been,' he said. 'Not that expert witnesses aren't sometimes useful,' he added.

'If Dupuy's glass was washed up, I wonder why Mrs. Dawes's glass wasn't as well,' I said. 'That would surely have been to the murderer's advantage; if at the same time he had more effectively got rid of the bottle we found in the garden we shouldn't have had any clues at all.'

'You can't expect a murderer to be able to have everything his own way,' Julian objected, very reasonably.

As we talked Julian had been driving slowly, but we had now reached Dawes's cottage. The door was opened by a woman whom I took to be the charwoman, Mrs. Butcher; she told us that Dawes was out. 'He's out at the school,' she said. 'He won't be back for half an hour.'

'We'll come in and wait, if we may,' Julian said, 'and as a matter of fact I'd like a word with you, Mrs. Butcher. Perhaps we could go into the sitting-room.'

Mrs. Butcher showed us in, and the Superintendent and I sat down while she stood near the door, looking as though she would seize the first opportunity that presented itself to escape from the room. But Julian began with some remarks about the weather and with some highly conventional words of sympathy about Mrs. Dawes's death, which seemed to put Mrs. Butcher rather more at her ease.

'Who could have done it?' she suddenly asked.

'Well, we don't quite know yet,' Julian answered, 'but it won't be long before we do.' This answer seemed to disappoint Mrs. Butcher, perhaps because it made her doubt the efficiency of the police, or perhaps because it gave her no material for future conversation with her neighbours. She told us a long story about a man who left his wife, of which the moral was that the police weren't able to do anything about that either. Then she got back to Mr. Dawes.

'He's taking it very hardly,' she said.

'Yes, I'm sure,' said Julian.

'He never did like those parties,' Mrs. Butcher said. 'But Mrs. Dawes used to go regularly.'

'Did Mr. Dawes always go with her?' Julian asked.

'Oh yes,' she answered, 'Mrs. Dawes didn't like going alone.'

'She didn't get anyone else to take her, then?'

'Not except when Mr. Dawes was away.'

'And was he often away?'

'Mr. Dawes goes to London sometimes; it's to do with his work.'

'That's a long way to go, isn't it?'

'Well, London's London, I suppose.'

'Yes, I suppose so,' Julian had to agree. 'But when did he last go to London?'

'Now let me see.' Mrs. Butcher thought for a moment. 'It would be three weeks ago.'

'Did Mrs. Dawes go to a party then?' Julian asked. I could not quite see the point of all these questions, but afterwards I concluded that he was trying to find some evidence of discord between Mr. and Mrs. Dawes, perhaps about the bottle parties and the people whom Mrs. Dawes was likely to meet there. His method seemed to be to ask a great number of harmless and apparently aimless questions in the hope that one of them at least might expose the true relations of the people into whose lives he was inquiring. Mrs. Butcher told us that Mrs. Dawes did not go to a party when Dawes was in London three weeks ago.

'Not then, she didn't go,' Mrs. Butcher said. 'As far as I remember it was at the end of the winter term, as they call it—Oh, no, it was at the beginning of the holidays—Mr. Dawes was away and Mr. Dupuy came and fetched Mrs. Dawes to go to a party. It was at the headmaster's and I wondered Mr. Dawes didn't feel he ought to stay behind and go to it.'

'Were you here at the time?' Julian asked.

'I was washing up after dinner when Mr. Dupuy came for Mrs. Dawes.'

'Didn't Mrs. Dawes go to any parties between the beginning of last holidays and the party at Dr. Hickman's where she took the poison? I understood these parties were a regular thing at the school?'

'She did go to one at the beginning of this summer term,' Mrs. Butcher said. 'But Mr. Dawes took her to that. She told me about it next day because she had a headache; she said it was at Mr. Rimmle's and he'd given her something nasty to drink. But Mr. Dawes didn't have a headache at all.'

I concluded that Dawes had been wise enough not to touch Rimmle's vodka. No doubt Mrs. Dawes had felt that she ought to try some as it was Rimmle's party.

'Mrs. Dawes didn't like being alone, I think you said?' Julian continued. 'Did she see much of Mr. Dupuy when Mr. Dawes was at work?'

'Mr. Dupuy and others used to come sometimes. And why not?'

'Oh, no reason why not,' Julian reassured her. 'Who else used to come?'

'There was a good many. Mrs. Dawes liked company more than Mr. Dawes.'

'But you wouldn't say,' Julian asked, 'that any one of them came more than the others?'

'Mrs. Dawes always had a lot of friends,' Mrs. Butcher said, and was obviously not going to say any more on this subject however delicately Julian might insinuate his questions.

'Well now, to change the subject,' Julian said. 'Where did Mr. Dawes get his wine, or was it Mrs. Dawes who ordered it?'

'Mrs. Dawes did most of the ordering, of course. There was some bottles of wine came sometimes from Cromptons.'

'And I suppose there are some bottles in the house now?'

'There's some claret bottles in the cupboard in the kitchen that haven't been opened yet.'

'And is there any sherry?'

'Not now there isn't.'

'Then there has been sherry at some time in the past?'

'There was some came in the winter. The empties are still in the shed by the coal-cellar.'

'We'd better have a look at them,' Julian said.

Mrs. Butcher took us round by the back of the house and opened the door of a little shed where we saw some dusty bottles. The Superintendent counted them; there were nine and their labels told us that they had once contained 'Genuine Fino' Sherry.

'Ordered a dozen at a time?' asked Julian.

'I don't know for certain,' Mrs. Butcher said.

'There aren't any more about?' asked Julian.

'Not as far as I know,' Mrs. Butcher answered.

'Oh well,' Julian said, 'if there were any more they may have been used for something else or thrown away. You don't know anything about it?' he asked.

'I've never seen any other bottles,' Mrs. Butcher said.

We went back to the sitting-room and Julian, after tactfully dismissing Mrs. Butcher, sat down again to wait for Dawes.

'I can't imagine why there should be three bottles missing,' I said.

'Perhaps they were given away, or perhaps only nine were ordered, three-quarters of a dozen...' Julian suggested.

'You could find that out from Cromptons,' I said.

There was a telephone in the room and Julian decided to ring up Cromptons while he was waiting. After a little while, the people in the shop were able to look up the order and find that a dozen bottles had been sent to Mrs. Dawes in December of last year.

'Perhaps the other three were a Christmas present to somebody,' I suggested.

'I'll ask Mr. Dawes,' said Julian.

'Would that be any good?' I asked.

'Well, if he should lie about it,' Julian said, 'then we'll know where we are.'

'He's only got to say he gave them away to a rag-and-bone man, and you would have very little hope of tracing them any further.'

'There isn't a rag-and-bone man round here. In fact it's very difficult to get rid of anything you can't burn in the garden. It's one of our difficulties round here; people throw things on to each other's land and then there's trouble. A good many people throw their worst rubbish into a sort of hollow in a spinney not far from here.'

'Dawes isn't likely to have thrown three empty bottles away and then have kept the rest,' I said.

'No,' said Julian. 'It's a funny thing,' he continued in a meditative voice, 'I saw a great bath in that spinney the other day. I should like to know how that got there. It couldn't have been carried to the place; much too heavy. And yet you can't imagine people putting a bath in the back of a motor car and carrying it a long way simply in order to chuck it on to a heap of rubbish. At least, I've never seen anyone doing such a thing.'

'It's like that other mystery of the countryside,' I said. 'How do hansom cabs get driven into the middle of a field and then get left there for ever? It's lucky a detective doesn't have to solve every mystery he comes across.'

'I like to know why things happen,' Julian said. 'I suppose that's why I'm in my job. But unfortunately only a small part of my job is finding out why things happen. If I could stop working on a case when I've ceased to feel curious about it mine would be a much more interesting job. It's getting everything in order and having all the evidence ready that makes the work.'

I was about to express my sympathy when the door opened and Dawes came abruptly into the room, looking very indignant. He stared at Julian and then, with even more marked disapproval, at me.

'Where the feast is,' he said, 'there shall the vultures be gathered together.'

The quotation—at least I presume it was a quotation—left both Julian and me in astonished silence. But Julian was the first to recover himself.

'I'm sorry you should take it like that, Sir,' he said. The use of the word 'Sir,' as I have often noticed before, can be curiously soothing, no doubt because it gratifies one's vanity, even in moments of great anger or extreme distress, perhaps even especially then, to be addressed in this ceremonial fashion. On the other hand, by a very slight change of intonation, the word can be made to sound like an insult, as we know from the habitual use that Dr. Johnson made of it. Julian used the word with a masterly and immediate effect, and Dawes was patient again.

'I'm sorry,' he said, 'I oughtn't to have said that. But I thought I had already told the police everything they could possibly want to know. And I can't imagine why you should have brought Hardwicke with you. I should have thought a little privacy in these matters...'

There was nothing for me to do but to offer to go, and Julian made as yet no effort to excuse or explain my presence. But as I was on the point of going Dawes again interrupted.

'Now that you're here, you'd better stay,' he said. 'I'd rather everybody heard what I've got to say. I don't want anything hidden and I imagine you can be trusted to tell everyone in the school...'

There was a note of excitement in Dawes's voice and Julian interrupted him before he could say anything further.

'I'm sure Mr. Hardwicke won't repeat anything,' he said. 'I wouldn't have brought him along to see you, only I wanted you to hear from him what your wife said to him. You see it was to Mr. Hardwicke that your wife spoke of there being some connection between the fires at Scrope House and a possible Nazi spy. Now I think you told me that you knew nothing at all either about the fires or about any spy among the refugees, so I thought you'd better hear directly from Mr. Hardwicke what your wife said. It might, perhaps, lead you to remember some little detail you'd forgotten, if you see what I mean.'

Thus prompted, I described as accurately as I could remember my conversation with Mrs. Dawes on the occasion when I had had tea at her house, and I also told Dawes what she had said in the note she wrote to me on the day of the party.

'I'm afraid that doesn't make me remember anything,' Dawes said. 'Why should it?'

'Your wife didn't say anything more to you about this Mr. Rosenberg, did she?' Julian asked. 'She seems to have been a bit suspicious about him.'

'But I've already told you,' Dawes answered, 'that I didn't altogether share my wife's political interests. I respected her work and she respected mine, but we each did our own work separately.'

'No, Sir, I quite understand,' Julian said. 'Politics aren't the same for everyone, are they?'

I suspect that Julian must have cultivated his gift for uttering such disarming imbecilities and there is no doubt that they helped to produce a restful atmosphere. He then proceeded to ask whether Mrs. Dawes could have made any enemies through her political activities, and tried to find out what exactly these political activities were. Dawes gave very brief and often non-committal replies and I even wondered whether he was being deliberately vague in order to avoid exposing any of the secrets of the revolutionary politicians at Scrope House to the hired thugs of the boss class; this, I believe, is the proper term for the police in such circles.

Julian was still rambling on, or at least it seemed to me that he was rambling, when he suddenly changed the subject to the nine bottles in the shed by the coal-cellar. Dawes seemed to know nothing whatever about them and only dimly remembered, as he told us, that his wife had from time to time ordered a dozen bottles of sherry from Cromptons. Neither could he tell us whether she had given away any bottles of sherry at Christmas time or whether they had been got rid of in any other way. Julian accepted his unhelpful answers without any complaint, and then rose to take his leave. Before we went Dawes apologized to me for what he called his asperity at the beginning of the interview.

'The truth is,' he said, 'I was hoping there wouldn't be any more of these endless questions, and then when I saw Julian I knew we should have to go over all the same ground again.'

I really felt very sorry for Dawes and would willingly have excused a much greater display of irritation; I expressed my sympathy as best I could.

'You see what we're up against,' Julian said, as we left the house. 'Everybody answers my questions and I can't complain that they're not co-operating with the police, but these sort of people don't talk freely. Now when I was working in a suburban district it was almost too easy; the women were left alone all day and they would pour out all their troubles to the man who was selling vacuum cleaners, provided they thought he had a sympathetic face. Everybody *wanted* to talk, either about themselves or about their neighbours. But here it's like trying to get into a little ring of people; they may perhaps talk freely to each other, but the very last thing they would think of doing would be to give anything away to an outsider. I assure you any gang of crooks would be more open than these people.'

It had seemed to me that the lives of most of the people at Scrope House were an open book; they freely disclosed and discussed details of their lives which would have been considered a shameful secret in more conventional circles. But no doubt they never thought of talking to a policeman as they talked to their friends and acquaintances; they would as soon have made a confidant of the dustman. It was too delicate a matter to explain to Julian why he could not be admitted to the gossip of the Scrope House people, and probably unnecessary, because he must have understood very well. Instead I asked what he was going to do next.

'Are you going to look for the other two bottles?' I asked. 'Do you think it safe to assume that the bottle I found in Hickman's garden was one of the three that are missing from Dawes's shed?'

'I'll tell my men to keep their eyes open,' Julian said, 'but it's no good looking for them without having any idea where to look.'

'Do you think,' I continued, 'that Rosenberg could have been a spy, as Mrs. Dawes seems to have thought?'

'Why don't you ask him?' said Julian.

'Surely that would be much too simple?' I said.

'You'd be surprised,' Julian answered, 'if you knew how often people tell you what you want to know when you ask a direct question. That's mostly our method, anyway.'

'I don't see how it can work,' I said. 'I knew a Russian once who was applying to be naturalized. The police came round to try and find out if he was a communist, so they asked him what he thought of Russia. You couldn't be more direct than that.'

'Well, what did he say?' Julian asked.

'He said it was a beautiful country and he often dreamt of those great rolling steppes.'

Julian remained unimpressed. 'Refusing to answer,' he said. 'Well, that was suspicious in itself, wasn't it?'

'Your colleagues don't seem to have thought so,' I said. 'They naturalized him all right and, after all, he was a communist. It's like the questions they ask when you want to get into America. Who's going to admit that he's a polygamist in answer to a question which so obviously expects the answer "no"?'

'Well, you try it with Rosenberg,' Julian advised. 'Perhaps he would be more willing to tell you than me. By the way,' he continued, 'Colonel Redder was telling me that you wanted some more questions asked about the fire at Walton's farm. We made a few inquiries ourselves, of course, but the trouble is that Smallbones, that's the constable there, has never managed to get on good terms with the man who keeps that pub by the farm.'

'Why should that make it more difficult?' I asked in some surprise.

'But it's the most important thing of all,' said Julian, 'especially for a village constable. If the landlord's willing to help, the constable can find out almost anything he wants to know; otherwise he's stuck. Of course the police have the right to enter licensed premises at any time of the day or night and they've always got some hold over a landlord, but if the landlord doesn't get on with the constable it's much less likely that he'll pass on anything he's heard. These things work much better when everyone's friendly; landlords aren't nearly so willing to oblige if you show your hand and suggest they should tell you something under a threat. It puts their backs up.'

'Do you mean that you expect a pub-keeper to repeat what he's heard his customers say?' I asked.

'We expect it all right,' said Julian. 'But we don't always get what we expect. However, that's not the point. I gather you don't want any more inquiries about the fire in the neighbourhood; what you suggested to Colonel Redder was that Smallbones should go and ask Walton himself some awkward questions.'

'Yes,' I said, 'that was my idea, if you think it would be all right.'

'There'd be no harm in trying it,' Julian said, 'if you think it would help you with the Scrope House fires, though I don't quite see why you think that. There's no hurry about it, I suppose? There've been no more fires lately, and everyone's very busy with this murder case.'

I did not think it would be wise to try and hurry the police, so I left it at that.

Chapter Nine

Acting on the Superintendent's advice, I made an appointment to see Rosenberg in his lodgings. I found myself in what seemed to be a positive caricature of a parlour in a seaside lodging house.

'You're looking at my room,' Rosenberg said. 'It's exactly as I found it; I didn't have to touch it up at all. It's beautifully English, isn't it? The English are so tolerant, even of the most incongruous colours, the most discordantly irrelevant objects. My landlady must have a very beautiful nature, I often think; she doesn't even object to the final incongruity of putting me in the midst of her so parochial interior. Do you know what that is?' he added, pointing to a large ball of crumpled and variously coloured paper which hung from the ceiling in the middle of the room.

'No,' I said, 'but I suppose it's some kind of ornament.'

'Severely practical, I assure you,' Rosenberg said. 'It's a fly-rest.'

'A fly-rest?'

'Yes, for the flies to deposit their excrement on, so that they shan't leave it about in the rest of the room. I don't understand why the flies should be obliging enough to use it, but apparently they are. My landlady tells me that in her time you seldom saw a house without a fly-rest in it and she says she can't understand why anything so useful should have gone out. I can't either.'

After some more polite conversation I approached the question which had brought me to see him, though perhaps not quite so directly as Julian had recommended. I began talking about Mrs. Dawes and about the periodical which she had helped to run.

'She told me,' I said, 'that you had written two articles for her, about the Axis I think it was, and that you were going to let her have a third. She wondered when you were going to let her have it, but I suppose you must have been too busy. She seemed to be surprised that you hadn't written it, but no doubt there's some quite simple explanation?'

Rosenberg looked sharply at me and was evidently considering what to answer. I waited with some excitement for him to speak, but he only asked why I wanted to know.

'You didn't have anything to do with Mrs. Dawes's periodical, did you?' he added.

'No, no,' I replied, 'but Mrs. Dawes seemed to attach some importance to the fact that you hadn't written the third article. I've no doubt she was rather a mystery-monger...'

'Hadn't you better tell me,' Rosenberg interrupted, 'exactly what it is you want to know?'

This was precisely what Julian had recommended, and so I thought I had better make a clean breast, however apologetically, of Mrs. Dawes's devastating suspicions. Rosenberg did not seem to be in the least taken back.

'Yes, I see,' he said. 'Well, I rather expected it.'

'What did you expect?' I asked.

'I'd better explain everything to you,' he said. 'You're rather innocent about politics, perhaps?'

'Oh, I don't know,' I protested.

'Oh yes,' Rosenberg said. 'It's very pleasant, of course, and to be innocent is one of the most agreeable luxuries of the average liberal Englishman, but I should think you would sometimes find it difficult to understand the modern world.'

I was not altogether comfortable under this patronage, but

perhaps Rosenberg, as a political refugee, had some reason to look upon anyone who was not a refugee as a foolish optimist.

'You see,' he went on, 'my first two articles were on the subject of the peace front against the Axis and, of course, I was recommending an immediate alliance and military agreement with Russia. But before I'd written my third article I'd changed my mind.'

'Good Lord,' I exclaimed. 'But why?'

'That, I am afraid, is what the innocent English of the left will find it hard to understand. I feel pretty sure there's going to be an agreement between Germany and Russia.'

'But surely that's unthinkable,' I said.

'Well, a few people are thinking it,' he answered, 'though no one will listen to them here. However, that's only to do with the general situation. The real point is that I've resigned from the Communist Party, and that means I'm probably in for some trouble.'

'But good Heavens,' I said. 'I should have thought it was much simpler and safer for a refugee in England not to be a communist.'

'That's where you're wrong,' he said. 'The communists are quite prepared to make as much trouble as they can for anyone who leaves the C.P. and it's not very difficult to make trouble for a refugee.'

'But I don't see what they can do in England,' I said. 'After all they've no power here.'

'You don't need power in order to make trouble,' he answered. 'If there's a communist working in one of the refugee organizations, and there usually is, he can hold up my letters. Or he can go about denouncing me as a Nazi agent planted by the Gestapo among the genuine refugees. I heard of a case the other day of a man in Austria, working underground, of course, who left the party. They published his name in a Paris newspaper and accused him there of being a Nazi spy. The Nazis knew, of course, that he wasn't one of their spies and promptly arrested him for being a communist, which was precisely what the communists intended.'

'But surely,' I said, 'you can't think that Susan Dawes would be so inconceivably base. The worst you could say about her, I should have thought, was that she was a rather silly enthusiast.'

'My dear Hardwicke,' Rosenberg said, 'that's where your innocence comes in. Once you get the idea that any action is justifiable if it's for the good of the party anything can happen. The ordinary rules mean nothing at all; it's quite incredible, until you see it happen, how quickly a charming, perhaps rather silly enthusiast, as you put it, will develop into a ruthless Machiavellian. As it happens, I think they soon get a taste for Machiavellian conduct for its own sake, and I think I can see why this should be. What the young like above all is to be, as they imagine, ruthlessly logical. Whatever idea they get into their heads, it doesn't matter whether it's psycho-analysis, or logical positivisim, or even the notions of their favourite novelist, they apply it in season and out of season with an absurd and often fantastic rigidity. I remember myself when we all read Proust and derived from him the notion that no two people could ever be in love with each other; if somebody fell in love with you, it followed automatically that you must fall out of love with them; however much in love you were before, you lost interest when your feelings were reciprocated. Well, if the young like to believe this, it does no harm at all, but only makes a few pleasing obstacles to enliven the course of a love affair which, in spite of Proust, will most probably come to a successful conclusion, though for biological rather than intellectual reasons.'

'Does Proust really make any such statement?' I asked.

'I don't know,' Rosenberg answered. 'He may do, but it doesn't matter; we all thought he did in those fortunate days. But to go on with my point; if you carry out the precepts of the communist party in the same ruthlessly logical way, if you feel that where ordinary morality is insulted or ordinary common sense ignored you are only showing your superiority to the muddled thinking of the rest of mankind, there is, unfortunately, nothing in biology to stop you. A communist positively enjoys voting for the conservatives and against the labour party, or with the Fascists and against the social democrats, because it is so beautifully logical when the key to this paradoxical conduct is supplied to the initiate. What all the more ruthless political parties do is to exploit the young when they are passing through this dangerous but most agreeable period of intoxication with ideas. It is very sad; they could be just as happy and much less harmful if they could occupy their minds, as until lately they used to do in England, by discussing the meaning of the word "good".'

'And if you want a decent political party,' Rosenberg concluded, 'that is, one that doesn't carry its immorality to fantastic extremes, I am afraid you must, as in England, keep politics out of the hands both of the young and of the intelligentsia. Though that also,' he added with a sigh, 'has its disadvantages.'

'But Mrs. Dawes wasn't as young as all that,' I protested.

'No,' Rosenberg agreed. 'But I'm not saying that she denounced me as a Nazi agent, either to you or to anyone else. She may possibly have been doing so, but equally she may only have passed on to you what she heard from someone else. She may have been as innocent as yourself; I don't think she was really an orthodox Marxist.'

'But who,' I asked, 'would have denounced you to her? Are there many communists at Scrope House?'

'Quite a few,' said Rosenberg. 'Rimmle's one, and I think Dupuy may be, though I'm not really sure that he's an actual party member. Or else it needn't necessarily have been anyone at Scrope House. There are plenty of people in London who might have done it.'

'Or else nobody may have denounced you after all,' I said.

'Oh, but I think they have,' said Rosenberg. 'This isn't the only time I've come across the suggestion that I am not what I seem to be.'

I must confess that I was shocked by the intrigues which Rosenberg attributed to the communists, though I considered it possible that he might be exaggerating and in the first flush of his loss of faith might be inclined to think too harshly of his old co-religionists. Previously I had had only one serious grievance against the communists, their mystical belief in dialectical materialism and their attempt to force every operation of nature and art into the mould of a progress by way of thesis and antithesis to synthesis. I particularly deplored any attempt to force science into such a mould and was distressed to find that several scientists in England had taken up with this fancy. They seem childishly pleased when they discover that light, for example, was once thought to be waves, which is the thesis, and then particles, which is the antithesis, and then a bit of both, which of course is the synthesis. According to Mr. Bernal 'there could hardly be a better example of the dialectical development in science than this', but it seems to me that you can impose that kind of pattern on any development if you care to try. You could easily have such a pattern in a detective story; the local police would say that the murderer was X, Scotland Yard would say that he was Y, and the private detective would conclude that X and Y were accomplices, receiving the order of Lenin for his truly orthodox solution. But, after all, such fancies are very harmless and even Rosenberg might consider it safe for the young to be allowed to play with them; what he had just suggested was far more alarming. I must have shown my bewilderment in my face and perhaps my incredulity that any such thing could happen in England's cosy and ornamental land, for Rosenberg looked quizzically at me as though he had guessed my thoughts.

'Yes, I know that it must be difficult for you to believe,' he said. 'I daresay you're prepared to believe anything about the Nazis, perhaps even about the communists in Russia, but you can't grasp the idea that people you actually know or might meet should behave in such a fashion. And it must be especially difficult in a place like this, so absurdly tolerant and with so many men of rather weak goodwill. I must confess that the whole of Scrope House and its whole system of education seems to me absurdly unprepared to stand the shock and the impact of the modern world. I feel that its tolerance is rather like that of my landlady; both she and Edgeworth are equally will-ing to accept any nonsense. For me, of course, both Scrope House and this fantastic room make the perfect rest cure; I am back in the nineteenth century, provincial and full of hope. But for you and the rest of the English liberals, such an atmosphere must be profoundly weakening and dangerous.'

I objected that the vagaries of Scrope House might not be what we had to defend, but were certainly a symptom of what we had to defend, and as such must not be cleared away for fear that more essential signs of freedom might go too and we should be left fighting for something we had destroyed ourselves. Rosenberg was familiar with this argument, and objected that if we preserved unessentials as well as essentials, if we insisted on the right to bring up children as though they were going to live in a Utopia of liberalism, we should be so encumbered that we could not fight at all. In fact, it was the usual argument of that particular period and as we could get no further I changed the subject. I said that it was very curious that someone should have mixed boracic powder with the atropine that Rimmle had lent him, and I asked him whether he had any idea what had really happened.

'Of course the whole point of the boracic,' he said, 'was to disguise the fact that the atropine had been taken. We were bound to find out in the end, but too late for either of us to remember how it had been taken. I am afraid I was rather careless, but I hadn't the slightest reason to suspect a thief in my laboratory. I am afraid I didn't always lock the door when I went out for a few minutes.'

'I heard that rather a lot of atropine had been taken,' I said, 'but I don't really know how much.'

'It was enough,' Rosenberg said, 'to poison a dozen people, at least.'

'Do you think the thief came prepared with his own boracic,' I asked, 'or did he find some in your laboratory?'

'I don't think I had any boracic powder immediately to hand in the laboratory,' Rosenberg said. 'I expect what happened was that he slipped in one day and saw the little bottle marked atropine, either in my own or in Rimmle's laboratory and then watched for his opportunity, perhaps at some time when he could see or know that Rimmle or I were elsewhere. He then came back with a little boracic in his pocket ready to substitute for what he had taken.'

'You don't remember anyone visiting you in your laboratory who might have had an opportunity to notice the atropine lying about?'

'I don't encourage visitors,' he answered. 'But I certainly don't remember anyone in particular. Perhaps the thief's first visit was made when I wasn't there. Or if it was taken from Rimmle's laboratory perhaps there was some boracic there; I should think there must have been—probably a first aid outfit or something.'

'It looks as if the whole thing was very deliberate,' I said.

'Oh, obviously,' said Rosenberg. 'And now that we know what the atropine was taken for, it's hardly likely that it was just picked up on the spur of the moment.'

'When the police interviewed you about it,' I said, 'did they see if there were any fingerprints on the atropine bottle?'

'Yes, they did,' said Rosenberg. 'But, as I pointed out at the time, both Rimmle and I had handled the bottle far too much after the atropine had been taken from it for there to be any other prints left on it.'

When I left Rosenberg I found Julian waiting for me in his car round a corner where he could not have been seen from Rosenberg's house.

'I didn't want Rosenberg to see that you were going to tell me everything he had said,' Julian remarked, and thus encouraged I gave him a condensed summary of Rosenberg's explanation of why Mrs. Dawes had suspected him of being a Nazi agent. I added that in my opinion it seemed a genuine explanation; unless evidence to the contrary turned up I did not see why it should not be believed.

'I've never had much to do with these communists,' Julian said, 'but according to all accounts that's nothing to what they'll do when they get their blood up.'

'I don't think it's a question of their getting their blood up,' I said, 'the surprising thing is what they can do in cold blood.'

'Well, that's one way of looking at it,' Julian said, and then told me what he had been doing.

'I've traced the missing bottles from Dawes's shed,' he said. 'Mrs. Dawes gave Mr. Dupuy three bottles of sherry for a present last Christmas, or so he says.'

'Is there any doubt about it?' I asked.

'Well, he can't produce the empties,' Julian answered. 'He says he threw them away at the end of his garden; there are a lot of other bottles there, but not the three sherry bottles.'

'Isn't that very suspicious?' I asked.

'Well, it would be if we knew that the bottle you found in Hickman's garden was definitely one of the three that Mrs. Dawes gave away. But of course we don't.'

'It seems a reasonable assumption,' I said. 'And it would explain what seems inexplicable otherwise, why Dupuy should say he had put the empties at the bottom of his garden when they aren't there now. They couldn't be there if he'd taken one of them with the poisoned sherry in it to Hickman's party.'

'But why should he not have left the other two there?' Julian asked.

'Perhaps he thought someone might notice them on his rubbish heap,' I said. 'He wouldn't want anyone to know that he had ever had this Genuine Fino stuff in the house—that is, if he was the murderer.'

'Then why should he tell me, as he did, and quite openly, that Mrs. Dawes had given him three bottles as a present?' Julian asked.

'I can't imagine,' I said. 'But perhaps he didn't know that Dawes wouldn't remember that Mrs. Dawes had given the three bottles to Dupuy.'

'Then why use that sherry at all?' Julian objected. 'Why not use some other kind of sherry which couldn't be connected with him? I don't suppose Mrs. Dawes only drank that particular kind of sherry; Dupuy could easily have bought some other kind in London or anywhere else where the sale wouldn't be traced to him.'

'It was certainly a mistake to tell you that Mrs. Dawes had given him the three bottles of Genuine Fino,' I said. 'But then murderers do make mistakes, don't they?'

'They do,' Julian answered, 'but it doesn't seem consistent, somehow. The murderer seems to have been very careful up to now and left us no real clues at all, but then he suddenly goes and tells me that he's had three bottles of the sherry we're looking for when he knows he can't produce the empties to back up his story. However, I admit it's suspicious and I shall certainly keep my eyes on Dupuy. As you say, murderers do make mistakes.'

'Perhaps he didn't expect you to ask him whether Mrs. Dawes had given him three bottles for a present,' I suggested. 'Perhaps he thought you knew more than you did and had to invent a story on the spur of the moment. Did he seem at all frightened when you asked him that question?'

'No, he didn't,' Julian said. 'But I don't set much store by that; my experience is that you never know how well a man can act until he's put to it.'

'How did you get the idea that he might have had some sherry from Mrs. Dawes?' I asked.

'I didn't,' Julian said. 'I went round to ask him if he remembered any better what he'd had to drink at Hickman's party. He still doesn't remember drinking anything but whisky, by the way. In fact he says he makes it a rule not to drink anything else; says it makes him feel better the next morning. I only asked him quite casually whether Mrs. Dawes had given him a bottle of sherry for a present at any time; I thought it might be just worth asking while I was there.'

'It certainly was a lucky question,' I said.

Chapter Ten

I found that Caroline was out to luncheon and I had to have my meal alone. She had, I remembered, been out to several meals lately, but although she had obviously been enjoying herself this did not prevent her from grumbling at me when she returned in the afternoon. I had spent my time, she complained, going about with Superintendent Julian and the Chief Constable, having every kind of exciting adventure, looking at finger-prints, following suspects, sniffing at poisons, and I know not what else. But when I was with her I was dull and secretive; if I thought I was going to make another Dr. Watson out of her she assured me that she was no more willing to assume the part than I was capable of acting that of Holmes. I apologized profoundly, though for what I was not quite sure, and hastily began to describe what had lately happened. I told her I was afraid there was beginning to be something of a case against Dupuy; he had been poisoned at the bottle party but couldn't find any coherent explanation of how it had happened, and he had admitted receiving some bottles of Genuine Fino sherry from Mrs. Dawes but had apparently told a lie about what he had done with the empties. It looked as if he had given himself a small and safe dose of atropine in order to divert suspicion from himself; it looked as if he had been taken aback by Julian's questions about Mrs. Dawes's present and had hastily told an ill-considered lie. There was no kind of proof against him, I said, but certainly some grounds for suspicion.

Caroline protested vigorously. She was sure that poor John, as she called him, was not and never could be a murderer; it was a ridiculous suspicion and absurd to condemn him because the poor boy didn't remember what he had done with some old empty bottles. Perhaps he had put them somewhere else, perhaps someone had taken them off his rubbish heap; some of the children might easily have found a use for empty bottles, or some of the villagers. I agreed with all this but explained that it was necessary to continue suspecting him at least as much as anyone else and, to turn the edge of her indignation, I asked her whether she had learnt anything in the course of her recent wanderings about the school.

'Nothing to do with the murder, I'm afraid,' Caroline answered. 'I certainly didn't hear anything against John Dupuy, if that's what you're suggesting.'

'No, no,' I protested.

'The only thing I heard was some discussion about that old affair of Dawes with some woman in London. Susan's murder brought the subject up again, I suppose, but only because we were wondering how she actually got on with her husband. It doesn't seem very relevant really.'

'No,' I agreed, 'but did you hear anything new about it?'

'I only heard some people remembering what an extraordinary amount of talk there had been about it. It was when I was out to tea yesterday.'

'You didn't find out whether it went on after Dawes's marriage, did you?' I asked.

'No,' Caroline answered, 'but of course it might have done. What I did hear was that Dawes had gone about telling everybody that he was conducting some secret affair.'

'But we knew that already,' I said.

'Yes, I know,' Caroline answered. 'But the point is that he used actually to describe some of the extraordinary things he did to keep the whole affair secret. Letters sent to a post-office, and how the post-office objected, and how eventually he used to leave notes inside books at the London Library; he had to be very careful to choose books that nobody else was likely to look at and he made one of his typical jokes, I was told, and said he put the letters inside books he'd written himself.'

'But who was he keeping the affair secret from?' I asked.

'Well, from the woman's husband, I suppose,' Caroline said.

'And did anybody explain why he was so open about his secret?' I asked.

'Well most people thought it was just part of his character,' Caroline said. 'But John suggested that there might also have been something he was trying to conceal by putting out a misleading story.'

'Yes, I see,' I said. 'And what do you suppose he was trying to conceal?'

'Well, it might have been the fact that he hadn't got a mistress at all,' Caroline suggested. 'But we've discussed that already. Or, as someone suggested, he might have been concealing the fact that when he went off to see his mistress he didn't go to London at all but somewhere else.'

'Yes, that's an interesting possibility,' I said. 'But rather vague, don't you think?'

'Dawes is going to London the day after to-morrow,' Caroline said.

'Oh is he? By Jove, I wonder… How do you know?'

'Oh he's told one or two people.'

'Has he now?' I asked.

'Yes, he's going by the 10.15, or so I heard,' Caroline replied. 'It's the train which meets the express at the junction. About the only train worth taking, of course, if he really is going to London. The adjourned inquest is to-morrow, but you knew that. Probably some more will come out then, as the first was what they call merely formal. Dawes has got to be there, of course; he couldn't go to town until after.'

'Isn't it rather odd that he should be going to town so soon anyway?' I asked.

'Well, perhaps,' Caroline said. 'That's really my point. Do you know,' she added and her voice betrayed some excitement, 'I think we ought to follow Dawes up to London or wherever he's going.'

'Probably the police will be doing that anyway,' I said.

'I shouldn't think so,' Caroline said. 'They've got nothing definite against him.'

'You can't be sure,' I said.

'Anyway, I think we ought to go, whatever the police do,' Caroline said.

'Rubbish,' I answered. 'I haven't any idea how to follow people. It requires training. I should be noticed at once.'

'It obviously only requires a little intelligence,' Caroline said. 'And anyway I shall be there to help you.'

'Then it will be all the easier for Dawes to see that he's being followed,' I pointed out.

'I thought of asking Dupuy to come too,' Caroline said, looking obstinately at me.

'Well, then,' I objected, 'Dawes is even more likely to notice us.'

But Caroline met every objection, though not always with rational argument. She pointed out that Dawes was short-sighted and would never wear spectacles unless it was absolutely necessary, so that he would not notice even if he was followed by a crowd. She wanted me to take this opportunity of observing Dupuy as well, and she was sure, she told me, that when I knew him a little better I would see that he could not possibly be a criminal. And she suggested that if I did not bestir myself Mrs. Eakins would be writing to her old friend the Home Secretary, Scotland Yard would come down, and I should not be allowed to have anything more to do with the case.

I was not impressed by this last argument, but I did reflect that if Caroline was really determined to drag Dupuy up to town with her, it might not be advisable to let them go alone. He was, I had always thought, a very impressionable young man and naturally I was by no means certain of Caroline's affections. But the prospect of trailing—I believe this is the proper word—the unfortunate Dawes all over the place, after the fashion of the detectives who procure evidence for divorce, did not appeal to me. It would be just like Caroline to insist on some kind of disguise or pursue some elaborate manœuvre which would turn the whole very sordid pursuit into an uproarious but highly embarrassing farce.

The next day the adjourned inquest was held in Scropeham in a dingy hall. I went in at the beginning, but after I had sampled the peculiar flavour of the ceremony and had observed the solemn jury, the local journalists pretending to be hard-boiled, the coroner speaking in a very low voice so as to avoid all sensationalism, the police very attentively playing up to his mood, I decided that I would be unlikely to learn anything much from the inquest and that the evidence would probably amount to no more than a slow recapitulation of what I already knew. I left as Hickman was describing what had happened at his house; he was being made to explain, very laboriously, what a bottle party was, and the coroner did not seem to approve. After all, I reflected, if anything important came out I could read about it later or get it from Julian. I went off to the Red Dragon, which seemed the most promising hotel in Scropeham, though excessively Tudor within and black and white outside, and waited in the lounge with a drink. I went back to the inquest when I thought it might be ending but it was not, and I hung about outside in the hope of catching Julian when it was all over. He must have left by another door, for I missed him; instead I was myself caught by a journalist from London who said that he had met me somewhere before and suggested we might lunch together at the Red Dragon.

It is generally believed that journalists infest the scene of every crime, pestering everyone in the neighbourhood to allay their insatiable curiosity. But where, and in what newspapers, can you read all the thrilling revelations that ought surely to result from such impertinent inquiries? Photographs, one may suspect, are sometimes obtained by unscrupulous devices and when the trial is over one may sometimes be offered embarrassing statements by sorrowing relations. But on the whole I am inclined to think that the curiosity of the Press has been much exaggerated and I am sure that nothing happens in this country which is in the least like what one sees in American films. Here everyone is much too frightened of the law of libel, or of contempt of court, or of questions in the House of Commons, or at the very least of a letter to *The Times*, so that the difficulty is to get anything into the newspapers, not to keep it out of them. At any rate my acquaintance—he reminded me that his name was Graham—seemed to have been chosen by his newspaper for his tact and discretion rather than for his capacity for intruding. He asked me none but the most general questions about Scrope House School and scarcely referred to the crime; when I asked him if he had any ideas about the murder of Mrs. Dawes he seemed to be quite uninterested. It was his business, I discovered, to sort out the statements of the police and the reports of the inquest so that they made a coherent account; it was a severely technical task and he complained bitterly of the trouble the police often gave him by putting out such muddled and unprintable stuff. 'Not that the news agencies are much better,' he conceded, and he then proceeded to complain of the subeditors who, when he had at last got a paragraph into some sort of order, often made a mess of it again. I asked him why he bothered to come all this way from London when he could just as well employ his talent for adjusting the cadence of a paragraph at home.

'Why indeed?' he asked. 'But there it is. There's a tradition that a descriptive writer ought to be on the spot, and sometimes I can get a bit in about the landscape, or about the kind of house the murder was committed in. But they usually cut that out. However, I did think I might put in something about progressive schools, though I don't know whether it would be allowed. I gather they're going to keep this business as quiet as they can; Mrs. Eakins seems to have a bit of a pull and anyway we don't think it fair to give the impression that just because the school's a modern one it's the sort of place where the staff go about murdering each other. No, I daresay I'd do better to concentrate on the landscape, the moors you know, and perhaps a bit about what Scrope House was like in the eighteenth century. I'm going to look up the house in the County History if they've got it in the library here.'

I asked Graham if he had met Superintendent Julian.

'Oh yes,' he answered, 'I got on all right with him. He's a free-mason, of course.'

I did not follow the connection of his thoughts and said so.

'You can't get on in my job without being a freemason,' Graham replied. 'All the chief London police are freemasons and a good many in the provinces. It's really one of the chief drawbacks to my profession; it's rather expensive, you know, the subscriptions and all the dinners. But you can't expect the police to tell you anything if you're not a freemason.'

'I thought you didn't want them to tell you anything,' I objected.

'Oh well, it's always useful to be on good terms with the police,' he said. 'They can always make things difficult for you if they want.'

Since Graham appeared to be so trustworthy I told him how we had found a bottle with a little poisoned sherry in it in Hickman's garden and how difficult we found it to understand why only two people in the party had been poisoned. It seemed to me just possible that a man who had reported so many crimes might have a new idea.

'I don't think the police issued any statement about that,' he said.

'Oh, didn't they?' I asked.

'No, I'm sure they didn't,' Graham said. 'And nothing came out about it at the inquest. I'm afraid we couldn't touch that. Definitely not the sort of the thing that ought to be published.' I felt as if I had been indulging in what is now called Careless Talk and had been properly reproved.

That evening, when I had made another vain attempt to persuade Caroline to give up her notion of following Dawes to London, or wherever else he might be going, we had to make plans for the next day. It would be necessary, she thought, and I had to agree with her, to be at the station half an hour or so before the train started, in order that we might not meet Dawes on the platform. If we got there early we could lurk in the waiting- or refreshment-room and then jump into the train just before it started. I suggested that Dawes might also come into the refreshment-or waiting-room, and what should we do then? Caroline answered that we should have to pass it off somehow, which left me with grave misgivings. But, after all, if we were caught at the very beginning of our enterprise and had to give it up there would be no harm done. Thus we had to arrange for an intolerably early start, ordering breakfast at a quarter past eight and rising positively at dawn. We gave our instructions to Noakes and asked him to tell Mrs. Eakins, who had now gone into strict retirement again after the first excitement of Mrs. Dawes's murder had passed off, that we would be away on business for a day and a night at least, and conceivably for longer. Dupuy, it was arranged, was to call for us at the Dower House five minutes before the car was to start.

The next morning Caroline was inevitably not up in time and I debated whether I should let her go on sleeping and call the whole thing off, but I knew that she would make a fuss if I did not see that she caught the train, so I sent several messages to her room and eventually roused her with five minutes to spare for a scrambled breakfast. This meant that it was not until we were in the car with Dupuy that I was able to show her a letter which had come for me by post that morning; I was not quite sure that I ought to have shown it to her in front of Dupuy. It was without any signature, printed in the conventional capital letters which are intended to disguise the writer's handwriting, there was a local postmark, and it read:—

'Thou wretched, rash, intruding fool, farewell.'

At first I thought that Caroline was suitably impressed by this alarming message, but after gazing at it for a moment she began to laugh and then handed the letter to Dupuy, who was also amused.

'It's all very well,' I said, 'but it may be important.'

'I'm sorry,' Caroline said. 'But you must admit that it's rather funny to get it just when we're starting.'

'It doesn't look as if there was much chance of being able to follow Dawes without being seen,' Dupuy said.

'I suppose Dawes must have written it,' Caroline said, 'but how on earth did he find out? Did you tell anyone,' she added, turning to Dupuy, 'that we were going up to town to-day?'

'Well, I had to tell Edgeworth, of course,' Dupuy answered, 'and I had to let my class know I shouldn't be there and arrange for someone else to take my place. Richards is taking them; I don't think you've met him, have you?'

'No,' I said. 'But no doubt he'll turn out to be a great friend of Dawes.' I was extremely annoyed that our expedition should have been so well advertised.

'But even if Dawes has been told that John was going to town,' Caroline said, 'there's no reason why he should suspect that John was going with us and certainly no reason why he should suspect that he himself was going to be followed.'

'That's true,' said Dupuy.

'Let me have a look at the letter again,' Caroline said. 'It's from *Hamlet*, isn't it.'

'Oh yes, it's *Hamlet* all right,' I said. 'Now where did I hear…?'

Caroline's remark had vaguely reminded me of something and I tried to trace the lost connection in my mind, but since I was trying to remember I inevitably lost the connection all the more.

'No doubt it will come in time,' I continued. 'But as to *Hamlet*, is there any special reason why it should be quoted at the moment? Is the play being acted in the school, or anything?'

'I've no doubt Dawes has read *Hamlet*,' said Caroline.

'Yes, of course,' I said, 'but I wondered if there could be any special reason.'

'I believe his class have been reading it lately,' Dupuy said. 'I'm not sure, but I can find out if you really think it worth while.'

He was obviously unable to understand why I should look for a special reason for quoting from a play which consists almost entirely of well-known quotations.

We reached the station nearly half an hour before the train was due and made at once for the refreshment room. Dupuy kept watch by the window while Caroline and I had a cup of coffee each, at my request, to provide a reason for going into the room. I was glad that Dupuy should have decided to stand by the window; if I had had to stand there I should have felt very uncomfortable, wondering what the girl behind the counter would be thinking of me and whether she would object to an intruder who used the room without buying any refreshments. It is this timidity, or perhaps it might be better described as delicacy of feeling, which makes me so unsuited to the assertive profession of detective. Dupuy, however, seemed quite brazen and contented to wait there for some twenty minutes until he saw Dawes walking on the platform and beckoned us over to point him out. We all gazed through the window, as though expecting I know not what illumination; the hunt was, as Caroline ventured to put it in this moment of excitement, up.

Chapter Eleven

We waited in the refreshment-room until the train came in and we could see that Dawes had entered a carriage; there was an awkward moment when he seemed to be looking towards the refreshment-room window, from which we were looking out, but as Caroline had predicted he was not wearing his glasses and she assured us that he would be unable to recognize anybody at a distance of more than a few feet. We ourselves did not venture out until the train was just due to start and then we had no time to choose our carriage. When we had time to look round we saw that we had a fellow-passenger, a hawk-eyed Scotchman reading *Exchange and Mart*. In this sombre and disapproving presence we were constrained to silence and each of us, I make no doubt, felt embarrassed as we contemplated the preposterous adventure that lay before us; it was unfortunate that we were unable to exorcise our embarrassment by any open conversation.

But we soon slowed down for the next local station and one of us had to lean out of the window to make sure that Dawes did not leave the train, a procedure which seemed to puzzle the Scotchman, and so at each station until we reached the junction. There Dupuy jumped out before the train had entirely stopped so that he could see Dawes getting out of his carriage and not lose him in the crowd. Soon he waved to us to come on; this was a critical moment, for the London train would be in in ten minutes but there might be other trains, either from this or another platform, and it was essential to see that Dawes did not go by any of them. Actually he merely paced the platform, reading what seemed to be a very small pocket edition of some eminent work of literature, and we were able to watch him unobserved until the London train came in. This train, as Dupuy pointed out, would have a restaurant car, and it was important for us to find a carriage that would not be between the restaurant car and whatever carriage Dawes himself might choose; otherwise he might pass our carriage on the way down the corridor to get a meal. As it turned out, this meant that we had to get into a crowded part of the train and to separate, each finding a seat in a different carriage.

I was not sorry to be alone and to be able to read in peace, but actually my fellow passengers were so talkative that I found it hard to pay attention to my book. They were, I discovered, commercial travellers and two of them were returning rather disconsolately to London after a tour of the northern counties. I listened vaguely to their accounts of astonishing strokes of business and heard how one of them, a traveller in paper as it seemed, had accidentally met a butcher and had been given a large order for a great deal of grease-proof paper.

But I had to listen more closely when I found that the travellers were talking about Scropeham and Scrope House. The paper man, it seemed, had tried to get some orders from the school and had found everyone there most unsympathetic. It was obvious that his friends were anxious to hear anything that he could tell them about a place where there had lately been so exciting a murder.

'Funny place,' the traveller in paper was saying. 'Girls and boys together. Not very up-to-date, I shouldn't call it, more like one of these council schools. I don't know how they manage, not when the kids are as old as that. No idea of doing business either. By the way,' he continued, 'I saw one of the chaps from the school, when I went along the corridor just now. The drawing master there, I believe he is. I once tried him with some cartridge paper samples but he wouldn't look at it. Didn't seem to be half good enough for him. Don't know what they use there, I'm sure; put the kids to draw on gold leaf, I shouldn't wonder.'

'Daresay this murder won't do them any good,' said another traveller.

'They don't seem to know who did it yet,' said another.

'I've heard,' the traveller in paper said, 'that it's one of these cases where the police know who it is but can't prove it.'

It occurred to me that as Sinclair was in the train he might, perhaps, see Dawes in the restaurant car and Caroline and me in our several seats; he might then wonder why we were all going to town. Perhaps I was unduly suspicious but I was suffering from a guilty conscience and naturally feared that anyone who looked at me would detect my intention. I thought that at any rate it could do no harm if I had a casual word with Sinclair and found a plausible reason for running up to town. I went along the corridor and, as it happened, noticed that there was a seat vacant by Sinclair's side. I sat down and asked him if he was going up to town. He seemed rather annoyed; no doubt he was one of those many people who dislike talking in the train.

'Obviously,' he replied, and I apologized, reminding him that it was customary when Englishmen were crossing the Atlantic and met on the boat to ask each other if they were going to America. He was not impressed by this argument, but he did tell me that he was going up to town to take up some children's paintings for a combined exhibition of the work of school-children from a large number of schools. I then explained that I was going to meet an American who had done some work on identical twins; I thought it better to tell a barefaced lie and one that would never be exposed, so I embroidered it by explaining that the American thought he had found an interesting correspondence in the electro-encephalograms of identical twins; some such discovery had in fact been lately made and I thought it unlikely that Sinclair had heard of it. Caroline, I said, was coming up with me in case there should be any notes to take or papers to collect from my rooms. As to Dupuy, I thought it unnecessary to invent a story for him; I merely mentioned that I had noticed that he was on the train. Sinclair did not seem in the least interested in these elaborate, perhaps rather suspiciously over-elaborate, explanations. In fact the only thing that seemed to interest him at all was the work of his pupils, about which he talked, though not very freely, for a while. I remembered that Mrs. Dawes had described him as a lonely man who wanted company but did not like it when he got it. I returned, after expressing my hope that the children's pictures would look well in the exhibition, and again attempted to read without attending too closely to the conversation of the commercial travellers. Perhaps I ought really to have listened, if by doing so I could have acquired something of their superb assurance, a quality which, as I was beginning more and more to fear, is absolutely indispensable in a private detective. The snack luncheon in a box, which Caroline had thoughtfully purchased at the junction so that we might not be driven to the restaurant-car and a possible meeting with Dawes, did very little to enliven the journey.

I am glad to say that at King's Cross there was no question of having to exclaim 'Follow that taxi', a possibility which I had been dreading at intervals during the journey. Dawes was not the man to take a taxi except in a grave emergency, and after I had met Caroline and Dupuy on the platform, we were able to see him make for the Tube. There was, it is true, a moment when we feared that we had lost him in the crowd, but we were soon reassured by the sight of his hat, a hat that had evidently been kept for visits to London and looked discordantly smart by contrast with the rest of his dim and scholarly costume. At the booking office Caroline had the presence of mind to ask for three eightpenny tickets as we followed Dawes at no great distance; we could not know how far he was going and it was essential that we should not be checked by having to pay any excess fare on our tickets. There was a considerable crowd on the platform waiting for the train and we hastily conferred together and decided that I had better travel in the same carriage as Dawes, since he knew Dupuy better than me while, as to Caroline, it was more likely that he would let his eyes rest on a woman than on a man. I was to try to signal to them when Dawes got out of the train. If by chance I should be separated from my companions while I was following Dawes we were to meet for dinner at the hotel where we were to stay for the night, or if I could not get away at dinner time, still later that night.

Accordingly I followed Dawes into the train and stood at the other end of the carriage with my back turned towards him, looking occasionally over my shoulder and only venturing to turn round when I saw that he had his eyes fixed on his little leather-bound book. He got out at Russell Square and I stumbled after him through the crowded carriage. As I followed him down the platform past the carriage where Caroline and Dupuy were sitting I rapped on the window but did not succeed in attracting their attention though I did attract the attention, most embarrassingly, of several other people in the carriage and one young woman gave a start and a giggle; I do think that Caroline might have been more alert. There was nothing for it but to go on alone, which was just what I had feared might happen all along.

As it turned out, it was not too bad at the beginning. Dawes went into Russell Square, a large and empty space across which I could follow him at a discreet distance, without any risk of being seen by my short-sighted quarry—that is, if he really were short-sighted and this was not merely an invention by Caroline designed to lure me up to town. This painful thought came into my mind when we had crossed the square and were proceeding down a short street whose name I forget; I immediately walked more slowly and put another ten yards between myself and Dawes. But then I thought again and decided that this was too bad to be true; as Dawes turned to the right at the end of the street I came up closer to him. He turned in at the British Museum, went inside, glanced at the clock in the entrance hall, and entered the reading-room.

I have never had a ticket for the reading-room; no doubt I ought to have one and it certainly looks bad, but there it is and at any rate it is not the best place to go for scientific papers. I might have got in, but this would have meant making a fuss and perhaps attracting Dawes's attention. So I stood disconsolate by the picture-postcards, wondering whether Dawes would remain in the reading-room until closing time. That would mean a wait of an hour and a half and I had a good mind to give the whole thing up. Nothing could be more innocent than a visit to the reading-room and no doubt this was the sole reason for his journey to town; he was merely trying to get on with some work, poor fellow. But why had he looked so attentively at the clock? Doubtless, my common sense told me, in order to see how long he had before closing time, but doubtless, the detective lurking within me suggested, because he was going to meet someone at the Museum in a fairly short while. It might be in the reading-room or it might be elsewhere, but in any case it would be worth waiting. I stayed on by the postcards and had plenty of time to reflect on the extraordinary capriciousness of the British Museum, which provides a great many postcards, coloured reproductions of Chinese pictures, expensive volumes of reproductions of anonymous dotted prints, but, unlike every other museum in Europe, refuses to supply the ordinary public with photographs of even its more obvious and eminent exhibits. The stimulus of adventure had made me bold and I ventured to ask the young woman behind the counter for a photograph of my favourite piece of Etruscan sculpture; I hope this annoyed the Museum, but I doubt if the reproach was really felt. In about twenty minutes, when I had exhausted the interest of everything in the entrance hall and was wondering whether it would be safe to pay a brief visit to the illuminated manuscripts—not that manuscripts are really my cup of tea—Dawes came out of the reading-room and I ducked behind a pillar.

He went up the stairs and I made my way cautiously after him; we passed through the fascinating chaos of perhaps the most interesting and certainly the worst arranged ethnological collection in Europe and eventually reached the Print Room. The British Museum is a good place in which to follow a suspect; it is positively made for loitering with intent and if the suspect should look round there is always something behind which to hide, but I was certainly nervous of being observed in the Print Room. However, Dawes made straight for the other end of the room and while he was contemplating the Chinese pictures I was able to make use of the screens and bays which are thoughtfully provided there and so get closer to him without, as I hoped, any risk of being seen. I took up what seemed to be a good strategic position behind a screen on which was displayed a German engraving of remarkable ugliness but interesting, as its label informed me, because it was a hitherto unknown state of a work by the Master of the Gadarene Swine. If anyone had noticed the rapt attention with which I had inspected this production he might well have been suspicious, but the only other visitors in the Print Room, besides Dawes himself, were two small Japanese who were not likely to cause me any trouble. In about five minutes a personable young woman came into the room and made straight for Dawes; they were soon engaged in earnest conversation and from their manner I could tell that they were certainly intimate friends. I went on listening and snooping and from what scraps of conversation I managed to overhear I was led to suspect the worst.

At this point a door which I had not noticed before was opened and a pale young man came into the room. After a moment's reflection I was able to place him; I had met him at dinner somewhere a year or so ago, Harty, as I now remembered, by name, though presumably not by nature. The two Japanese also observed him and came up to him.

'Please,' they said, 'we want to see dirty pictures.'

'What, again?' asked Harty, but they said nothing in answer.

'Oh, very well then' he continued. 'If you'll go in by that door, I'll come in a minute.'

The Japanese went through the door, preserving the inscrutable mask of the Orient, and Harty proceeded towards a show-case, wrote something in a notebook, and returned to his room. On the way back he seemed to catch Dawes's eye and nodded at him. I waited until Dawes and the young woman had their backs turned towards me and were so intent on their conversation that they were unlikely to notice what any other visitor to the Museum might be doing; I then crept towards the door and as casually as I could manage, though I am afraid I could not altogether shake off the air of a conspirator, I opened it and went inside. Perhaps I ought to have knocked, but I was not going to risk it.

I introduced myself to Harty; I was not sure whether he remembered me but he was quite friendly and, I should think, very glad to have a little distraction from the dull duty of making a catalogue, or whatever it is that people do in museums. He looked rather impressive at his handsome desk and the whole room was formidably academic in appearance, but the Japanese did not appear to be troubled by the atmosphere; they were seated at a table in a corner with some coloured prints, presumably from their own country, which they had taken from a portfolio in front of them. I wanted to take a closer look over their shoulder, but I did not think this would make a good impression on Harty. We had a little desultory conversation and then I mentioned Dawes.

'By the way,' I said, 'I thought I caught sight of Richard Dawes in the Print Room. Isn't he one of the people from Scrope House?'

'Oh yes,' Harty answered. 'I met him when I was down there once. Do you know the place at all?'

'Oh yes, a little,' I said. 'Do you go there often?'

'No,' he answered, 'I've only spent a week-end there, like most people.'

'You don't know the girl Dawes is with, I suppose?' I asked. 'Does she come from Scrope House, too?'

'Oh no,' Harty answered. 'She's Isobel Walker. You know, the girl who runs that shop where they sell instructional toys invented by psycho-analysts. And very curious some of them are.'

'Have you got any in the Museum?' I said. 'I should like to see one.'

'No, but we ought to have some. You'll have to look in at the shop, though if you do you won't get out again without at least an hour of insufferable ennui.'

Harty seemed to have an inexhaustible fund of gossip and we continued in this vein for some minutes, until I took my leave. No doubt he must have wondered why I had paid him a visit, since we hardly knew each other, but I couldn't help that; he may only have thought that I was at a loose end.

When I came into the Print Room Dawes and Miss Walker had left and, to tell the truth, I had rather hoped that they wouldn't be there. I might, of course, have hurried out of the Museum and caught up with them in the street; but it seemed to me that I had both learnt and had enough. It would be very easy to say that Dawes had taken a taxi outside Russell Square Station and that I had lost him because there was no other taxi for me to take.

'Took a taxi, did he?' Caroline said, when we had met again at our hotel. 'I thought we'd agreed that it wasn't in his nature to take taxis. That's rather suspicious, isn't it?'

'Why?' I asked.

'Perhaps he saw you after all,' said Caroline, 'and took that means of getting away from you.'

'Perhaps,' I said.

It was a pity that I could not ask Caroline what sort of person Isobel Walker was—she would almost certainly have known all about her—but I was determined to keep my information to myself, at any rate for the time being. It was too serious a matter to run the risk of letting everybody at Scrope House gossip about it, and I don't think that Caroline or Dupuy were at all seriously disappointed by what must have appeared to them an extremely meagre result of our expedition to town. Caroline, as it seemed to me, had merely wanted an excuse for a trip to London and she should have been satisfied. As for Dupuy, he may have been disappointed that he was unable to divert suspicion from himself by attracting more suspicion towards Dawes, but as far as I could tell from his actual demeanour he had been quite happy to make the journey for the sake of Caroline's company. And so we had dinner, went to a cinema, returned to our hotel, and arrived back at Scrope House the next day.

Chapter Twelve

I soon found there was no reason to fear that our expedition to London had aroused too much interest at Scrope House. Mrs. Eakins, I had thought, might have imagined that I was neglecting my duties and others might have imagined that in following Dawes I was going too eagerly about them; actually they were all much too busy to wonder what I had been doing. For on the day after that of my return there was to be the first cricket match which Scrope House had ever played against another school. Not long after we had got back to the Dower House Edgeworth arrived to arrange with Mrs. Eakins about to-morrow's entertainment of the spectators at the cricket match and of the Scrope House eleven and the visiting team from Seadale School. He invited Caroline and me to watch the match from privileged seats in front of the pavilion and I was glad to see that I was still considered a distinguished visitor to the school. But I was surprised, and could not help saying so, to learn that the emancipated children of Scrope House should indulge in what, according to the *Encyclopædia Britannica*, 'may be called the national summer pastime of the English race.'

'Oh, it's not my idea, of course,' Edgeworth said. 'But the children wanted to play cricket and I didn't see that there was anything I could do about it. As a matter of fact I was rather surprised myself but, after all, there's no great harm in it.'

'No, no, of course not,' I reassured him.

'I expect some of them had been talking to children from other schools in the holidays,' he continued, 'and they may have felt a little ashamed of not having any cricket of their own to talk about. I think that must be the explanation, or something like it. It began with a very solemn deputation to ask me to have a pitch prepared; I said they must put it to the vote at the next meeting of the children's general council. I thought that would stop it, but it didn't; cricket got through by a small majority. I rather think all the refugees must have voted for it because they thought it would please the English. I spoke myself, of course, though I didn't vote; I said that I very much hoped they wouldn't try to persuade any children to play cricket who mightn't really want to. Naturally that was what I was afraid of.'

'I don't really see,' I said, 'why there should be more chance of tyranny in connection with cricket than with net-ball, or stool-ball, or whatever it is that they play at progressive schools.'

'Nevertheless it is so,' said Edgeworth, 'though I admit there's no obvious reason why.'

'Perhaps,' I said, 'it's because of the immense moral importance attached to cricket and all its rules, particularly to the unofficial and unwritten rules. The bowler, for example, must never stump the batsman at his end if he should go outside his crease, that is, not unless he gives the batsman fair warning; otherwise it would be considered a dirty trick, though there's actually nothing in the rules against it. No, cricket is a ritual which binds the upper-middle classes together, inducing a feeling both of solidarity and of virtue. Rulers of the world unite; you have nothing to lose but your wickets. And naturally, if you won't play, it's as bad as being a Trotskyite in Russia or a Calvinist in Rome. It's a communion, a sacrament, a love-feast, in which the participators are enabled to perform the most delicate acts of sacrifice for the greater good of the community, the congregation, or, as the cricketers themselves would put it, of the game. Observe, for example, how willingly the batting side will lend one of its members to the fielding side if any of them should be injured, and how scrupulously he will work to run or catch his own side out. Inevitably, and like the Christians of old, they set great store by the text, "compel them to come in."'

'Dear me,' said Edgeworth, 'I wish we'd had you to speak at the general council. I've no doubt you would have carried the majority with you and saved me a great deal of trouble. It's certainly a great nuisance arranging all the pomps and ceremonies of this infernal match. Do you know that they actually want me to call for three cheers for the Seadale eleven when the match is over? Most embarrassing.'

'I should have thought,' I said, 'that the captain of the Scrope House eleven ought to do that. I have an idea that's the rule.'

'Is that really so?' Edgeworth asked. 'Well, I'll certainly tell him you said so. You don't mind my quoting you as an authority?'

'Not at all,' I answered, 'only too glad to be of assistance. By the way,' I continued, 'I wouldn't mind betting that Crossley and Mandeville were on that deputation you were talking about.'

Crossley and Mandeville were the two boys with whom Caroline and I had talked on our way back from Walton's farm.

'Well, yes, they were,' Edgeworth answered. 'But how on earth did you know?'

I smiled in what must have seemed to him a painfully self-satisfied manner.

It was a beautiful day for the match, so fine and warm that Mrs. Eakins, as her secretary told us after breakfast, thought it would do her no harm to watch the cricket for an hour or so before lunch. If we wished we could drive out with her to the cricket field; the match was to begin at eleven-thirty and we would start soon after eleven. Accordingly Mrs. Eakins was wrapped and muffled and hoisted into the car, while we watched from the steps by the front door. She took a parasol to protect her from the sun, an umbrella in case it should rain, a shooting-stick because this might be considered a sporting event, a manuscript book bound in hand-printed Italian wallpaper, a copy of the cricketer's almanack, quite new and evidently bought for the occasion, and two pairs of field-glasses. What with her rugs and her parcels and, in spite of the compression exerted by the world's most expensive corsets, the body of Mrs. Eakins herself, there was no room for anyone else on the back seat of the car, so Caroline and I sat on the folding seats while the secretary travelled in front with the chauffeur. This meant that there was no room for a footman to ride beside the chauffeur, although it had been arranged that on this ceremonial occasion there should be one, and Mrs. Eakins had to dismiss the man who was standing attentively by. But, after all, Miss Stanhope would be far more useful in any emergency.

The cricket ground was some way from the school, an agreeable field, with a background of handsome elms, very impressive in the sunlight. 'Cricket is so English,' Mrs. Eakins said, as the ground came in view; her intonation made it impossible to judge whether or no she used the word 'English' as a term of endearment, and it was characteristic of her to leave this doubt in one's mind; by refusing to commit herself, by enclosing quite ordinary words in scarcely percep-tible inverted commas, she contrived to invest the simplest remarks with a no doubt quite spurious air of subtlety. Before I could return a suitably ambiguous answer in the same vein we had stopped and it was time for Mrs. Eakins to be pried, very slowly and gently, out of the motor. I was conscious that a large company were watching this process but while it continued Mrs. Eakins seemed quite unaware of anything except herself and her belongings; the very instant that it was over she changed in the twinkling of an eye and became an overpoweringly gracious hostess, uttering affectionate but nicely calculated greetings with astonishing rapidity. Once again I was amazed at the latent vitality which only showed itself at such a time. Normally sessile, an appropriate stimulus would turn her into an active and free-swimming creature; the mature barnacle could on occasion revert to its larval form.

Caroline and I quickly removed ourselves from the more immediate orbit of Mrs. Eakins; Caroline found several friends to talk to and I had leisure to observe the assembled company, who were waiting, rather impatiently, for the arrival of the Seadale eleven; they appeared to have been delayed on the road. Dawes was not, of course, present, but most of the staff of Scrope House were there, together with a number of strangers whom I took to be visitors from Seadale. The Scrope House eleven were fiddling about by the door of the pavilion, a small wooden building hastily erected and in itself proclaiming that cricket was a side-show at Scrope House; I was interested to notice that there were two girls in the eleven and also my old friend Crossley, though not, as far as I could see, his companion, Mandeville. Colonel Redder and his wife were there, dressed as for a garden party. Deck-chairs were provided for all the official or distinguished spectators, but such children from Scrope House as wanted to watch the match, and of these there was no great number, had brought camp-stools and were distributed round the field. There were also some other visitors outside the enclosure in front of the pavilion and among these I thought I caught sight of Superintendent Julian, and also, as far as I could see from a distance, of the farmer Walton and his son. It was a Saturday and no doubt this was a whole holiday at the grammar school, so that the boy was free to watch the match. Julian and Walton, I thought, must have been genuine lovers of cricket to come, apparently without invitation, and I hoped that the play would be worth their attention.

Edgeworth beckoned to me when he saw me and introduced me to an impressive figure, a clergyman dressed in artfully careless tweeds, perhaps rather theatrically handsome, Dr. Borrodale, as he told me, the headmaster of Seadale School. I had the impression that Edgeworth had been glad to interrupt an awkward conversation and had called me over for that express purpose. The two headmasters appeared to be extremely suspicious of each other, though hiding their feelings under a mask of assumed affability.

I once had an uncle who was a clergyman and with whom I used occasionally to go for country walks. If we ever met another clergyman in the road, a clergyman whom my uncle did not know, I used to notice how covertly but closely they would observe each other, after the fashion of dogs meeting for the first time, though my uncle's cloth naturally forbade that more thorough inspection which is permitted among dogs. No doubt schoolmasters have as good reason as clergymen to stare out of the corner of the eye, to sniff with discreet nostrils, when they meet their fellows, but Edgeworth and Borrodale had better reason than most. Seadale School, I had already learnt, was one of those minor public schools which are never quite sure of their status. Fifty years ago it might almost have been described as a grammar school, and it offered its pupils little more than a classical education and some useful knowledge; thirty years ago its first attempts to better itself, under a headmaster with a considerable reputation as an alpine climber, were checked by one or two unfortunate scandals. It was generally agreed that the school suffered from what is known in academic circles as a bad tone. After the retirement of the alpine climber Dr. Borrodale was appointed. He had been enthusiastically recommended by a number of knowledgeable dons, there was no risk that he would falter in his purpose, he had submitted to the customary ordeal of two years in charge of a boys' club in Bethnal Green, and his fixed preference for the children of the upper classes had been quite unaffected by this test. By lowering the intellectual and raising the social standard required of prospective pupils, by offering scholarships to children of distinguished parentage who might not have succeeded in passing the common entrance examination at better known schools, he had worked wonders for Seadale. Moreover he had proceeded with exemplary tact. Once captured, a valuable pupil was never unduly favoured, and the principles on which he made his choice were never openly exposed; it was only possible to infer them from the result. Edgeworth, on the other hand, chose his pupils for very different reasons; what he preferred in a candidate for admission to Scrope House was a thoroughly interesting neurosis, such as a total incapacity for any kind of washing, and a high I.Q. Thus the only entrance examination for Scrope House was an intelligence test specially devised by an American psychologist. The antipathy resulting from the possession of such very different principles of selection, and such very different systems of education, was increased by the fact that Edgeworth had recently contributed to a symposium on progressive schools and Borrodale to a symposium on public schools; each had made unpleasant jokes at the expense of the most cherished beliefs of the other. It was evident that the cricket match between Seadale and Scrope House was beginning to be regarded by the two headmasters as a symbolic struggle between two implacably opposed parties. It was to be a trial by combat, not the less momentous because Edgeworth, at any rate, would be unlikely to admit that it was capable of deciding the issue.

At last the Seadale eleven arrived in a charabanc, with two schoolmasters to guard them; they had to explain, under the disapproving eye of their headmaster, that they had been delayed by a puncture. The eleven boys were so beautifully dressed, in white trousers and striped blazers of violent colour, with caps to match, that as with a row of chorus girls one scarcely noticed any difference in their polished and confident faces; it was as if the type had been conveniently stamped out in a set of eleven. Each face flickered with the same consternation when they saw the Scrope House eleven and observed that they were all differently dressed, only one or two in white trousers, and with no cricket colours at all, except that one boy wore an M.C.C. blazer which it was unlikely that he had any right to wear. The presence of the two girls—when they first saw them the Seadale boys must have supposed that they had nothing to do with the Scrope House eleven—proved the final shock, and I am afraid that for the moment they forgot their manners, whispering among themselves and even tittering aloud, until they once again observed that Dr. Borrodale's eye was upon them.

Seadale won the toss and decided to go in first; the weather and still more the pitch, which altogether lacked the perfection to which they were accustomed on their own ground, made this an obvious decision. The pitch had not been adequately rolled, there were many plantains, and the Seadale captain, inspecting the ground with a morose and supercilious eye, even wondered whether it had been recently played on. No doubt it had been; it had probably not occurred to the careless amateurs of Scrope House that it might be prudent to shift the stumps a little to right or left of the ground disturbed by their last game. The supporters of Seadale were indignant when they saw how lively and unpredictable this made the Scrope House bowling—though it is true that their own bowlers would have an even greater advantage when their turn came—but Edgeworth had no regard for their feelings. When Borrodale made an ironic comment, Edgeworth at once launched into a lament for the old days of really exciting cricket, when every ground except the very best was as imperfect as his own.

'Of course,' he conceded,' the fatal predominance of the defence over the attack is never so disastrous in inferior as in first-class cricket. You seldom get Maginot line cricket in school or village matches, which is why I infinitely prefer them. But if the pitch isn't first-class either, then defence and attack are really balanced; you get, as it were, a war of movement instead of a war of attrition and anything can happen.'

'Anything indeed,' Borrodale answered, but Edgeworth disregarded him.

'It's curious,' he said, 'how the Maginot line seems to have exerted its fatal influence over every game in recent years; I believe it's much the same with chess.'

'You ought to get your team to use those bats you see in old prints,' Borrodale said, in a by no means agreeable voice.

'Ah, no,' Edgeworth answered. 'Those bats were used when the bowling was quite different and the ball was trundled along the ground. Against modern bowling you couldn't defend your wicket at all with a curved bat and that would be as bad as defending it too well.'

'I did not intend my suggestion to be taken seriously,' Borrodale replied.

The effect of the pitch showed itself in the first few overs. The Scrope House captain had put on a fast and a fairly slow bowler; in his very first over the slow bowler pitched a ball into what appeared to be a hole filled with dust; the ball scarcely bounced at all, but trickled slowly along the ground. The batsman stopped it with an expression of haughty disgust and it was as if a child had thrown a brightly painted rubber ball on to the pitch at the most critical moment of a test match and the captain of the Australian eleven had had to remove it. In the next over a fast ball of good length hit a plantain or some other obstacle and bounced almost vertically upwards. The batsman attempted to play it, though it might just have been safe to leave it alone; the inevitable result was that it sailed directly into the air and immediately over his head. The bowler and point ran to get below it and even the wicket-keeper, so great was his excitement, rushed in front of his wicket to gaze upwards at the ball as it dropped from a great height. It was fortunate that he did so, for point and bowler collided disastrously and while they were wondering if they had suddenly been assaulted the wicket-keeper was able to catch the ball.

'I suppose that would be "caught at wicket",' said Borrodale, an obscure but apparently effective sneer.

The next man in had evidently been so impressed by his predecessor's fate that he determined to take every precaution. He took guard
with precision and ceremony and spent at least two minutes patting
down refractory hummocks with his bat and poking at plantains in
his immediate neighbourhood. When at last he was ready to play he
steadily blocked every ball or ignored it if he thought this was safe; his
example seemed to affect the other batsman, so that for a number of
overs there was very little happening, except for an occasional bye or
a very discreet hit to leg for one. In fact the headmasters were left to
do all the scoring for their respective schools. Borrodale commented
on the remarkably small number of Scrope House children who had
turned out to see the match. Edgeworth replied that of course they
could all have come if they had wished but no doubt they had found
something better to do and quite a number preferred to get on with
their work. To judge by the effect of this on Borrodale, it was as
good as a boundary for Scrope House.

When this monotonous play had finally exhausted the patience
of the spectators and only Mrs. Eakins could be seen still showing
a bright but presumably simulated interest in the game, the Scrope
House captain decided to change the bowling. We were all excited,
and no one, I am sure, more than Borrodale, to see that he was putting
on one of the two girls in the eleven. She was a charming creature
with two pigtails of dark hair, very neat and precise in figure and in
all her movements, and it was obvious that she took her bowling very
seriously. She measured exactly the length of her run and dropped
a handkerchief to mark its limit; she altered the disposition of the
field, waving cover-point about five feet to the right of where he was
standing before and putting three instead of two in the slips. Her
delivery was curious, with many apparently deliberate hoppings and
skippings, and as the ball left her hand she had the attention of the
whole field and of all the spectators upon her. But her first ball was,
catastrophically, a wide, and the gasp of horror from every throat

would have unnerved any less armed and impregnable Amazon. She returned with entire composure to the spot marked by her handkerchief, executed a sharp and military right-about-turn, and once again ran with precisely the same irregular and jerky movements towards the crease. The ball was quite a good one but the batsman, who no doubt felt himself infinitely superior to a female bowler whose first ball was a wide, came out and took it full toss. The ball soared away towards the trees and the batsman leant negligently on his bat; it was the kind of hit which could not be mistaken for anything but a boundary. Again the bowler walked slowly to her mark, again she turned sharply round, flapped her way forward, and, with every eye upon her, bowled an outrageous long hop. The batsman had prepared himself to come out and take as before a ball of much better length; he did not quite recover himself in time and was cleanly bowled.

'I've never seen a wicket taken by a worse ball,' Borrodale said, and Edgeworth had to agree.

The next batsman, it appeared, was the most cherished virtuoso of the Seadale eleven. 'That's Clifton,' Borrodale said. 'He comes of a cricketing family, of course, but I'm not sure that he isn't going to be even better than his father.' A late cut for two showed that Borrodale's pride was not misplaced; the bowler rearranged the field, but once again Clifton made almost the same stroke and with beautiful precision placed the ball where the fielders in their new positions could not reach it. The last ball of the over broke eccentrically to leg and Clifton left it alone. But the bowler seemed to have recovered her nerve—for in spite of her apparent composure one had to assume from the quality of her bowling that she had not been feeling quite herself. Long-hop or no, she had taken a wicket, and the last three balls of the over were entirely respectable.

It was the fast bowler who had been kept on at the other end and Clifton's partner was determined to continue playing as cautiously as ever, leaving it to Clifton himself to make the runs. Several times he managed to make one run at the beginning of an over in order to leave the bowling to Clifton, but otherwise he blocked or evaded every ball. The score mounted quietly but impressively, the bowlers were several times changed, but Clifton remained unassailable and Scrope House began to rest all its hopes on the well-known effect of the luncheon interval. Shortly before one o'clock Clifton's partner was neatly caught in the slips, but this did little to cheer the supporters of Scrope House. Seadale, it was felt, would have an unlimited supply of sound and stolid batsmen who would be ready to eschew all adventures and exist to oblige their hero; whatever else you might think of them, it was obvious that they would have cultivated the team spirit. When it was time for lunch Clifton was only six runs from his half-century and the score was 73 for three wickets; Seadale was doing a great deal too well.

It is to be hoped that their luncheon did something to compensate the visitors for the asperities of the cricket-ground and the degrading slovenliness of the Scrope House eleven. It was cold salmon with cucumber, cold chicken and salad, and strawberries and cream with an ice on the top; as far as I can remember this was exactly the kind of lunch I had most enjoyed as a boy, though on this occasion, and especially when my palate had been so amply indulged at Mrs. Eakins's table, I did not find it altogether to my taste. Lunch was in a large marquee, with the two elevens at a long table—I was interested to notice that Crossley had seated himself next to Clifton and was obviously absorbing with rapt attention the authentic flavour of a genuine public school—while the rest of us sat at smaller tables. The elevens were given cider cup—very mild, as Edgeworth carefully explained—but we had a really excellent claret which must, I should think, have come from Mrs. Eakins's cellar. Edgeworth, Borrodale, and I shared a table, and when Borrodale had drunk a glass or two of the claret he became much more cheerful and enthusiastically praised the wine. He seemed, in fact, to be one of those wine-maniacs whose fuss about vintages and decanting, about the kind of glass from which you should take your liquor, and so on and so forth, with every kind of preposterous rule and shibboleth, has always seemed to me to be an exercise for the snobbery far rather than for the sensibility of the toper. If you want to train your sensibility I should have thought the study of one of the arts would be far more useful, but wine-maniacs will often tolerate the most frightful assaults on all but the particular sense they have chosen to cultivate. Dons, for example, are usually quite happy to sip their priceless vintages in full view of the Herkomers which hang in their college halls. I am all, of course, for alcohol when used as a sociable drug, but that is quite a different matter; it was the drug in Mrs. Eakins's claret, rather than the delicate opulence of its bouquet, which now made Borrodale so good-humoured.

He had a stock of quotations from the librettos of the operas of Gilbert and Sullivan and from *The Wrong Box* which he evidently kept for his hours of relaxation, and he praised these works in a fashion which I found exasperating, especially as he did so with the air of showing how broad-minded he was. Since Edgeworth was not ready with any rejoinder I decided that I would do my best for the honour of his school. I said that I had lately heard some extracts from Gilbert and Sullivan's operas on a friend's gramophone and had been frankly appalled by their undisguised vulgarity and intolerable coarseness of fibre. As to *The Wrong Box*, I said that no doubt it was the best of Stevenson's novels, and certainly the most readable, but I had always believed that this was because Stevenson had had Lloyd Osborn to collaborate with him in this work and no doubt to correct his style. The claret was not having quite the same effect on me as on Borrodale, though I suppose something must be allowed for the fact that he had given me an opportunity to retort, rather unfairly, to the pastors and masters with whom I had had differences in my youth. I should think schoolmasters must often have to suffer such acts of vicarious revenge.

Chapter Thirteen

We finished lunch before the two elevens had had their second helpings of strawberries and we left the marquee before them. When I got outside I noticed that a number of the Scrope House children were waiting for the afternoon's cricket to begin; they had had a less spectacular lunch in another tent. I came on the small boy whom I had met in the school studio, where I had seen him painting with profound concentration. Now he had a butterfly net in his hand and was gazing sadly into the air at an insect which had flown far beyond the reach of his net.

'What was it?' I asked him, and he looked round with a start.

'I thought it might be a white admiral, or even a purple emperor,' he said.

'Are white admirals common round here?' I asked.

'No,' he answered, 'very rare, but not so rare as purple emperors. I shouldn't think it could have been a purple emperor... not really.'

'Oh, I wouldn't say that,' I said, but I could see that he did not really care for any too obvious illusion.

'I got a silver-washed fritillary the other day,' he said, falling back on the more solid satisfactions offered by reality.

'Is this a good place for butterflies,' I asked him, 'or have you come to paint a picture of the cricket match?'

'Oh, I wouldn't paint a picture of a cricket match,' he answered. 'Not unless it was an imaginary one, that is.'

'I see. What have you been painting lately?'

'I finished two pictures yesterday for the exhibition.'

'Is that the exhibition in London?' I asked.

'Yes,' he said. 'It's the first we've sent pictures to. They had to be posted off this morning. They went by registered post. Do you think they'll give me five pounds if they're lost? That's what you get if a registered letter's lost, isn't it?'

'Oh, I should think so,' I said, 'though they probably won't be lost. But didn't Mr. Sinclair take the pictures up to town on Thursday?'

'Oh yes, he did, of course, but those were only the ones that were ready then. I had to do a lot more to mine and so had Sally Thomson and Peter Green and Robert Plowright... There's the cricket beginning,' he added.

'So it is. Do you think they'll get Clifton out soon?'

'I don't know. He's very tall, isn't he?'

A butterfly caught his eye and he made after it, but soon returned.

'It was only a green-veined white,' he said.

'What'll you do,' I asked, 'if you see a butterfly fly across the cricket pitch?'

'It'd be difficult, wouldn't it?' he said. 'If it was a cabbage white, it wouldn't matter, but I couldn't very well miss a purple emperor, could I?'

'No, indeed,' I answered, and, after saying good-bye, made my way back to the seats in front of the pavilion. I couldn't help wishing that a purple emperor, real or imaginary, might flutter across the pitch; it would be a lovely situation for Dr. Borrodale and the Seadale eleven, while I felt sure that the butterfly-catcher would be able to carry it off with complete aplomb.

In the first over there was nothing to suggest that Clifton's efficiency had been impaired by his luncheon; a drive through mid-off gave him three runs and left him to face the bowling in the next over. There was a new bowler at this end; as is the amiable custom of teams which play cricket for pleasure it seemed that almost everybody in the Scrope House eleven was going to be allowed to bowl for at least one over. The new bowler's first ball was a yorker which Clifton played without scoring, and the rest, though the bowler kept a reasonably good length, were nothing to disturb any batsman of the most ordinary competence. Even the pitch seemed to be behaving itself, and for all that one could tell Clifton might have been playing on a perfect wicket; if he had been at all uncomfortable after lunch the new bowler had given him his chance to play himself in and, incidentally, to reach his fifty with a couple of two's off the last two balls of the over. Nor was there any hope that he might prove overconfident, for the next two overs passed without incident and it began to look as if there was no hope for Scrope House and very much as if Clifton might carry his bat. Once again the bowling was changed, with the pig-tailed girl back again in place of the last bowler, for in this emergency the Scrope House captain could not follow his plan of evenly distributing the bowling in regular rotation amongst all who might like to try their hand. The girl had now changed to the other end and had the advantage of what little wind there was; it was not much but whether for this or for some other reason she was now distinctly faster. The third ball of the over completely baffled Clifton, and this without any adventitious aid from the wicket; he came out of his ground, was badly deceived in the flight, and failed to connect. The girl had to be allowed all the credit for dismissing Clifton, even by Dr. Borrodale.

'A very good ball,' he admitted. 'Let's see, that's 82 for four wickets and it's just a quarter past two. I hope we shan't have to declare.'

Their lunch may have made no difference to the agility of the little victims, as the poet Gray would so reasonably have thought them, who were playing out there in the sunshine. But the grateful shade which had now reached the space in front of the pavilion, the scent of grass cuttings mixed with oil from the mower, the humming of insects and the distant sound of bat meeting ball, combined with the warm claret within us to keep us all at our ease in the deck-chairs. Mrs. Eakins had already left to take her nap, perhaps in her bedroom, perhaps in the Italian garden—it would depend on how she felt when she got back to the Dower House—Edgeworth and Borrodale were no longer alert in defence or attack, the butterfly-catcher left his prey undisturbed, and for myself I was soon half and at moments wholly asleep. I may have missed many prodigies of cricket, but no one suggested that anything very exciting had happened when at last I was able to give attention to my neighbours and to the game. Seadale, as I saw from the scoring board, had made a hundred and thirty-eight and there was now only one wicket to fall. Within a few minutes the last wicket had been taken for three more runs.

'What time are stumps drawn?' I asked in a still sleepy voice.

'At half-past six,' Edgeworth answered. 'It's a quarter past three now. I suppose we shall play for a draw, though I hope not.'

Before his team went out to take the field, Borrodale had a word with the Seadale captain and I overheard him saying that they must be careful not to bowl too fast on a bumpy ground when the two girls were batting. This sounded ominous and when, in fact, I saw the Seadale bowlers at work I felt that Scrope House had not much chance even for a draw. They may or may not have decided to play for one, but their intentions were hardly discoverable from their play; the first wicket fell in the second over, with only a bye to begin the score, and the second not much later, after another bye had been run and a ball had been snicked for two between the slips, where it ought really to have been caught.

This would not, of course, have been recognized as fast bowling by really good cricketers, but any bowling which is faster than one is used to can be sufficiently alarming. Even Crossley, who went in next, was visibly nervous and was not in the least comforted when Edgeworth called out to him as he passed to remind him that he was only playing a game. It was a remark which Edgeworth could hardly have resisted making, for Crossley's expression was comically resolute and solemn, he carried his bat with an air of supporting the whole destiny of his school, his hair had been most carefully smoothed and greased, and his pads, unlike those of the rest of the eleven, had been beautifully whitened for the occasion. But it was not what was required to reassure Crossley; it would have been better to fall in with his mood and if possible to suggest that his equipment was entirely adequate for so serious and formal an occasion. Edgeworth must have recognized his mistake as soon as he made it.

'I am afraid,' he said, 'that I don't quite know how to manage that boy. No doubt,' he added reflectively, 'it's because he always rubs me up the wrong way.'

'He looks all right,' Borrodale said. 'Well turned-out, at any rate. Is he a good bat?'

'I don't know, I'm sure,' said Edgeworth.

This hardly seemed to me the moment for discussing what was the right approach to Crossley since, as I saw it, he was suffering from an excessive respect for precisely those values and standards that Borrodale thought most suitable for adolescence. I therefore held my tongue and watched Crossley supporting the white man's burden in the field. He was by no means a natural or inspired bat, his style was not easy, but he must have taken trouble and practised a good deal; he played by rule and tried to do the right thing. Unfortunately, when he had made no more than eight, he sent up a particularly feeble catch to short leg; the ball had come higher than he expected and his rather slow working mind had not enabled him to make the quick adjustment that was required. It was as if he had given the ball to the fields-man on a spoon, and when he returned to the pavilion his chagrin was evident. When he had taken off his pads he wandered away from the pavilion by himself.

Scrope House was now making a rather better stand, though there was still very little scoring. It is true that they had the advantage of being accustomed to their own kind of pitch, which had now become even more erratic than when Seadale was batting, but as against this they were up against unusually competent bowling and it looked as if the most they could hope for was a purely defensive stand which would almost certainly not last until stumps were drawn. Borrodale had every reason for complacency as he watched the batsmen only just holding their own through a number of maiden overs.

'It looks,' he said to Edgeworth, 'as though your theory about the advantages of a rough wicket wasn't altogether sound. You could hardly call this a very lively game or a war of movement.'

'They've got to get their eye in,' Edgeworth answered, but unfortunately at this moment a thoroughly timid and evasive stroke gave the bowler an easy catch. However he dropped it, as even the most accomplished cricketers sometimes will, and Borrodale had to make apologetic noises. When the score had reached thirty-four by slow and seldom creditable stages, another wicket fell and a curious figure left the pavilion, his trousers not only grey but baggy and stained, the rest of his clothes even shabbier than those of most of the Scrope House eleven. He wore a felt hat to protect his head against the sun.

'Who's that?' Borrodale asked.

'That's Apfelbaum,' said Edgeworth. 'It's curious he should have taken up cricket.'

'Very curious,' Borrodale said. 'And who is Apfelbaum?'

'You've probably heard of his father,' Edgeworth said.

'No, I haven't,' Borrodale said.

'Oh, haven't you seen any of his plays?' Edgeworth asked. 'They've been translated and one or two of them were put on at that communist theatre, what's its name?'

Borrodale grunted; he wasn't going to trouble to protest against the assumption that he might be the sort of person who would spend his time watching seditious plays.

Apfelbaum made no great impression at the beginning of his innings and one or two overs proceeded without incident, but his subsequent performance was so interesting that I afterwards took the trouble to ask some questions about him. It was from Rosenberg that I got my information; the two exiles had naturally been drawn together and Rosenberg had watched with benevolent interest over what he considered Apfelbaum's rather erratic enthusiasms. I gathered that he had arrived one day and asked Rosenberg why only the English played cricket; it was not, he pointed out, as though the peoples of other countries were not equally interested in most other games, but cricket they seldom if ever attempted. Rosenberg was delighted to consider this problem; he was, as I had already discovered, one of those numerous foreigners who enjoy explaining the English. Apfelbaum listened politely to the suggestion that so extremely dull a game and at the same time one that offered so many opportunities for nice distinctions of conduct, for subtle interprepations of 'the unwritten law', was obviously made for the English. Who but the English, Rosenberg asked, would discuss so interminably the obscure ethics of body-line bowling and who but they would consider reprehensible a practice against which there is no rule and which makes it possible for them to win the game? Apfelbaum agreed, but was not really interested in this aspect of the matter; what he really wanted to know was not why only the English would, but whether only the English could, play cricket. It turned out that he had formed an attachment for one of the girls at Scrope House but feared that she was unable to take a foreigner seriously. She herself was an enthusiast for cricket—she was, in fact, the pig-tailed girl whose bowling had at last sent Clifton back to the pavilion—and it had occurred to Apfelbaum that if he took up cricket it might establish his common humanity in her eyes. Rosenberg thought the whole idea very silly and considered that cricket was a waste of time for a clever and promising boy. And as to his love affair, it was, of course, no more than an adolescent and wholly innocent passion, but not the less likely to distract his mind. He had much better concentrate on his mathematics, in which he was very likely to do well, but if he were really determined there could be no possible reason why cricket should be beyond his capacity. Of course, he could do as well as any Englishman; he might do better, because he would probably apply himself more seriously to the game. The English, Rosenberg concluded, were apt to have apparently serious emotions about trivial matters, but even to such frivolities they found it difficult to apply their minds seriously. Apfelbaum had better begin by grasping the theory and history of the game; a good bibliography of the subject could no doubt be found in any encyclopædia; Rosenberg would be interested to know whether the new Italian encyclopædia was better informed on this subject than the *Encyclopædia Britannica*.

Apfelbaum proceeded patiently and earnestly with his reading and for some time perplexed everybody who met him with difficult inquiries. Buttonholing the schoolmaster who gave casual instruction in cricket, a certain Mr. Wilkins, he would ask what was the difference between playing and hitting a ball, a distinction which he had met in a report of a cricket match but which the unfortunate Wilkins was quite unable to understand. Very soon Apfelbaum was able to overwhelm the pig-tailed girl with his learning and to criticize every ball that she bowled, every stroke that she made, with deadly precision. Distressed by this omniscience she suggested that Apfelbaum had better see what he could do himself, and let her do the criticizing. This seemed reasonable, so he took her place at the nets and she proceeded to bowl for him. He was at first in some difficulty, because the description which he had read of the process of keeping a straight bat had seemed, to a mind trained in geometry, most ambiguously framed; he was not quite sure how the bat should be held in order that, as the authorities put it, it should be equally opposite to the trajectory of the ball. He argued with the girl and she with him; she was even less capable of making a clear statement than the book he had consulted, but eventually, by watching what she instinctively did, he was able to understand the process both in theory and in practice. She bowled to him for about ten minutes while he accustomed himself to the use of an unfamiliar instrument, and he then directed her to bowl in turn each variety of ball about which he had read in his books. He was amazed to find that she could not deliver any kind of ball to order and pointed out that this would certainly retard his education in cricket, since it was probable that she would waste time by sending down balls which he already knew how to manage. However he kept her at it until she was exhausted; when she insisted on stopping he pointed out that there were several strokes in which he had had insufficient practice.

The next day he procured the services of Mr. Wilkins and asked him to demonstrate Larwood's method of bowling against the Australians in 1932–33; Wilkins did his best, but Apfelbaum was profoundly dissatisfied with the result, though in the process he certainly gained experience of faster bowling than he was likely to encounter from the Seadale bowlers, for Wilkins got exasperated by Apfelbaum's persistence and bowled as fiercely as when in the past he had played for his college. It did him no good; Apfelbaum still insisted that almost every day he should spend several exhausting hours at the nets. He did not greatly care for playing in the casual games which were occasionally arranged at Scrope House; they wasted time which could have been spent on more intensive practice. He had not yet taken up bowling, but was meditating a comprehensive study of this art in the near future.

Apfelbaum was the only member of the Scrope House eleven who seriously regretted the irregularity of the pitch; it was apt to disturb his calculations. There was, however, as he had already foreseen, a method of cutting out this unpredictable element in the bowling, though in order to apply it it would be necessary to get his eye in.

For this reason he played with great caution for several overs and during this time yet another wicket fell; his new partner proved to be the pig-tailed girl. Mindful of Borrodale's instructions and wishing to make a demonstration against the ridiculous notion of letting girls play in serious matches, the bowler behaved disgracefully; his first ball to the girl was an under-arm lob. The insult went home and the girl's blush of mortification could be seen from the pavilion; in her distress she could do no more than block the ball. Apfelbaum, though not often interested in other people's feelings, had had his perception quickened by love and resented the bowler's gesture almost as much as did the girl herself. He waited until he had to face this same bowler, in the next over but one, and then decided to put into practice his method of cutting out the unpredictable influence of the wicket; he came right out of his ground and took the ball full toss. He frowned slightly when he observed the result of his stroke, doubtless because if the ground had been larger he might have given a catch to a fieldsman standing just on the boundary line. His emotions had for the moment mastered his intellect and he had perhaps got a trifle too much under the ball; he decided that this should not happen again. Thereafter the bowlers could do nothing with him; if they attempted to baffle him by any considerable variation of the length they only succeeded in bowling long-hops and soon learnt the folly of that.

You never know what will happen in cricket—great men have trodden on their wicket and the best batsmen in England have made strokes that would disgrace a village player. But apart from such accidents, it was soon obvious that Scrope House could only lose if all the remaining batsmen were out before Apfelbaum had made the required score. Unfortunately this seemed only too likely to happen. 'I can't think,' Edgeworth said, 'why we didn't put Apfelbaum in first,' but as this had not been done it was certain to be a very near thing. The bowlers, in this new and urgent situation, were no longer bowling

under-arm to the pig-tailed girl, Apfelbaum was running her off her
feet, and she was only able to keep her end up for three more overs,
during which the score mounted to fifty-eight. She would probably
not have stayed in so long if the bowlers had not remembered their
headmaster's instructions and had not still in some measure respected
her sex; it was as a bowler rather than for her batting that she had
been included in the team. Six wickets had now fallen and Edgeworth
himself instructed the remaining batsmen to play for safety and to
give Apfelbaum every possible opportunity to take the bowling. 'But
for Heaven's sake don't run him out,' he added, and I was amused
to see how very seriously he was taking the game. He was shocked
when the next batsman himself made several hits, and horrified when
he insisted on taking two runs though he could easily have taken one
and so have left the bowling to Apfelbaum. However he did rather
better than his predecessor and when eventually he was caught and
bowled he had himself made nine, two more byes had been run, and
Apfelbaum's contribution had raised the score to eighty-five.

The next batsman appeared to be terrified by his responsibility and
was all but bowled first ball, but by the mercy of providence this was
the last ball of the over and when the eighth wicket fell Apfelbaum
had made twelve more runs. The second girl of the Scrope House
eleven went in next and once again the Seadale bowlers had most
reluctantly to exercise their chivalry; she was smaller than the pig-
tailed girl, she had not bowled, there was no reason to think that she
could play cricket at all, and though there could be no question of
any more under-arm bowling her opponents were very gentle with
her. She resisted the temptation of slow and easy balls and for some
time took no risks; Apfelbaum went remorselessly on and the score
had reached a hundred and nineteen when she succumbed to the offer
of a particularly easy ball and hit it, with considerable style, for an
admirable two. This was too much for the bowler's patience; if she
could play cricket after all she could not expect to be so expensively

indulged and so, regardless of his headmaster's possible disapproval, the bowler sent down a fast one. This only surprised the wicket-keeper, produced a bye, and gave Apfelbaum the bowling, but he lost it again with a three and the last ball of the over took away the girl's middle stump.

'I wonder,' Edgeworth said, 'whether Apfelbaum realizes what the score is,' and he instructed the last man in to draw Apfelbaum's attention to the extreme urgency of the situation. 'He's got to make fourteen to win,' he said. 'You'd better tell him. And whatever you do, keep in for another five minutes.' Possibly Apfelbaum was not really interested in winning the match, but the Seadale captain was well aware that the next few minutes would decide the issue and in this crisis he decided once again to change the bowling. A slow and cunning bowler might prevent Apfelbaum from scoring as quickly as before and give more time in which to get his partner out. It looked as if the plan might work, and perhaps even better than the Seadale captain had any right to expect; Apfelbaum played the first ball with caution, and off the second he sent up what seemed to be an easy catch in the direction of cover-point. It was all right, because the field were standing so far out, in expectation of Apfelbaum's usual standard of play, that no one had time to reach the ball, but it was an appalling moment for the spectators. The bowler waved to his field to come further in, and they came forward, licking their lips. This may have annoyed Apfelbaum, though I doubt if he was capable of so childish an emotion. At any rate he hit the next four balls for four each, the first to leg and well over the fielders' heads, the next three, when every one was in the deep field again, exactly where the ball would most comfortably reach the boundary without any risk of interference. The minute tip of the tail of the Scrope House eleven, relieved of all responsibility, hit out wildly at the first ball of the next over and sat down on his wicket. Scrope House had won the first innings by two runs.

'The match was certainly full of incident,' Borrodale remarked, 'but I don't know that it could be precisely called cricket.'

'Would you prefer to call it football?' Edgeworth asked, a childish repartee, but one that came naturally to him in his present mood of boyish exuberance.

Chapter Fourteen

B ut this nerve-racking day was not over, nor were all its events yet revealed. It had been decided that the Seadale eleven should go in to bat during the hour or so that remained for play. 'It's the sporting thing to do,' said Borrodale, and so it was done, but I felt that to watch this pointless even though sporting performance would be very much of an anticlimax and I therefore persuaded Caroline to walk back with me to the Dower House. When we had had a rather late tea it was still so fine and warm that I decided I would take a book into the garden. I read it, of course, but I also meditated and my reflections were started by Borrodale's use of the word 'sporting'. It is an odious word, at any rate when it issues with entirely false joviality from a mouth which seems to have been made to shut like a rat-trap, but it was curious to observe that Borrowdale had, after all, most strictly regarded the rules and regulations of his contest with Edgeworth. The two headmasters had spent the day in scrapping with each other, but though Edgeworth must often have tried Borrodale beyond endurance, and I myself, I am afraid, often did my best to get under his guard, he had still treated the contest as a game rather than as open war. For at any moment, if he had chosen to break the rules, Borrodale could have won the easiest of victories; he had only to refer, however obliquely, to the murder which had so recently disgraced Scrope House and he had only to suggest, however softly, that this crime was no advertisement for the absence of discipline in which the school took so much pride. But this would not have been sporting, this would not have been cricket, and even though the real cricket on the field was proceeding with a shocking lack of decorum Borrodale was not going to break his own rules. I must admit that I saw some advantages in the discipline that results from organized and compulsory games.

So far Edgeworth, and everyone else connected with the school, had succeeded pretty well in concealing their fears for the reputation of Scrope House; to behave as if the murder was merely an awkward irrelevance was obviously the right procedure, but I was beginning to doubt whether this composure could be much longer sustained. It was becoming more and more necessary that the facts about the murder of Mrs. Dawes should be discovered; at the moment the murder remained a charge against the whole system and morals of Scrope House, an unanswered and unanswerable charge. While it was not precisely formulated no defence could be made, but when the facts were known, however disastrous they might prove to be, Scrope House would at least know what it had to face. Borrodale might think it unsporting to mention the murder and draw the obvious conclusion when actually in Edgeworth's company; elsewhere he and many others could not fail to do so.

When I had come to this unhappy point in my meditation and had in consequence decided that I must now make a really determined effort to solve the mystery, Caroline arrived with news of another crushing and unexpected blow to the reputation of the school; like a messenger in a Greek tragedy she came just when the chorus had decided that the situation could not be more hopeless than it was. She had just taken a message for me on the telephone informing me that the cricket pavilion was in flames.

'The fires have begun again,' she exclaimed. 'You really must do something this time.'

'Yes, but what?' I asked.

'I've borrowed Miss Stanhope's bicycle,' she said. 'I'm going straight off to the cricket field. You'd better see if you can get another bicycle and come straight after me.'

The bicycle seemed a good idea, and I managed to get one from Noakes, but I did not follow Caroline. Instead I rode as fast as I could to Walton's farm, but left the bicycle in a ditch when I was nearly there, and for the rest of the way strolled gently up the lane until I reached the farmyard. There I leant negligently against a gate as though enjoying the cool of the evening. For some time I contemplated, with as innocent an expression as I could manage, the laborious efforts of a sow who wanted to break down a fence to reach her children; they had wickedly crept through a gap through which their mother was too fat to pass. Presently Walton appeared and let the sow through by another gate. I wished him a polite good evening.

'There's a lot of interesting things to see in a farmyard,' I added. 'I don't wonder country people are supposed to spend all their time leaning over gates.'

'There's nothing interesting here,' he answered. 'Not for a bloody detective.'

This was very satisfactory, but of course I had to make a gentle protest. It was disregarded.

'Still I'm glad,' Walton continued, 'that you've come to see for yourself instead of setting Smallbones on to me.'

'Who's Smallbones?' I asked.

'Oh, nobody you'd know,' Walton answered. 'Nobody you've ever heard of.'

'I think I may have heard the name, but I can't exactly place it,' I said. 'I certainly don't know anybody of that name.'

'Whether you know him or not,' Walton retorted, 'I know him and he knows me and he told me it was your idea to start the police asking a lot of questions I've answered a hundred times already. If you've been paid by that crazy school to try and shove the blame for the fact they can't manage their own boys on to me, you'd better go back and tell them what they can do about it.'

'I don't quite know what you're talking about,' I said.

'Oh no,' Walton answered. 'Oh no, of course not.' His irony was portentous.

'I suppose Smallbones is the village policeman,' I said, because, as a matter of fact, I had just remembered that he was.

'Holmes, this is marvellous,' Walton replied, and I must say that I felt this was distinctly a score. But it did not look as if Walton would be content to keep the controversy on this level of polite irony for much longer; he was getting very red in the face and I really began to fear that he would go for me with his pitchfork. But he controlled himself enough to try another insinuation.

'Any way,' he said, 'if you'd been doing your business properly and watching that bunch of lunatics as you're paid to do, they wouldn't have burnt down their own cricket pavilion.'

'How did you hear about that?' I asked.

'It's all over the place,' he replied. 'If you think you can keep that sort of thing quiet you're much mistaken and you can tell those bloody schoolmasters I said so. Why, if you go to the top of that hill you can see the fire for yourself.'

I went to the top of the hill to see the fire for myself. I don't know if Walton expected me to do this but he made no effort to detain me in any further conversation. In order, if possible, to leave in a friendly manner I mentioned that I had seen Walton and his son at the cricket match; he growled out something about being a busy man and not being able to stay till the end of the first innings; it wasn't what he called cricket, anyway, and he and his son had left early in the afternoon because they had work to do at the farm. On my way up the hill I noticed Ted Walton hard at work cleaning out a fowlhouse. When I got to the top I found some difficulty in observing the fire but at last

I noticed a small amount of smoke going up beyond a distant clump of trees which were presumably the elms that shaded the pavilion. It was not an interesting sight and if I had not known what it was I might have taken it for a bonfire in the distance. On my way back I dropped in at the pub which I had visited before when I had gone to Walton's farm with Caroline. While I drank my half-pint I asked the landlord if he had heard of the fire at the cricket pavilion; after all, I reflected, Walton was perfectly right when he suggested that you could not hope to keep such things quiet, and the landlord was certainly interested to hear the news. I found that Caroline had returned to the Dower House before me; she also had been disappointed by the unspectacular nature of the fire. I suggested that perhaps she had not been in time to see the fire at its worst and that it had made more of a show before she arrived, but she was positive that she had missed nothing. She told me that, as far as she could gather, it had broken out soon after the Seadale eleven had left, after a late tea with the Scrope House eleven. There was nothing to show who had started the fire; it was first noticed by the groundsman when he was tidying up after everyone had left.

Later that evening Edgeworth rang me up and asked me to go round and see him. I was shown into his study where he received me rather solemnly and I realized that even with the best will in the world he could not help assuming the conventional air of severity which is expected of headmasters when they receive people in their studies.

'I very much hoped,' he said, 'that we had seen the last of these fires. I thought the mere fact that you were known to be on the look out might have stopped them.'

This did not seem very complimentary to my powers as a detective. Apparently I had only been employed as a warning, like the detective who shows himself, very obviously, at wedding receptions.

'I really don't know what to do now,' Edgeworth said, discarding the grand magisterial manner.

'I suppose there's no doubt this fire has considerably narrowed the field of suspects,' I said.

'Yes, but if so, that makes it even worse,' Edgeworth answered.

'Why?' I asked.

'Well, obviously,' he answered. 'If there's a dozen or so children, any of whom might have started the fire, each of them is bound to be seriously suspected, whereas if the suspicion is distributed over the whole school it falls more lightly on any individual.'

'All the same,' I said, 'let's consider who these dozen or so suspects are.'

'It's not quite definite,' Edgeworth said, 'but I must say it looks as if someone in the cricket eleven must have done it. There may have been someone else hanging about, but as far as I know everyone else went off while the elevens were having their tea, and afterwards, when the Seadale eleven had left, the Scrope House eleven had to pack up their cricket things and so on. Nobody else had any reason for hanging about the pavilion.'

'Not unless their reason was that they wanted to burn it down,' I said.

'Yes, of course,' Edgeworth answered. 'But I have made some inquiries and so far nobody claims to have seen anyone else about the place. I rather specially stressed the possibility of another person hanging about because I didn't want the eleven to think that I necessarily suspected one of their number.'

'If you knew who started the fire, what would you do?' I asked.

'Why, of course,' Edgeworth said, 'I should leave it all to Hickman.'

'Well,' I answered, 'I've got an idea about the fires but I can't say that I've got definite proof, though I think it makes a plausible theory. The question is, if I tell you my suspicions, will it make matters worse for you? How would you manage if you suspected a boy without having unassailable proof of his guilt?'

Edgeworth seemed to shy at the word 'guilt'.

'It might be rather difficult,' he said, 'but I don't know that it isn't worse to have to suspect eleven children. I'd rather know what you think.'

'I believe the conventional method of dealing with such situations,' I said, 'is to deliver a lecture to all the suspects, to tell them that you are giving the culprit a certain time in which to own up, but that otherwise all the suspects will be punished.'

'Yes,' Edgeworth answered, 'I know. It happened once at my school when I was a boy and it is also, I believe, the method of invading armies against acts of sabotage by the civilian population of an occupied country.'

'Quite so,' I said. From this, and from what I already knew of Edgeworth, I felt that I was justified in taking the risk.

'I'd better begin,' I said, 'with what I've learnt or surmised about Crossley's character, and to some extent about Mandeville's. Crossley is the stronger character of the two and the older; he probably has a great deal of influence over Mandeville. You probably know that he's passionately interested in the ways of conventional and public schools. I expect that he's read a great many school stories and talked to boys from other schools—I'm sure that he's talked to one particular boy from another school, but we'll come to that later. From all this he's come away with the notion that he's missing all the adventures of boyhood by coming to a soppy place like Scrope House. He doesn't like the company of girls, he doesn't like the absence of organized games, or the very few opportunities which Scrope House gives to him of displaying his superior toughness, his masculinity, his capacity for undergoing ordeals. He is, in fact, a young savage, with all the savage's passion for conventions. Deprived of these conventions in reality he dwells on them in fantasy. He lives an imaginary school story in which he himself is the hero, in which he is at once conventional and daring; the very conventions of this imaginary school would give him his opportunity to be daring. He likes to imagine himself what, in another walk of life, would be called "wide"; it is a quality much admired by criminals and a great many, I believe, commit their crimes in order to appear knowledgeable to their fellows, sophisticated, the sort of person who can't be taken in. But the atmosphere of Scrope House and the way in which it is run gives him no opportunity to indulge this need of his nature; even if he should succeed in impressing some of his companions, as presumably he has impressed his friend Mandeville, there is never any general or official approval for qualities which, in another environment, might have made him a prefect and a swell.'

'Yes, I've noticed something like that,' said Edgeworth. 'But how do the fires come in?'

'Well, in the first place,' I answered, 'I should say they were a demonstration against Scrope House and a desperate attempt to break its non-existent rules. You give him no opportunity of proving his masculinity by any of the usual puberty initiation ceremonies that do so much to add to the gaiety of public schools; he can't undergo any tests of strength or endurance with the full and complete approval of his fellows. He's been pushed into too civilized, too adult a world before he's ready for it. Probably at another school, after a supremely successful career, he would become one of those pathetic old boys who haunt the scenes of their early triumphs, perpetually yearning to re-enter the womb of their *alma mater*. Are there savages, I wonder, who even in old age haunt the huts where growing boys are segregated and where they undergo their ordeals of initiation? Almost certainly, I should think, though I can't for the moment remember coming across any instance of what would be a most interesting parallel.

'But to get back to Crossley as he is at the moment; look at what happened to-day. He takes immense trouble to dress himself properly for cricket, to observe all its rituals, and as far as possible to learn how to play this most difficult game. And then, in the first place, he gets no more credit for being in the eleven than if, at the University, he had won his half-blue for chess. And next, his own innings brings him no distinction but ends with him sending up a most childish catch, the result, I should not be surprised, of his growing irritation and profound disgust with the whole affair. On top of that, the most obviously shabby and disreputable member of the eleven, a miserable intellectual, a scug, a sap, a swot, the kind of boy who has been ridiculed in a hundred school stories and in even more schools, goes and plays with effortless brilliance and, almost single-handed, wins the match. Is it any wonder that he should choose this occasion for yet another of his gestures?'

'Yes,' said Edgeworth, 'I am inclined to agree with your diagnosis of Crossley's character, but I don't agree that pyromania can be deduced from it as a necessary and inevitable symptom. Would you, I mean, expect it to follow, if you didn't know that it had already happened, from the fact that there was such a boy in such a situation as you describe? Would you expect it as a doctor who found measles spots inside the mouth would also expect to find a raised temperature?'

'No, of course not,' I said. 'But at any rate the causes of this particular pyromania seem to me less and not more mysterious than the causes of pyromania in general. When Crossley sets fire to things he's doing something dangerous, something which he hopes the whole school will be forced to recognize as a daring feat, even though it refuses to recognize all the feats which, in his imaginary world of the ideal public school, would meet with instant and public approval. At the same time, the gesture expresses his hostility against the school and against the society which refuses him all the normal opportunities of winning the approval of his fellow creatures for the qualities which he knows he possesses. As I say, in another state of society, and if he had been born in the East End or lived in Soho, he might have taken to crime as just such a means of winning distinction, as just such a gesture against the society which deprived him of all easier ways of making a name for himself. However, I think that there is also an important practical reason for the fires. You remember that before any of the fires began in the school, Walton's farm buildings and haystacks were burnt down?'

'Yes,' said Edgeworth, 'but that might easily have been an accident. There's surely no reason for thinking that Crossley started the fire at Walton's farm. If he did, it rather looks as if this contradicted your whole theory. Why should he have wanted to make a gesture against Walton?'

'Exactly,' I said, 'and I'm sure he was not responsible for this fire. In fact I feel pretty sure that Walton himself burnt the buildings and haystacks down, in order to get the insurance money.'

'I don't understand what you're getting at,' Edgeworth said.

'I'll come to the point quite soon,' I replied. 'There seems to have been some general suspicion that Walton started his own fire; there was talk in the village and the police made some inquiries but found there was nothing that could justify them in taking any action. Walton must have heard of these suspicions and was no doubt extremely worried by them. His son, Ted Walton, was a friend of Crossley and Mandeville; they first met him when they did some work at Walton's farm and he entertained them with stories of his own school, the grammar school at Scropeham. He enormously impressed them with these stories, some of which may have been imaginary, and Crossley began to look to Ted Walton as yet another hero of a school story; he acquired in Crossley's eyes all the prestige of the Fifth Form at St. Dominic's, and moreover Ted was the older boy and mature for his years. They probably discussed the fire at Walton's farm and after that got on to the subject of fires at school; a fire is a very usual incident in school stories. Ted Walton may have seen that Crossley was unusually interested in the subject; he probably dared Crossley—I believe "dared" is the correct word—to start a fire at Scrope House. Crossley may have demurred at first, but the idea sank in because it appealed to him as a means of making his own protest against Scrope House; when he had actually started his first fire he was sustained by Ted Walton's whole-hearted approval of this feat. It was an obvious but quite ingenious method of diverting suspicion from Ted Walton's father; if there was a pyromaniac at Scrope House, and if children from the school had been working on the farm, then it was natural to suspect that one of them had set fire to the buildings and the haystacks. And, of course, a good many people, including you yourself, did actually suspect this.'

'Yes,' said Edgeworth, 'but this is all pure speculation on your part.'

'There's more to come,' I answered. 'When I first heard that Walton had been suspected of setting fire to his own buildings I arranged that the local policeman should go and bother him again with some more inquiries about the fires. I didn't think these questions would produce any useful answers, but I thought they might stir Walton up. And so, in fact, they did. Smallbones, the village policeman, turned out to be a friend of Walton's and very improperly but very satisfactorily told Walton that the school detective employed to look for a pyromaniac at Scrope House had suggested more inquiries into the origin of the fires at the farm. Ted Walton was then put to work again. He had given up inciting Crossley to any more conflagrations when suspicion of his father appeared to be dying down, but now that it had risen again he tried the same trick. But first he must have warned Crossley and Mandeville about the interfering detective at Scrope House. I received one morning an anonymous letter which must, I think, have come from Crossley or Mandeville. It was a quotation from *Hamlet*—"Thou wretched, rash, intruding fool, farewell"—which came on the very day that I was going up to town. This led me to misunderstand the purpose of the quotation; I thought that it referred to my journey to town and must have been written with knowledge of it, but I think the letter really expressed a wish for me to leave and not the writer's satisfaction at my actual departure. After a while I remembered that when I first met Crossley and Mandeville, near Walton's farm, Mandeville quoted another line from *Hamlet* with a flourish. Had he, perhaps, been in Dawes's class when it was reading *Hamlet* this term?'

'Yes,' Edgeworth replied. 'But anyone can quote *Hamlet*.'

'Of course,' I conceded. 'But let me go on. The anonymous letter did not frighten me away—it would be amusing to know exactly why Crossley and Mandeville imagined it would alarm me—and it was time for another fire which should focus attention on the school and away from the farm. Crossley, you may remember, went off by himself immediately after his innings was over and perhaps he saw Ted Walton then, on some other part of the cricket ground, or perhaps Ted Walton had already suggested that the pavilion should be burnt down and Crossley was confirmed in his resolution by his discomfiture during the match. At any rate Ted Walton was lucky and Crossley was in exactly the right mood for another inflammatory protest.

'As soon as I heard of the fire I went off to Walton's farm where I found that Walton had had remarkably early news of the fire at the pavilion. He told me, when I asked him where he had got his information, that the news was all over the place, but no one in the pub near by had heard it. He also said that you could see the fire from the top of the hill above the farm, and I went up myself to look; it was an extremely inconspicuous sight and I don't think anyone would have noticed it if they hadn't been on the look out for it. By the way, it looks as if Ted Walton had been very careful to suggest that Crossley should do no harm with his fires or run anyone into danger; for this purpose the pavilion was an obvious choice and the other fires were almost as safe.'

'Yes,' Edgeworth said. 'I suppose you must be right. At any rate it all holds together. It's my job, of course, and not yours, but have you any idea how I should proceed? It would be easier to get on with curing Crossley if I could somehow get him to admit, to himself rather than to me, that he needed treatment.'

'Oddly enough,' I said, 'he would probably be only too glad if you did threaten to punish the rest of the eleven unless the culprit came forward. In his present state of mind this would strike him as exactly the right way for a headmaster to behave, it would be in strict accordance with all the school stories, and what is more it would give him an opportunity to make the spectacular yet highly conventional gesture of owning up.'

'Yes, I daresay,' said Edgeworth, 'but I can't undermine my whole system and upset the whole school for the sake of Crossley; besides, this would suggest that I thought him a culprit, as you put it, a criminal, in fact, and this would only increase the sense of guilt which has probably induced his neurosis.'

'Well,' I said, 'another alternative would be to put the responsibility on to someone else. Let him go to a public school and there he'll be treated as he wants to be treated. Or, more probably, he would not find even the best, or the worst, public school up to the standard of the imaginary school he has created in his own mind. The disappointment might be very good for him, a gentle shock to bring him back to reality.'

'No,' Edgeworth answered. 'I should like to succeed with him on my own ground. I can't turn him out just because I've failed with him so far. And, if you're right about Crossley, he'll be one of the most interesting cases I've ever handled. I couldn't think of losing him. By the way,' he continued, 'how would it be if you were to have a talk with him? He might be more willing to speak to an outsider; it might be less embarrassing for him.'

'I don't think that would do,' I said. 'I think I'm as capable as the next man of understanding how human beings work, but I have to have time to think deliberately and quietly about them. I altogether lack that intuitive understanding which enables one to say the right thing on the spur of the moment—it's that intuitive sympathy which makes a good schoolmaster.'

'Perhaps you're right,' Edgeworth said. 'And what would you advise me to do about Walton?' he asked, but continued without waiting for me to reply. 'Naturally I'll see to it that we don't send any more children to work on his farm. It's a pity, because it was much the most convenient farm and for certain types there's nothing like a little work on the land.'

'I don't see there's anything else you can do,' I said. 'The police probably wouldn't take any action on the little evidence we could give them, even if Crossley should choose to give Ted Walton away; he would be very unwilling to do so, because it would so obviously be sneaking, but even if you persuaded him you would only be giving him as well as Walton away to the police. Besides, I shouldn't think you'd want Walton to be prosecuted; if he were it would only advertise the fact that there was a pyromaniac at Scrope House, and you may be sure that Walton would do his best to attract attention away from himself and towards the school. That would be his best defence.'

'Oh, we must avoid a prosecution at all costs,' Edgeworth said with a shudder. 'But do you think,' he continued, 'that Walton will continue to make mischief even if we leave him severely alone?'

'I should think,' I said, 'that he'd have the sense to keep quiet. He'll soon be able to infer that you know all about what he's been doing, though a word of advice to keep his son away from Scrope House might rub this fact in.'

'I feel sorry for Ted Walton,' Edgeworth said.

'Yes, of course,' I said, 'but he's not your responsibility.' I was afraid that Edgeworth might begin wondering what he could do to cure Ted Walton and might perhaps offer him a scholarship to Scrope House on the strength of his interesting delinquency. I was careful not to remind Edgeworth that Crossley and Mandeville had been present, in their capacity as members of Hickman's quartet, at the party when Mrs. Dawes had been murdered. Nor did I refer to the possibility that Susan might just conceivably have known something about the fires which her death prevented her from revealing. I felt that Edgeworth had quite enough worries for the moment.

Chapter Fifteen

I returned to give Caroline an abbreviated account of the theory I had propounded to Edgeworth. She was, I must say, most satisfactorily and flatteringly impressed. When we had thoroughly discussed my solution she put forward an ingenious idea of her own.

'Do you think,' she said, 'that the booby trap we came on when we were driving to Scrope House—you remember the parcel with a jar of water in it—was the work of Crossley and Mandeville?'

'Undoubtedly,' I said. 'Like many other masterpieces it was, as they say, signed all over.'

'I don't know,' Caroline said. 'It was a more poetic joke than might be expected from Crossley, if your analysis of his character is right.'

'Poetic?' I said. 'Now is that the right word? Yes, perhaps it is; perhaps it was Mandeville's idea rather than Crossley's. Mandeville is certainly the more childish of the two boys, and therefore the more inclined to poetic ideas; he may be equally rebellious but not, I am inclined to think, because he really wants to belong to a more conventional society than that of Scrope House. I had the impression, when we were talking to the two boys, that Mandeville was not so deadly serious as Crossley; he was amused rather than impressed by the details of public life that I gave him. Yes, as I see it, Mandeville is attracted by Crossley's fantasies about public schools, you might almost call it Crossley's mythology, but he doesn't take them so seriously; in fact he likes these fantasies just because they are fantastic, and he may well be one of those children who live in a dream world of their own making. He'll probably turn into one of those modern poets who create a mythology based on their private or their public school, if that kind of poetry is still being written when he grows up. You know the kind of thing; the class war, revolution and counter-revolution, civil war between Communists and Fascists, all in terms of a grotesque parody of life in an English school. Disconcerting and surrealist practical jokes would certainly appeal to such a mind. Wasn't it Tennyson, by the way, who said that some revolution—the French revolution of 'forty-eight, perhaps—was no more serious than a schoolboys' barring out? I suppose Auden and the rest of the poets of this school would think Tennyson was recommending this particular revolution as a specially good subject for poetry.'

'Really,' Caroline interrupted, 'you ought to tell fortunes. You've revealed Mandeville's character and predicted his future career on the strength of the one word "poetic" which I used to describe a booby trap for which he was very likely not responsible.'

'Yes,' I said, 'I'm sorry. But since I've taken up detection I've acquired a taste for speculation. I hope it won't unfit me for my proper work. Any way, I'm not going to bother about who actually arranged that booby trap; it would be too much like hard work.'

Next day I was received in audience by Mrs. Eakins, in order that she might congratulate me on the apparent success of my first mission to Scrope House. Edgeworth had told her about my theory and she gave me my due allowance of flattery, ending up with her promise that Colonel Redder should hear of my achievement and that she was sure he would be most relieved to know that this mystery, at any rate, had been cleared up. It was as if Colonel Redder had been my superior officer and Mrs. Eakins was going to make a handsome report to him of his subordinate's zeal and efficiency. A little of her goodwill towards me even splashed over on to Caroline; 'Miss Fisher,' she said, 'always keeps herself so nice and fresh.' It was as if Mrs. Eakins was thinking how satisfactory it was and how consoling that the middle classes, in spite of everything, were able to find each other sexually attractive.

All this was not quite so gratifying as Mrs. Eakins intended, but this did not worry me; what did disturb me was to think of what the Chief Constable might conceive to be his duty when he heard of Crossley's habit of setting fire to things. As I happened to know from my study of the histories of criminal twins, the law is not in the habit of making the fine distinction between pyromania and arson which it readily allows between kleptomania and theft. Both arson and theft may equally be committed to satisfy an unconscious emotional need; neither crime can be automatically assumed to have gain for its object. But the damage which results equally from pyromania as from arson is so great that the law probably feels that it cannot afford, even to the most approved pyromaniacs, that gentle censure which is given to those who get away with a few silk stockings and can prove that they have no need of them. Would Colonel Redder, I wondered, think it his duty to the insurance companies, and to property in general, to make an extremely awkward investigation of the whole affair? I tried to point out this danger to Mrs. Eakins, but she brushed my advice aside.

'I think you can leave it to me,' she said, with a note of impatience in her voice,' to handle this little matter as it should be handled. And of course,' she added, 'I shan't say anything about what you've found out about that dreadful man Walton, unless I can see that it is *quite* safe to do so.'

With this unsatisfactory assurance I had to be content, but I comforted myself with the reflection that, after all, Mrs. Eakins could not be quite such a goose as she appeared. Indubitably she had a pull, and a pull is neither gained nor retained without the exercise of some dexterity.

This reflection proved to be sound. The next day I was invited to lunch with Colonel Redder, and when I reached his house he began at once on the subject of the fires.

'Damn good piece of work that, my boy,' he said, and I smirked. 'But mind you,' he continued, 'I don't want to talk about that now, in fact I want to know as little about it as possible, eh?' A most singular look of low but benevolent cunning appeared on his face. 'The insurance is the point,' he added, 'but I am sure we can trust Mrs. Eakins to put things right. Got a head on her shoulders, that good lady has, though I expect all those ushers often wish they weren't bossed by a woman. But then an usher's not much more than a nursemaid, any way.'

As Colonel Redder had so obviously just been bossed by the same woman, I felt that this was hardly fair, but made no comment. Luncheon began with a strange accident. The Colonel poured himself out a whisky and soda and I thought I would have one too, but when I took a drink it tasted extremely weak and odd. My delicate sense of propriety prevented me from saying anything, and besides, for all I knew, this might have been some special kind of military or Indian whisky with which Colonel Redder would expect me to be familiar, a Rajah's tipple or a stingah or what not. But the Colonel himself took a sip and immediately spluttered.

'What the devil's the matter with this whisky?' he demanded. 'Is there anything wrong with yours, Hardwicke?'

The parlourmaid looked alarmed and Mrs. Redder said that only the same kind as usual had been ordered.

'You'd better go to another shop, then,' Colonel Redder said, but then he recollected himself and began to organize. He took up the decanter, smelt it, and then poured himself out a small quantity of its contents in a wine-glass and tasted it.

'It's sherry,' he said, in great astonishment.

'Oh yes, Sir,' the parlourmaid said, 'I can easily explain that. The two decanters are just the same to look at.'

Mrs. Redder soothed her husband down and told the parlourmaid to fetch the other decanter. 'I'll pour your whisky out for you this time,' she said. 'Men are so helpless, aren't they, Mr. Hardwicke?'

'Good God,' said Colonel Redder, 'do you think someone's been trying to give us poisoned sherry instead of whisky?'

'Oh don't say such things,' Mrs. Redder said. 'You know it's only an accident.'

'I dare say,' Colonel Redder said, 'but if that girl's going to make mistakes like that she'll be giving me weed-killer instead of sugar next time. Nasty stuff, poison.'

Mrs. Redder then took the conversation in hand and with an obvious exercise of tact began to talk about the cricket match between Seadale and Scrope House. The Colonel also remembered his duty as a host and did his best to make polite conversation, but there was evidently still something on his mind. Finally he put an end to our aimless chatter.

'Sorry to talk shop,' he said, 'but the fact is something's just occurred to me. Do you think that man Dupuy could have been poisoned like that at the bottle party? Do you think he could have poured out a sherry and soda for himself instead of a whisky and soda? They look much the same, after all. And what's more, he wouldn't have taken a lethal dose in that way; there wouldn't have been enough of the sherry to kill him.'

'Dupuy did say,' I answered, 'that he didn't remember drinking anything except whisky and soda at that party.'

'Yes, that's right,' Colonel Redder said, very pleased at this confirmation of his theory.

'But, of course, if Dupuy was the murderer what he says about himself is hardly evidence,' I pointed out.

'We didn't get anything on him, you know,' said Colonel Redder. 'No motive.'

'Oh well,' I said, 'let's assume he's telling the truth. But even then he wouldn't have finished up his drink when he found he'd given himself a sherry and soda by mistake. And if he'd only taken a first sip, just as you did, it wouldn't have made him as ill as he was.'

'He might have finished it off,' Colonel Redder objected, 'if he'd already had a good many over the eight.'

'I suppose he might,' I conceded, 'but it's not very likely, do you think?'

'I expect you're right,' Colonel Redder said. 'I can't imagine myself gulping down anything so nasty. No go then, eh?'

'Oh well, you never know,' I answered, by way of consolation.

After lunch Mrs. Redder left us and we moved to two leather arm-chairs by the fireplace. The Colonel then told me that Julian would soon be round and we could discuss the case of Mrs. Dawes again.

'I don't mind telling you we're up against it,' he said, 'but we won't go into all that until Julian gets here.'

Julian soon arrived and was put into a less comfortable chair than ours, no doubt for reasons of discipline.

'It's the usual thing,' Colonel Redder began. 'We know pretty well who it is, but we can't get any definite proof that would be anything like good enough for the public prosecutor. Oh yes, and we've had a letter from someone who agrees with us, too. It gives us a clear motive, of course, but that doesn't make things much easier.'

He handed me a letter, explaining that it had been sent down from London by Scotland Yard. It was addressed to Miss Isobel Walker, who, it appeared, had taken it to the police in London because she was so much alarmed by its contents. It was addressed and written in block capitals, written on paper so ordinary as to be untraceable, the postmark 'W.C. 1.' It read as follows:—

'Dawes murdered his wife in order to marry you, but he may
eventually murder you to marry someone else.'

Miss Walker, it seemed, had been very anxious to explain to the policeman who interviewed her that she was no more than a friend of Dawes and had only seen him since his wife's death because she knew him before and he had come to her for sympathy. She was, she added, a friend of both Mr. and Mrs. Dawes.

'That's all rot, of course,' Colonel Redder said. 'She's bound to say something of the kind. But all the same she's cleared herself of any suspicion of being an accomplice of Dawes; I daresay she was, but we couldn't prosecute her after she'd taken the letter to Scotland Yard.'

'That's why she took it to Scotland Yard,' said Julian.

'I wonder who wrote the letter,' I said.

'Oh just some malicious idiot,' Colonel Redder answered. 'You'd be surprised at the number of such letters we're always getting. Naturally we're trying to find out all about this girl and how often Dawes was seeing her before his wife's death. Scotland Yard's looking after the London end of it for us, but whether we get any definite evidence for the public prosecutor depends entirely on how careful they managed to be.'

'I take it your idea is that Dawes murdered his wife in order to marry this girl,' I said. 'But why couldn't they get a divorce?'

'Perhaps Mrs. Dawes wouldn't give him one,' Julian said.

'I don't think that's very likely,' I said. 'It's not in keeping with Mrs. Dawes's character, or her political opinions, or the sort of people she lived with.'

'You never know,' Colonel Redder said. 'When it comes to women there's no telling what they'll do. But it doesn't matter, any way. The point is that Mrs. Dawes had about five hundred a year of her own, and that goes to Dawes now, of course. If he'd lost that money by getting his wife to divorce him he'd have had to cut down all round—no more trips to town or abroad in the holidays, and I dare say this Walker girl wouldn't be willing to marry him if he could only offer her the sort of life that most of these ushers lead.'

I conceded that this was an important point and that Dawes certainly had a motive for killing his wife.

'But the motive doesn't really matter so much now,' Colonel Redder said. 'What we want to get at now is the method of the murder. If we could get all that business clear, if we could only find out exactly what Dawes did with the poison at the party, I've no doubt we could catch him out. And that,' he added impressively, 'is why I asked you to come here to-day. Julian's brought round all the statements and the analyst's reports and so forth, and perhaps if we have a look at them together we can get somewhere. Or, if you like, you can take the papers home with you and see if you can get an idea from them.'

I decided, for the moment, to have a look at the analysis of the dregs found in the bottle from Hickman's garden and in the glass from which Mrs. Dawes had drunk. The rest of the papers and the statements which the police had collected would have to be read at leisure when I was by myself. I did not expect to learn anything new from the analyst's report, the gist of which I had already been given several times, but I had to look at something since the papers had been so obligingly produced. And, in fact, I did notice a small and curious point; the proportion of poison to sherry was slightly less in Mrs. Dawes's glass than in the bottle I found in the garden. I showed this to Julian and asked him what he thought it meant.

'Yes, I noticed that,' he said, 'but there's nothing so wonderful about that. There's nothing in it, I'm afraid, because she might so easily have had a little sherry at the bottom of her glass which was left over from a previous drink; then when her glass was filled up again from the poisoned bottle the remains of the unpoisoned sherry already in the glass would have been enough to reduce the proportion of atropine in her drink. In fact, if you look at Hickman's statement you'll see that he says he actually remembers Dawes refilling a glass for his wife which already had a little sherry in it. Hickman asked Dawes if he wanted a clean glass; I suppose he didn't know Mrs. Dawes was only having the same again.'

'Well, there you are then,' Colonel Redder said. 'You've got something there; that shows it was then that Dawes gave his wife a glass of sherry from the poisoned bottle.'

'Very likely,' Julian said, 'but there's another though rather less probable explanation. She or someone else might have added a spot of unpoisoned sherry to the glass when she'd drunk a little of the poisoned sherry.'

'From another bottle, you mean?' I asked.

'Yes,' Julian answered. 'But I admit it's not so likely. It's quite possible that she should have had her glass filled up again when she'd drunk half the poisoned sherry in it. But if she'd done that there would have been a much smaller percentage of poison in the dregs, about half the percentage of poison that we found in the bottle, in fact. As it is, no more than a teaspoonful or so of unpoisoned sherry can have been added to the glass of poisoned sherry, and I can't see how that could happen. The only thing I've thought of is that there might have been a bottle which was all but empty, and to finish it off someone might have tipped the last tea-spoonful into Mrs. Dawes's glass. It's possible, but I shouldn't think very likely. And whichever way you look at it, it doesn't help us with our main problem, what happened to all the rest of the poisoned sherry. Mrs. Dawes had one glass, Dupuy must have had about a third of a glass, or a little less, and there was about half a glass in the bottle in the garden, but what happened to the rest? There must have been about six or seven of those small tumblers to the bottle.'

'Why shouldn't Mrs. Dawes have drunk the lot?' asked Colonel Redder.

'Oh, I naturally thought of that,' Julian answered. 'But she didn't. The post-mortem showed there wasn't all that poison in her, and her symptoms didn't agree, so the doctor said, with anything like so large a dose of atropine. Besides, that would have meant that one bottle had to be kept exclusively for Mrs. Dawes, with perhaps a tot for Mr. Dupuy, and I can't imagine how the murderer could have managed this without arousing suspicion. How did he prevent other people coming to the bar and pouring drinks from the poisoned bottle?'

'Well then, the rest of the bottle must have been poured out somewhere, perhaps in the garden,' Colonel Redder said.

'It doesn't make sense,' Julian objected. 'Why leave half a glass of poisoned sherry at the bottom of the bottle. Why not pour the lot away?'

'Perhaps the murderer was interrupted,' I said, 'and perhaps he had to stop before he'd finished pouring out the bottle. Whoever interrupted him might remember something, in that case, if you put it to him.'

'Well, it might have happened like that,' Julian said. 'But, of course I've already asked everybody if they remember seeing any-body with a bottle of sherry in the garden, and nobody remembers anything. I'm afraid that won't be any use to us. If it happened like that, we shan't get any further. But I don't believe it did happen like that; it seems absurd to bring a bottle of poisoned sherry, give about a glass and a quarter of it to Mrs. Dawes and Mr. Dupuy, and then waste the rest of it.'

After some more equally inconclusive discussion, it was decided that I should take away all the statements and reports and study them at my leisure. I had to promise to keep them entirely to myself and to lock them up when I was not actually reading them. In fact there was so much fuss about them that I went away feeling as though I had been entrusted with a secret plan for the invasion of Britain. I conscientiously read through all the statements but found nothing new in them, though they did refresh my memory of some conver-sations that I myself had heard and so enabled me to add more detail to this little narrative of my adventures of Scrope House. No doubt it was Mrs. Eakins's report of my prowess as a detective which had persuaded the police to let me have these documents, but I was really more grateful to Colonel Redder's parlourmaid. Her mistake with the decanters made me notice the fact that sherry and whisky can be much the same colour and this gave me an idea which in turn led to another and in the end rather more important idea about the way in which the murder had been committed. For the moment I did not see how this new idea could be checked, and I decided to wait for an inspiration. It might be as well, I considered, to leave the mechanics of the crime on one side for the moment and to inspect the character of the murderer.

The police seemed very certain of Dawes's guilt, and if they were right his writings would certainly be interesting and relevant documents in which it was just possible that he might inadvertently have exposed his character. This was to presume that a murderer has something permanent in his character, perhaps some overmastering vanity or some insensibility, which makes him recognizable as a potential murderer even before he has committed his crime. But this presumption might in some instances be true and it would certainly look well if I could say that I had spotted the murderer after one glance at his poems. I therefore collected Dawes's three volumes of verse from Mrs. Eakins's library and began to read them with a new interest. One might advise all poets, at any rate those that have no more talent than poor Dawes, to commit an atrocious crime; scarcely anything else would compel the attention of even the most unwilling reader as my attention was now compelled. It was as good as reading the poems, of which so far I have only come across one brief extract, of Rudolph Valentino.

Nearly all the poems were dated, a small touch of vanity which certainly made my task easier than that of the critics who propose to reconstruct Shakespeare's life from the evidence of his sonnets.

But in other ways Dawes had not been so obliging as Shakespeare; he had not, for example, taken the trouble to distinguish the various women to whom his poems were addressed, or who were described in them, by the colour of their hair. Here were no dark ladies, but all a universal monochrome. One, it was true, was described as having on one occasion worn a yellow hat, but how could you tell whether this was the same woman as she who was said to have 'Smiled so gaily on deceit'? And who deceived her, was it Dawes or another man? The poem, most exasperatingly, did not say. I looked at the poems which dated from the period when Dawes must have been courting Susan, but I cannot honestly say that I recognized her in any of them, nor was there anything in more recent poems to suggest that they were concerned with a woman who worked in a shop for the sale of toys designed by psycho-analysts.

But it was Dawes whom I hoped to recognize and not his women, so I read with special attention all the many verses on the subject of love cut short by death. Was there, I wondered, any significance in his obvious relish for this subject and did he write so often on the brevity of life—almost the whole of one volume in particular, published just over two years ago, dealt with this subject—because he himself was prepared to make it a good deal shorter for anyone who got in his way? It was a pleasing idea, and it amused me to think of a murderer sitting down to write a lyric on the impermanence of flowers, the decay of the rose, the withering of the lily, with special reference to the corpse in the trunk upstairs. It is a courteous assassin who will thus compose his victim's epitaph. But, on the whole, I did not think that the police would be impressed by such evidence. No doubt the obvious step would be to consider when Dawes wrote most poems about death—there were far too many for each of them to have reference to a single and separate fatality—and then to look for someone who might have been murdered about this time. But no—such fancies would not do; so much sentimentality might make one suspicious of Dawes's entire sincerity, but that was all. Samuel Butler, it may be remembered, once deduced from the painful ambiguities in one of Wordsworth's poems that he must have done away with his Lucy, probably in conjunction with his friends Southey and Coleridge. With this awful warning in mind I decided to put Dawes's poems aside.

But at any rate, since the police now knew about Dawes and Isobel Walker, this could no longer be considered as dangerous a secret as before and I felt myself at liberty to ask Caroline if she had any information about this young woman. I still thought it prudent to ask her not to repeat to anyone at Scrope House what I now told her, by way of an explanation of my question, about Dawes's appointment with Isobel Walker in the British Museum. Caroline's first thought was that I had iniquitously tricked her by withholding what she called vital information. 'Vital to whom or what?' I naturally asked, but she paid no attention.

'So you made us all toil up to London,' she protested, 'and let us come back again thinking the whole thing had been a failure. And to think of all the lies you told about losing Dawes because you could not find a taxi!'

I waited until her indignation might be overcome by her desire to show how much inside information she possessed.

'I should never have thought,' she eventually said, 'that Isobel Walker would have suited Dawes. I shouldn't wonder if it wasn't all a stupid mistake.'

'What's she like?' I asked.

'Oh, you know the sort of thing,' Caroline answered. 'Hardworking and stupid at bottom—believes everything she's told as long as it sounds like advanced psychology—won't allow her child to be house-trained, even at five years old.'

'I didn't know she was married,' I said.

'She's not,' Caroline answered.

It turned out that Miss Walker, in Caroline's opinion, regarded an illegitimate child as the necessary flower of a blameless life and had obtained one as a matter of principle. I asked whether Dawes was the father and was told that he was not; I think I was told who the man was—Miss Walker made no secret about it—but I have forgotten and it is irrelevant.

It was really surprising, Caroline thought, that so obvious a goose should appeal to a man like Dawes, who prided himself on his extreme and disillusioned scepticism. But, as I pointed out, Dawes's scepticism did not go as far as he thought and he probably liked having an easy opportunity for exercising it. I could well imagine him listening, with his sad and disillusioned smile, to the eager prattling of Miss Walker and feeling himself a tremendous fellow because he did not believe every word of it. As I saw it, he imagined himself to be witheringly sceptical because he never took up with any intellectual fashion until all his acquaintances were thoroughly used to it and even tired of it. His mind moved rather slowly and this gave him plenty of time to exercise his dry wit on an intellectual fashion while his friends were absorbing it, but in the end he always came under its influence. His wife, for example, had taken up politics long before he had done so, at the time when all the intelligentsia were becoming political, but politics got him in the end and as he was slowly moving towards a complete agreement with Susan's views he was no longer able to feel any sublime detachment when she talked about them. He could no longer experience in her company the old delicious sensation of intellectual eminence and it seemed to me very natural that he should turn to Miss Walker, whose crude statements about psychology he could now so exquisitely and so complacently doubt.

'And so,' Caroline said, bringing my interpretation down with a bump '—and so Dawes murdered his wife because he was beginning to agree with her opinions.'

Chapter Sixteen

I t did not look as though I should find the murderer by speculating about his character, though this method had worked fairly well when I was looking for a pyromaniac. Colonel Redder, as so often, was obviously right, and to get any further it would be necessary to reconstruct the murderer's method and to try to find out exactly what he had done at the bottle party. I had now reached a point where, as I saw it, everything would depend on a more exact scrutiny of the dregs in the bottle and the glass. This might well lead to nothing, and if so I was stuck, but there was a faint hope. The analyst's report certainly did not give me the information that I wanted and so I rang up Julian; I asked him if the analyst had told him anything not included in his report and when I heard that he had not I asked if it would be possible for me to see the analyst himself.

'What, old Hopkins!' Julian exclaimed. 'You can certainly see him if you want to, but he's very old, you know, and rather slow.'

'Excellent,' I said, because if the analyst was a dotard he might easily have overlooked some important detail. I arranged to visit Hopkins in his laboratory at Scropeham the next day. I found that he was certainly old and at first he seemed more interested in questioning my right to make any inquiries at all than in answering them. But eventually I got him to listen to me.

'What I want to know,' I said, 'is whether you could possibly detect any difference between two bottles of the same kind of sherry.'

'I never drink sherry,' Hopkins replied. 'It affects my liver.'

'No, no,' I said. 'What I mean is—if you analysed two samples from different bottles of the same kind of sherry would you expect to find any difference at all between them? They might, for example, have been bottled from the same cask, but one might have come first from the cask and the other last. Or they might have come from different casks and there might be some variation in the quality. You see what I mean? What I want you to do, if you will be so very kind, is to look for some such difference between the sherry that was found in Mrs. Dawes's glass and the sherry that was found in the bottle that the police sent you, the bottle in which you found atropine.'

'I've only got very small quantities of the liquid,' Hopkins answered, 'and do you really expect me to make an organic analysis of the esters and so forth in it? I've already found the atropine—what more do you want?'

'Well,' I said, 'perhaps you could begin with something easier. There might be a very small variation in the alcohol content of the two samples, if they came from different bottles, and I suppose you could detect that.'

'I suppose I might,' Hopkins answered, 'though I can't think why the police couldn't ask me about this when I made my first analysis, if they're so keen on it now.'

'Well, they are frightfully keen on it at the moment,' I said.

'It's pretty hopeless,' Hopkins said, 'especially with such small quantities, but I suppose I'd better try. I can't imagine what the police think they're getting at—just making work for others, no doubt. They've no idea what's possible and what isn't nowadays. Scientific detection, it's called, which only means that a lot of ignorant people think I can perform miracles and do all their work for them. And why should they send you? Too lazy to come themselves, I suppose.'

I left him in the enjoyment of this singularly perverse misconception of why I had come to badger him and I thanked him profusely, on behalf of the police, for his willingness to help. I watched him procure two vessels containing liquid from the glass and from the bottle; they were locked in a cupboard and he took so long about opening it that I felt sure I was in for a long wait before the analysis was ended. And if he was unable to find any difference in the alcohol content of the two samples, if I had to ask him to look for some other kind of difference between them, how exasperated the old man would be and how strongly I would then have to exercise my powers of persuasion! I might, of course, have gone off to enjoy myself elsewhere but I thought it safer to watch over him and if necessary prod him on to his work.

And then, after all this fuss, and though Hopkins proceeded with remarkable solemnity and a great air of mystification, I found there was nothing to it; I know nothing about chemistry and have forgotten the very little I learnt in my first year at the University but even I could tell that Hopkins was only taking the specific gravity of the two liquids. The quantities were small enough, at any rate of the sherry left at the bottom of Mrs. Dawes's glass, to make this a task of some little delicacy, but he was emphatically not performing one of the miracles of modern science.

The result of the test surprised me and I think even succeeded in stirring Hopkins to some faint interest in what he had been doing; there was quite a lot more alcohol in the liquid from the bottle than in the liquid from Mrs. Dawes's glass.

'It shows how unreliable all these shops are nowadays,' Hopkins said. 'You never know what you're buying. One bottle of sherry will put you under the table and the next is practically lemonade.'

'But surely it's not such a big variation as that,' I protested.

'You young men have no sense of humour,' Hopkins said. 'But all the same the difference is appreciable, quite appreciable.'

He seemed much more cheerful now, doubtless because he had succeeded in making a joke which I appeared not to have understood. I looked again at the figures he had jotted down and gave myself up to meditation, while Hopkins coughed impatiently, as though he wanted to be rid of me.

'Look here,' I eventually said, 'if I brought you two more samples of sherry this afternoon, would you be able to test them in the same way? I should be most awfully obliged if you would.'

Hopkins finally agreed, though only after a good deal of grumbling, and I left him. I went at once to the wine-merchants at Scropeham, where I bought a bottle of the same 'Genuine Fino' sherry and then I asked the chauffeur—I had succeeded in borrowing Mrs. Eakins's car for this important expedition—to drive to Colonel Redder's house. Fortunately I found him in and I asked him if he would be kind enough to give me some of the 'Genuine Fino' sherry he had given me before, if he still had some in the house. I reminded him that he had once given me a glass because it was the same kind of sherry as that in which the poison was found.

'Oh yes,' Colonel Redder said, 'as a matter of fact that's the same kind that was in the decanter when the parlourmaid made that ridiculous mistake at lunch the other day. There's still a few glasses in the decanter. But what d'you want it for? Always glad to give my friends a drink, of course, but…?' He hesitated between politeness and curiosity.

'Oh no, I don't want a drink,' I said. 'I want to get it analysed.'

'Good Lord,' Colonel Redder said. 'So you do think someone was trying to poison us at lunch the other day?'

'Very unlikely,' I said, and after obtaining a sample of the sherry in a medicine bottle I took my leave, in what I conceived to be the traditional manner of the Private Investigator, explaining nothing. I gave my new bottle of sherry and Colonel Redder's sample to Hopkins, telling him that these two samples had been obtained from the shop at a considerable interval of time, so that they ought to vary in alcohol content as much as the two previously analysed samples, supposing that such variations were the rule rather than the exception. He went to work on them and in the end found scarcely any difference of alcohol content.

'It's not conclusive,' I said, in order to take my revenge for Hopkins's disobliging manner. 'What we ought to do is to take the specific gravity of at least a hundred samples. Then we could be sure what degree of variation in alcohol content we might normally expect.'

I spent the evening considering these results and grumbling at Caroline whenever she interrupted my thoughts with her conversation. I remembered that there had been a slightly smaller proportion of atropine in Mrs. Dawes's glass than in the bottle found in the garden and for a moment I wondered whether this would account for the variation of alcohol content in the two samples. The more atropine you put in, the smaller percentage of alcohol in the resultant mixture. But it was, of course, a foolish idea, because there ought, in that case, to have been a larger percentage of atropine in the sherry found at the bottom of Mrs. Dawes's glass in order to account for the smaller percentage of alcohol in the same place; Julian had told me that there was, in fact, a slightly smaller percentage of atropine in the sherry found in the glass than in the sherry found in the bottle. Yet, though foolish, the idea was useful because it suggested that there were two ways of looking at the problem; a variation in the percentage of alcohol might result from a corresponding variation in the percentage of some other fluid.

The next morning I had yet another idea and foresaw a possibility which might arise from the observed difference between the sherry in the glass and the sherry in the bottle. I looked up some details in the statements which Julian had given me and then I rang up Rimmle—you will remember that he professed to teach chemistry at Scrope House—to ask him if he would mind if I searched his garden. He seemed very much surprised, but I said that it was only a matter of routine, vaguely remembering that this was supposed to be what the police said on such occasions. 'It's nothing but a back-yard with a small lawn,' Rimmle told me. 'You won't want to dig up the lawn, I hope? I can assure you that there aren't any bodies under it.' I said that I was not looking for bodies and eventually he consented, though he hoped I would not mind looking round by myself, as he was just starting for his laboratory. Before I left the Dower House I wondered whether I ought to tell Julian what I was doing and ask him if he would like to accompany me, but then I remembered that he might feel he ought to be provided with a search-warrant and, any way, his presence would make everything much more complicated and official.

Rimmle was quite right; his garden was only a backyard and its only ornament was a small square of grass. There seemed to be nowhere where anything could be concealed, unless something had been buried, and I was not going to dig the whole place up on the chance that the remote possibility I had in mind might turn out to be a fact. I looked into an outhouse, where I saw a bicycle but that was not what I was looking for; I asked Rimmle's servant, a girl who had been watching me with ill-concealed curiosity from the kitchen window, whether I could use the telephone. Then I rang up Edgeworth to ask him whether I could search his garden. He had, of course, to consent and actually he seemed much impressed by the fact that I had proposed so very professional a course of action.

'I won't ask you why you want to search it,' he said. 'I wouldn't dream of asking you why. By all means search the garden.'

It was a much larger garden than Rimmle's, and a much longer job to search it, but I found nothing on the rubbish heap, behind a pile of wood, amongst the leaf-mould, or in any of the other obvious places in which to look. The potting-shed was equally useless, though dark and difficult to search. I prowled round the house and eventually found a coal-shed in which, besides coal, there were some garden tools which I should have thought would have been more conveniently kept in the potting-shed. There was also a shelf, and on it I found a bottle. I removed the cork and sniffed; it was paraffin. But when I took the bottle out into the light I saw some fragments of a familiar label and so felt justified in taking it away with me.

It would be tiresome to have to face old Hopkins again, I felt, and really quite unnecessary, so I rang up the police station at Scropeham and asked if I could speak to Superintendent Julian. He was in and I made an appointment with him for the afternoon. I brought the bottle of paraffin with me and told him where I had found it. I had expected him to be pleased, or at least amused, but instead he was horrified.

'Do you mean to say,' he exclaimed, 'that you picked up that bottle and brought it along with you? Good heavens, don't you realize that if anything should come of it you'll have to give evidence of finding it at the trial. And everyone will want to know why the police didn't find it themselves and we can't possibly explain that we called you in as a Private Detective; besides, we didn't call you in for that sort of thing. I don't know what we're going to do now.'

'I'm very sorry,' I said, 'but I had no idea...'

'We'll have to keep you out of it somehow,' Julian said, 'and I'm damned if I see how.'

'Perhaps,' I suggested, 'you might let me say that I just happened to be in Edgeworth's garden and came on this bottle. I thought it suspicious and brought it to you, just as anyone might bring something suspicious to the police station.'

'Yes,' Julian replied, 'that's all very well, but what are you going to say when you're asked why you thought a bottle of paraffin suspicious? And why do you think it's suspicious, anyway? What do you expect to find in it?'

'Atropine,' I answered.

Julian stared at me as though he thought I had gone mad.

'Oh, of course,' I hastily added, 'I should only expect to find a very little atropine; just a trace.

'I've no idea what you're talking about,' Julian said. 'Or do you think someone's been trying to poison Edgeworth? Is he in the habit of drinking paraffin? Or is it,' he asked, as though suddenly enlightened, 'is it medicinal paraffin?'

'No, I don't think so,' I said, 'and I don't think anyone has been trying to poison Edgeworth. I'm sorry to be so mysterious, but if I'm wrong I don't want to look more of a fool than is absolutely necessary. I suggest that you just get Hopkins to analyse the paraffin and then, if there's nothing in it, we can both forget all about it, which will be a relief to you and perhaps also to me.'

Julian reluctantly agreed to this course and as I took my leave of him he looked at me with eyes so wide open, with doubt and suspicion so clearly visible in his face, that I felt quite ashamed of myself.

'Cheer up,' I said. 'Probably there won't be any atropine in it.'

But there was, and, as I had suggested, no more than a trace. It was Julian who gave me this news; as soon as he had heard it himself he drove at once to the Dower House to ask me what the devil it all meant. Had I, he asked, got any definite evidence against Dawes?

'I don't think Dawes is the murderer,' I said. 'I'm not sure, but I think the bottle of paraffin ought to acquit him.'

'Why?' Julian asked. 'Do you mean that he couldn't have put atropine into the paraffin?'

'He wasn't there at the time,' I replied.

'At what time?' Julian asked.

'It's no good,' I said. 'I haven't got the thing straight in my own mind yet and if I try to explain it to you I'll only get both of us into a muddle. There's at least one vital point that I can't explain at all as yet.'

Julian had to be content with this and I think he was the more willing to stop asking questions because he thought I was merely indulging in wild speculation. I don't know how he explained to himself the presence of atropine in the paraffin, but perhaps he thought it was just an irrelevant accident. After all, in a lawless place like Scrope House, where atropine was left about without proper precautions, anything might happen.

I returned to the problem of the diminution of alcohol in the sherry that Mrs. Dawes had drunk and I spent at least an hour suggesting various unlikely explanations to myself. I even rang up the wine-merchants at Scropeham and asked them if they could think of any reason why some of their bottles of sherry should be more dilute than others. But they were quite useless and, in fact, they seemed to take my inquiry as a personal insult. They protested again and again that they had sold hundreds of bottles of their 'Genuine Fino' and had never received a single complaint. I explained that I was not complaining, but it was no good, so I rang off, leaving them still indignant. And then, quite suddenly, I hit on a possible explanation. To make sure, not that my hypothesis was actually sound, but that there was some reason for pursuing it, I should have to talk to a chemist. Not Hopkins, I decided, for I had been disturbed by Superintendent Julian's tetchiness, and even by the irritability of the wine-merchants, so that I was in no mood for any more black looks. Rimmle would be much better, I thought, and so I went round to his laboratory, where I found him busy with some calculations in a note-book. Three or four children were also in the laboratory so I had to ask him if I could speak to him alone. He seemed annoyed by the interruption but glad of an opportunity to get rid of his pupils. 'How would it be,' he said to the children, 'if you went out into the beautiful sunshine?' The children seemed unwilling to go out into the beautiful sunshine, but after Rimmle had alternately coaxed and scolded them they went.

'Have you come to tell me what you found in my garden?' Rimmle asked.

I had almost forgotten that I had made a search of his garden, but I explained that I had found nothing there. He seemed disappointed.

'Well, what is it?' he asked.

'Have you got any atropine here?' I asked.

'No,' he answered. 'I chucked it away; I thought it too dangerous to keep about the place after what happened. Is anything wrong?'

'No,' I said, 'it's all right. I only wanted to know how you would dissolve the stuff in sherry, or in water, for that matter.'

'You'd just put it in,' Rimmle said.

'Yes, I suppose so,' I said. 'But would it take any time to dissolve?'

'Not long,' Rimmle answered.

'Yes, but would it take an appreciable time?' I asked. 'The powder wouldn't just disappear instantaneously if you put it into a glass of sherry, would it?'

'Most powders take a little time to dissolve,' Rimmle said, 'Some of it is apt to float on the surface of the liquid. You have to stir it in.'

He obligingly took a little powder from a bottle in front of him and after filling a glass with water dropped the powder in. Sure enough, some of it floated on the surface, and Rimmle had to stir it for some little time before it was all dissolved.

'A remarkably simple experiment,' he said.

'Yes, I know,' I said, 'but it's so important that I thought I'd better consult the expert. And are you sure,' I added, 'that powdered atrophine would behave in the same way?'

'Of course it would,' Rimmle answered. 'Any fine powder will behave like that.'

'And your atropine was a fine powder?'

'Yes, it was,' Rimmle answered.

Chapter Seventeen

As Colonel Redder had said—it was really most interesting to find how often he was right—once we had learnt exactly how the poisoning was managed it was not difficult to find an indication that led straight to the murderer. After re-reading some of the statements the police had let me have, it all seemed fairly clear. But I was not ready to publish my conclusions; I remembered too well an occasion when I had published some results in a scientific journal before I had adequately verified them. I had been very properly trounced and contradicted by one of my colleagues and what I suffered then was present in my mind as a warning on this occasion. Besides I did not yet understand the murderer's motive: I believe it is true that motive does not have to be established when a murderer is tried but I could not be satisfied without knowing it. Could it be politics? It was not beyond the bounds of possibility, since Susan was certainly inclined to make mischief with her rumours and suspicions. Could it be something to do with the fires at Scrope House? I could see no reasonable connection with them. At this moment my eye was caught by the three volumes of Dawes's verses lying on the table by my side where I had put them when I last consulted them. I was amused to think how eagerly I had read them when I hoped that they would reveal a murderer's character and how rashly I had allowed myself to be lured into a close study of three whole volumes of execrable verse. 'Never again,' I said to myself, but I had scarcely said it when I found myself once again studying, with rapt attention, the second of these volumes, the volume published just over two years ago in which nearly every poem was concerned with the interruption of love by death.

I had suddenly remembered a coincidence of dates; two tragedies, it seemed, had occurred at the same time and it was possible that they might in reality be one and the same tragedy. It was certainly an interesting idea—I found that there was nothing in this volume of poetry to contradict it—and as I considered it I saw that it might explain a good deal. There was, for example, the floating suspicion that when Dawes was going so often to London, in the days before he married Susan, he had advertised a love affair with unnatural candour, as though there was something which the advertisement was meant to hide. I thought I could see now what he was hiding. And several other little points fell into place; there was, for instance, the fact that the little boy who painted and caught butterflies was able to send his pictures to town by registered post, there was the anonymous letter, accusing Dawes of murder, which Isobel Walker had taken to Scotland Yard.

I looked up from my meditation and caught Caroline's eye. 'The murder,' I said, 'was committed by the most unlikely person.'

'Was it?' she said. 'That's very conventional.'

'It's obviously in the murderer's interest,' I said, 'to appear to be the most unlikely person. And so all you have to do is to look for the most unlikely person.'

'There seems to be something wrong with that argument.' said Caroline.

'Well, as a matter of fact there is,' I answered. 'It doesn't follow that all those who are unlikely to have committed the crime have any particular interest in being thought the most unlikely person to have committed it. There's the Prime Minister, for example. But even if you overlook that point there's yet another fallacy—

'All murderers want to be thought the most unlikely person.

'This man wants to be thought the most unlikely person.

'Therefore this man is the murderer.

'The syllogism has, of course, an undistributed middle.'

'It doesn't seem to be much use, does it?' Caroline said.

But it was, alas, no longer possible to think of the murderer as a mere term in a syllogism. I had been interested and even amused while I had been able to regard my investigation as an abstract problem, but now it might be necessary for me to approach the murderer and consider him as a human being. I have never before felt myself and I hope I shall never again have to feel myself, possessed of the power of life and death over another human being. According to Lord Acton, 'all power corrupts, and absolute power corrupts absolutely,' and this I could well believe. It is surely only the most callous and insensitive who can accustom themselves to the habitual possession of such authority; even home secretaries, even the most conscientious home secretaries—can they be altogether good or amiable people? But by the same argument a murderer has taken the same power into his hands and has almost certainly been corrupted by it. However it was of no use for me to be drawn into a debate with myself about the justification of capital punishment; on such a subject all the arguments are known, all of them are platitudes, and a reasonable person can hardly be expected to make up his mind. Besides, I might very well be on the wrong track and the decision might never have to be made; I ought, at any rate, to ask several more questions before I took any more steps at all.

I remembered Julian's advice, to ask for what one wants to know quite directly and from the obvious person. If I took his advice I ought to go to Dawes and ask him point blank whether the motive I had assigned to the murderer was correct. But I could not imagine that he would answer me, not, at any rate, unless I disclosed so much else that my whole theory would be revealed, and at this stage that would hardly have been fair. I therefore decided to go by a more tortuous path.

I went round to Sinclair's house in the morning—it was a particularly beautiful day and a pleasant hour for a walk—and there I found him finishing a rather late breakfast. I said that I was sorry to bother him but hoped that he would not mind helping me with some few inquiries I was making.

'Do you want to search my garden?' he asked.

'Oh no,' I replied, 'not at all.'

'Why not?' he asked.

'Well, chiefly because I shouldn't expect to find anything there,' I said.

'I've been told that you've been asking rather a lot of questions lately,' Sinclair said. 'I suppose you must have some idea behind them.'

'Well yes, I think I have,' I said.

'Rimmle seemed to be very much amused,' Sinclair continued, 'by an experiment you asked him to do for you. He's made quite a good story out of it.'

I wished I had asked Rimmle to keep his mouth shut.

'Well what is it you want to know?' Sinclair asked.

At this point I found that I had not made any adequate plan for the interview but had trusted too much to a possible inspiration on the spur of the moment. When it came to it I had no inspiration, and so with nothing to say I desperately cast round in my mind for a harmless question. I saw that Sinclair was looking rather sharply at me and so I plunged.

'What did you really think of Susan Dawes?' I asked.

Sinclair seemed very much taken aback by this question, coming as it did after so long and uncomfortable a pause.

'What did I really think of Susan?' he repeated, and then, after an interval, 'I wasn't interested in Susan,' he replied.

'No, I thought perhaps you weren't,' I said.

'Why do you ask?' he said. 'Did some people think I was specially interested in her?'

'Oh, it was just an idea,' I said. 'You know how incessantly people gossip in this place.'

'Yes,' Sinclair said. 'But you thought I wasn't interested in her?'

'No, I didn't think you were,' I said. 'And I didn't think you were particularly interested in Isobel Walker.'

'Certainly I wasn't,' Sinclair said. 'I scarcely know her.'

'But you do know something about her?' I asked.

'Oh shut up,' Sinclair said. 'I've had enough of this.'

I felt no resentment at this speech, but stood there uncomfortably wondering whether I should say any more or whether, as I very much wished to do, I should take my leave. Sinclair eventually took the decision away from me.

'I'm not going to the studio this morning,' he said. 'I'm going for a walk. It's a beautiful day,' he added, 'I might go to the sea. Perhaps you'd like to come along with me. We can talk on the way, if necessary.'

I agreed, though I knew it was four or five miles to the sea and I had not prepared myself for so much exercise. Sinclair packed a towel and bathing-suit into a knapsack; he did not offer to lend me a bathing-suit and I did not ask him for one, partly because I am not very fond of bathing. We started our walk in silence and this grew long and awkward. Eventually Sinclair spoke.

'Don't let us have any more questions now,' he said. 'There'll be plenty of time for them later, if it's really necessary. It's an extraordinarily beautiful day.'

I discussed the weather and the landscape, which led Sinclair to talk about the light of the East coast, and to explain how suitable it was for painting, though not so good here as farther south. 'Still even so,' he said, 'it's one of the consolations for having to make my living by working at Scrope House.'

'Don't you enjoy teaching?' I asked.

'Up to a point,' he said.

With such desultory conversation we made our way to the sea, with many stretches of silent walking. When we reached the coast I found it was a beach of fine sand, with sand-dunes along the shore.

'The tide's up,' Sinclair said. 'I often come to bathe here.'

He changed into his bathing suit, but did not at once go into the water; he sat down on the sand, not very close to me, and again gave himself up to silent meditation. After two or three minutes he spoke.

'I think I'll go in now,' he said. 'By the way, I've left a letter in the top drawer of my bureau in the sitting-room. That'll have to do instead of answering your questions.'

He got up and walked a few paces towards the sea, but then turned round. 'I wish Dawes could be made to see just how bad his poems are,' he said.

'I don't see how that could be done,' I said.

'No, it wouldn't be possible,' Sinclair answered.

He walked into the water and, when he was deep enough, swam out to sea. After a while I walked home.

I could now ask Dawes the question whose answer would complete my theory. I had an extraordinarily uncomfortable interview with him at his house, uncomfortable from the very beginning, when he protested that he was not going to answer any questions and that I was making an intolerable intrusion upon his privacy. I pointed out that he himself was very strongly suspected by the police and that it might be very difficult for him to clear himself unless I could be allowed to prove that he was not responsible for the crime.

'But it's incredible,' he said. 'Why should I be suspected?'

I pointed out that he had, in the eyes of the police, an undeniable motive for murdering his wife. He smiled in an unconvincing and awkward fashion and said that life was far more complicated than the police could be expected to know. This seemed to be true, but it was just because the police might not follow all the intricacies of Dawes's character, and of the whole situation, that he himself was in danger, and so I told him. He then said that he preferred to look after himself and could dispense with my services, but I suggested that he might reasonably wish the murderer of his wife not to be left at large.

'I don't think I want him hanged,' Dawes said. 'I don't think it would do any good.'

'But what about the school?' I asked. 'It's a terrible position for Edgeworth and for everyone else at Scrope House while the crime still remains a mystery.'

Dawes sighed, as though he thought my persistence a nuisance; it was a superior and exasperating sigh. 'Oh very well then,' he said. 'I suppose you'll have to have all your questions answered. What is it that you want to know?'

'I want to know the name of the woman you used to visit in London,' I said, 'about a year or rather less before you married.'

'But what on earth has that got to do with it?' he asked.

'Everything,' I said, 'or so I believe. If you'll tell me who she was, I can see at once whether she had anything to do with it. And there can't be any real reason for keeping it a secret now; I gather the woman's dead, in any case.'

'How did you know that?' Dawes asked.

'Your second volume of poems suggested that she died about the time that you wrote them,' I said.

'Really,' Dawes said, 'I'd no idea you'd been reading my poems or that I gave so much away in them. I suppose I ought to be flattered that you read them with so much attention.'

'You ought indeed,' I said, 'but I couldn't, of course, discover from the poems the name of the woman they were written about. I think I know now, but I want you to confirm it.'

'If you know already, I'm certainly not going to tell you,' Dawes said. 'But I'm quite sure you don't know,' he added.

I could not move him from this position even by pointing out that in my opinion this old love affair was the direct cause of the murder of Susan Dawes; he merely said that he was sure I was wrong. And so I had to play my last card, which I had hoped not to use.

'Ever since the death of his wife,' I said, 'Sinclair has been a very unhappy man; he has, I think, suffered agonies of jealousy, and now I think it very likely that he has killed himself.'

Dawes was genuinely startled and asked me several questions about the manner of Sinclair's death; I told him as little as possible.

'But it's incredible,' he said. 'It's so uncivilized.'

'Do you think so?'

'But of course.'

'Then it was Mrs. Sinclair whom you met in London—or elsewhere?'

'Yes it was; but we didn't actually go to London, of course.'

'Well, I'm glad you told me.'

'I can't believe you're right,' Dawes said. 'I can't understand how Sinclair can have made himself so miserable because his wife was unfaithful to him. After all, think of the sort of people she might have had an affair with. If Sinclair suspected that she was unfaithful I should have thought it would have been a relief to him to know that it was with someone who was, well, reasonable. He did know that it was with me, I suppose?'

'Yes, he knew,' I said.

'But think of the people who might have been her lover. It might have been someone who was old, or physically repulsive, or entirely uneducated. After all, that's surely the only reasonable cause for jealousy, if a woman prefers some horrible creature to oneself and one can't even begin to understand why she's attracted to him. I wish I had had a quiet talk with Sinclair.'

'You would have offered him what you've just said as a consolation?' I asked. 'You would have told him how grateful he ought to be that his wife chose you, rather than somebody unattractive, for her lover?'

'Well, I shouldn't have put it quite like that,' Dawes said. 'But I wish we could have had a reasonable talk together. I'm sure I could have made him see things in a different light. Yes, I blame myself for that; I wish I had brought things out into the open. But, of course, I never knew how much he knew; that's why I kept quiet. Oh, well, it's no good regretting the past, though one can't help it sometimes.' He sighed heavily. 'But what,' he continued, 'has this got to do with the death of my wife?'

'I'm afraid I shall have to explain that later,' I said.

Chapter Eighteen

I rang up Julian and told him that Sinclair had swum far out to sea and had not returned. I explained that I had lost sight of him when he was too far out for me to go in after him; in any case, I added, I was a very poor swimmer. I did not tell Julian about the letter which Sinclair had left in the bureau in his sitting-room since I thought this might make trouble for me; if Julian heard that I knew about this letter he might think that I knew of Sinclair's intention before he committed suicide. But I did go so far as to say that, if it were definitely discovered that Sinclair was dead, I presumed Julian would be making a search of his house; there was a possiblity, as I thought it safe to suggest, that he had killed himself and if so he might, like many suicides, have left a letter behind him. No doubt Julian would suspect that I had allowed Sinclair to kill himself, but this could do no harm if he had no definite proof, and I therefore decided to say as little as possible until the inquest was safely over. When Julian came round to see me he did ask whether I knew there would be a letter for the police in Sinclair's house, but I blandly denied all foreknowledge of it. Sinclair's body was found next day—it had been cast up on the shore by the incoming tide—and the inquest was soon held and safely over; I had no trouble in answering what questions the coroner asked me.

I now thought it would be safe to satisfy Julian's curiosity; he kept ringing me up or calling on me on one pretext or another, and so did Colonel Redder. I arranged that Julian and Redder should be asked to the Dower House and that Mrs. Eakins and Edgeworth should be present at the interview; I wanted a barrier against the indignation of the police, if it should so happen that they felt indignant. I also asked Caroline to be present and so, when they were all gathered together in the morning-room and Mrs. Eakins had been allowed time to exercise her talents as a hostess on this rather unsuitable occasion, I began my explanation.

'I must confess,' I said, 'that until quite lately I made very little progress. I was asked to come to Scrope House to find out who was responsible for the fires that had broken out from time to time in the school and I went on with this inquiry because it was useful in itself and because I hoped that it might somehow be connected with the mystery of Mrs. Dawes's death. There was some reason for thinking this; Mrs. Dawes was much concerned about these fires and put forward an elaborate theory attributing them, directly or indirectly, to Nazi agents working among the refugees at Scrope House. Shortly before her death she wrote to tell me that she had some important information to give me, but she died before I could learn what it was. I am inclined to think that her information would have proved unimportant; Mrs. Dawes seems to have suffered, like so many politicians of the extreme left, from delusions of persecution, and she had a taste for intrigue. But I have been told that a number of communists who recently left their party have been accused of being Nazi agents by their comrades who remained within the party; I think it very likely that someone had just succeeded in convincing Mrs. Dawes that one of these unfortunate ex-communists really was a Nazi agent.

'But of course, it is possible that her information was more directly concerned with the fires and when I found what I thought was an adequate explanation of the fires I had to consider the extremely distasteful possibility that the pyromaniac, if you can call him that, had taken steps to silence Mrs. Dawes. He had no alibi at the time of the murder. And then Dawes himself was an obvious suspect; he was present at Hickman's party, it is always assumed that a husband has a motive for wishing to be rid of his wife, and he was obviously not a very monogamous character.'

'Poor Dawes,' said Edgeworth. 'I never took anything he said very seriously. I thought he was merely a romantic.'

'I think you were right,' I said, 'but even romantics sometimes act as well as day-dream. However, there was also some reason for suspecting Dupuy, and in general it was a difficult case. I was in a confused state of mind and could not see my way ahead when Colonel Redder very kindly asked me to lunch and gave me the first hint of a useful approach to the problem.'

'Oh, did I?' said Colonel Redder.

'Yes', I said, and rather maliciously reminded him that he had given me a sherry and soda by mistake. The Colonel seemed hurt in his feelings but contented himself with staring at me.

'But you also suggested,' I hastened to add, 'that if only we could discover what the murderer had actually done at the bottle-party we should probably learn who he was. And so I had these two valuable hints.'

'I don't understand about the sherry and soda,' Julian said.

'Well,' I said, 'the difficulty we have been up against all the time is that we didn't know what had happened to the rest of the poisoned sherry. Some had gone into Mrs. Dawes's glass, some into Dupuy's, but of the rest only a little remained in the bottle I found in Hickman's garden. But then I saw that Dupuy need not necessarily have had a glass of sherry of his own; he himself said that, as far as he could remember, he had only drunk whisky at the party, and I think his memory was more or less accurate. What he did, I suggest, was to mistake Mrs. Dawes's glass of sherry for his own glass of whisky when the two exactly similar glasses were side by side. The sherry and whisky were much the same colour and so he drank enough from

Mrs. Dawes's glass to make himself ill, but he would naturally drink no more after one or two mouthfuls. It is quite natural he should forget this trivial accident, especially as he had probably made his mistake when he had already had too much to drink.

'Now this made it much more likely that the poisoned sherry had only been intended for Mrs. Dawes and suggested that the murderer had been very careful that no one else should drink it. What would be the safest way to ensure that no one else should touch the poisoned sherry? Obviously to put the poison straight into her glass, rather than to pour out a glass from a bottle of poisoned sherry. And it was certainly more probable that this had happened if Dupuy had not had another poisoned drink of his own. But this meant that Mrs. Dawes's drink had not come from the bottle in the garden, and what then was the bottle doing there? I decided I would wait for the answer to this question until I could find some method of demonstrating whether Mrs. Dawes's sherry actually had or had not come from the bottle in the garden. I thought it over and then conceived the idea that there might be some analysable difference between two samples of sherry of the same brand but from different bottles. I went off to see Hopkins the analyst, who was not at all hopeful—quite rightly, as it turned out—but eventually consented to test the two samples, from the bottle in the garden and from Mrs. Dawes's glass, for alcohol content. This was the simplest test that could be expected to show any variation in the quality of the two samples of sherry. We had already, as Superintendent Julian will remember, found a slight difference in the proportion of atropine in the two fluids, but the Superintendent found two ingenious explanations of this, although, if you come to think of it, a much simpler explanation is that the sherry in the glass had not come from the bottle. Well, Hopkins found an unexpectedly large variation of alcohol content in the two samples; there was a higher percentage of alcohol in the sherry from the bottle. I discovered that this was an unlikely variation when I got him to analyse two other samples of 'Genuine Fino' sherry; in these there was hardly any variation of alcohol content.

'Eventually I saw that there were two ways of looking at this difference of alcohol content; less alcohol implied more of something else and, most probably, this meant more water in the glass of sherry. There would, in fact, have been two or three teaspoonfuls of additional water in Mrs. Dawes's glass when it was full. Somebody must have put this water in, but why? I wondered whether Mrs. Dawes had been out in the garden when it was raining and had had her glass with her, but there was no rain that night; I even wondered whether someone could have spat into her glass.'

'Oh come,' Edgeworth protested, 'our parties weren't as bad as all that.'

'No, of course not,' I said. 'Well, while I was racking my brains to find some explanation for this addition of water, I had another idea. You will remember we found that three empty bottles were rather unaccountably missing from the pile of empty bottles in Dupuy's garden. There might be a hundred reasons why they had gone, but now I had the idea that the murderer, wanting an empty bottle into which to put half a glass of poisoned sherry, might have taken one from Dupuy's rubbish heap. It would make it much less likely that the bottle would ever be traced to him if he obtained it in this way. But why, I asked myself, should he have taken three bottles? Perhaps, I thought, he might have used the two others for the same purpose before but, as against this, there were not as far as I knew two more murders to be accounted for. But what if he had made all his preparations on two previous occasions and then, either because the circumstances were unpropitious or because his nerve failed him, decided not to put poison into Mrs. Dawes's glass? In favour of this, there was the fact that the poison had disappeared, either from Rimmle's or from Rosenberg's laboratory, a considerable time ago.

'I knew that bottle parties were an institution at Scrope House and I could imagine the murderer, at one or even two of these previous parties, putting his bottle in the garden a day or so before the party began and then for some reason failing to put poison into his victim's glass. What would he do then? He might have visited the garden on the day after the party, or he might just possibly have thought it safer and less likely to attract suspicion if he left the bottle where it was. All this was pure speculation, but I thought it worth making a search and so I went to Rimmle's garden, since it was he, as I learnt from Mrs. Butcher's statement to Superintendent Julian, who had given the party immediately before Hickman's. There was nothing in his garden, so I went to Mr. Edgeworth's and there I found a bottle, with the remains of a 'Genuine Fino' label on it, but unfortunately containing paraffin. Yet was it not just possible that a bottle containing some dregs of sherry had been picked up by the gardener, who might well have used it to keep paraffin in?'

'My gardener always uses paraffin to start his bonfires,' Edgeworth said. 'He takes it from the drum we keep in the house; it's an extravagant habit and the maids complain.'

'Quite so,' I said. 'Well, no doubt the gardener would pour away most of the dregs of sherry, but some might have remained and they might have been enough to leave a trace of atropine in the paraffin. As it happens it was so; Hopkins found a distinct trace. Thus it is possible that the murderer went to collect the bottle from Edgeworth's garden, but found it gone. It must have been rather an awkward moment for him but as nothing further happened no doubt he was reassured.

'But Mrs. Butcher, Dawes's servant, had told us that when Mr. Edgeworth gave a party, at the beginning of the Easter holidays, Dawes was away in town and he would not have made any preparations for poisoning his wife on that occasion. Unless we suppose that he had an accomplice, or that he had somehow faked an alibi in town, or that someone else had intended to murder Mrs. Dawes by precisely the same method which her husband had afterwards used, he must be innocent. And as yet I had no idea who the real murderer could be.

'I returned to the problem of the additional water in Mrs. Dawes's glass, and then at last I saw a reasonable explanation. If the murderer put powdered atropine into his victim's glass it would take some time for the fine powder to dissolve and some of it might remain floating on the surface for quite a while; there was an obvious risk that it would be noticed either by Mrs. Dawes herself or by someone else. It was obviously much safer to bring the powder, already dissolved in water, in a test-tube or a small bottle, and so to be able to pour it quickly into the glass without risk of attracting attention. But such a procedure would have been unnecessary when mixing atropine with the sherry that was to go into the bottle; this could be done at leisure and in the privacy of the murderer's own house. And so there was inevitably a larger proportion of water in Mrs. Dawes's sherry than in the sherry in the bottle in the garden. It was the murderer's one serious mistake.

'But then why on earth,' Julian asked, 'did the murderer contrive such an elaborate plan, in which there was an obvious risk of making some such mistake? What on earth was the point of the bottle in the garden?'

'Well, you must admit that it puzzled us all,' I said, 'and that was certainly an advantage.'

'It might not have puzzled us so much,' Julian said, 'if Dupuy had not taken some poisoned sherry by mistake.'

'Yes,' I agreed, 'though even then it would have been puzzling enough. But that was not, of course, the real reason; the real reason was a much better one, and it was when I first saw it that I knew who the murderer was. If you remember what Hickman told us when we visited his house on the morning after the party, or if you look at the statement the police got from him, you'll see the explanation.

Hickman told us that Sinclair opened a full bottle of 'Genuine Fino' sherry and that he said he was getting Mrs. Dawes a drink. He took trouble to draw Hickman's attention to this; he opened a new bottle when there were several already opened bottles before him on the table. According to Hickman, several other people had drinks from this same bottle and suffered no ill effects; thus it was clear that whichever of her drinks had poisoned Mrs. Dawes it was not the drink which Sinclair poured out on this occasion. At least, this was clear so long as we assumed that her sherry had come from the bottle of poisoned sherry in the garden and it was to implant this assumption firmly in our minds that he had placed the bottle in the garden where it would appear to have been hidden but in fact would easily be found.

'Actually, of course, this was the drink into which Sinclair poured the atropine from the test-tube or little bottle which he already had in his pocket. He would have arranged it so that the atropine in Mrs. Dawes's drink was mixed in nearly the same proportion as in the sherry in the bottle; he probably filled her glass with sherry up to a particular mark, the little circle which you often get near the top of the tumbler, so that his measurements might be more exact. Then if he had already put half such a glass of poisoned sherry in the bottle—he would have known that Hickman, like most of the other people at Scrope House, used this kind of glass at his parties—it would not have been difficult to get a nearly similar proportion of atropine in both bottle and glass. But, of course, it was very likely that there would be a slight difference of proportion and, in fact, the analyst found such a difference; it could be explained in other ways and thus was not particularly suspicious. Sinclair would have found an opportunity to pour in the poison as he carried Mrs. Dawes's glass out to the verandah where she was sitting and, after that, he would take particular pains not to have to pour out any other drink for Mrs. Dawes. He would have kept well away from the bar and, as

I happen to remember, he went home early. Thus he would certainly have been able to bring forward evidence that the only glass he had handed to Mrs. Dawes was obviously and demonstrably harmless. That is what I meant'—here I turned to Caroline—'when I said that the murder was committed by the most unlikely person. He also took the precaution of bringing to the party an old and expensive bottle of whisky which would naturally attract attention and establish yet a further absence of connection between himself and any bottle of poisoned sherry.

'Therefore Sinclair was probably the murderer. But why should he have wanted to kill Mrs. Dawes? There was certainly no obvious motive and all I could do was to look about for any kind of connection between Sinclair and Mr. or Mrs. Dawes. At one time I thought that Mrs. Dawes might be his mistress, but that was when I was wondering whether Dawes had killed his wife because she was unfaithful, and there was never any confirmation of this idea. I think the first thing that put me on the track of Sinclair's motive was a volume of Dawes's poems, published a little more than two years ago. I noticed in this particular volume an unusually large number of poems on the subject of early death. Here was poem after poem lamenting the fact that love should be thus interrupted; the imagery was conventional but none the less, at any rate to a detective, expressive enough. The theme was one on which Dawes had often employed his pen, but here far more often and far more urgently than in his other volumes. I naturally concluded that some two and a half years ago someone with whom Dawes was in love had died. This was before his marriage and I remembered that at this time there had been a great deal of talk, the echoes of which still reverberated, about some love affair which often took Dawes to London. Obviously, I thought, this much advertised love affair must have concluded in the tragedy which formed the theme of so many of the poems in his second volume. But I also remembered that Sinclair had lost his wife about this time; it suddenly occurred to me that the two tragedies might be one and the same and that Sinclair's wife had been Dawes's mistress. This was no more than a guess but I thought I would accept it for the moment and see what came of it. One thing it would immediately explain—the general impression that Dawes was advertising his visits to town in order to conceal something else. He was concealing the fact that his mistress did not live in London but at Scrope House and also the fact that he himself did not go to London, but to somewhere nearer on these occasions. This was the purpose of his markedly exhibitionist conversation, though the fact that he is an exhibitionist may have prompted him to use this curious expedient.

'Sinclair probably discovered his wife's infidelity after her death; otherwise there might have been an open scandal. Perhaps he found some letters from Dawes to his wife when he was going through her papers and, now I come to think of it, these letters might still be in the house. I don't think Sinclair would have destroyed them unless he did so shortly before he killed himself; he would have kept them to support his resolution and also as material upon which to feed his jealousy.'

'Oh yes,' Julian said. 'We found them all right. They were, well... rather...'

As he was hesitating for a suitable word Colonel Redder coughed in a disapproving fashion.

'Oh, I didn't mean anything like that,' Julian said. 'Full of poetry, and all that, if you see what I mean. I didn't know who the letters were addressed to, though; there were no envelopes with them. I wondered for a moment whether Sinclair could have been blackmailing Dawes.'

'I don't think he'd have done that,' I said. 'That was not the kind of revenge he would have taken. But you must imagine him an intensely jealous man, devoted to his wife and lost without her. He has already listened to all the talk at Scrope House about Dawes's mistress in London and then he suddenly discovers that the subject of all this romantic exhibitionism on the part of Dawes, of all this malicious gossip on the part of everyone else, was his own wife. She was dead, and there was nothing he could do about it; he could not step in and separate her from Dawes and start again. But Dawes was still writing and publishing his over-emotional, melodramatic poems, and Sinclair knew that they referred to his wife and to her death. And then, when Dawes had adequately paraded his meretricious grief—I am describing it as it must have seemed to Sinclair—he married Susan and proceeded to live happily ever after, still prating of the pleasures of love as the sole consolation for the miseries of human existence and still putting himself forward as a great lover. In spite of his shameless exposure of his sorrow Dawes was obviously unaffected by the loss which had destroyed Sinclair and it may even have seemed to Sinclair that Dawes was in some measure responsible for the death of Mrs. Sinclair. If she had taken more care of herself, so he might have argued, if she had not spent her time rushing about with Dawes, she might not have lowered her resistance and might not have caught the disease from which she died. That is possible, but at any rate Sinclair had every reason to think that Dawes, comfortably married six months after Mrs. Sinclair's death, was insolently, blatantly, callously, enjoying the happiness of which he had deprived Sinclair himself.

'For long he thought over the means of revenge. His natural instinct might be to kill Dawes, but unhappy as he himself was, probably considering the possibility of suicide—observe how little he clung to life at the end—he would have thought this no revenge at all. No, it would be better to reduce Dawes to the same state as his own. And how was that to be done? Obviously by depriving Dawes of his wife as he himself had been deprived of his own wife. To make the revenge perfectly symmetrical he would first have had to seduce Mrs. Dawes and then to have killed her, and it is just possible that Sinclair made some half-hearted attempts at this—Mrs.

Dawes once told me that Sinclair used to pay her unexpected and rather inexplicable visits—but you cannot make love convincingly from motives of pure hate.

'He took the atropine from Rimmle's or Rosenberg's laboratory when the opportunity arose and what had previously been a fantasy, a morbid preoccupation of his unhappy mind, was brought so many stages nearer to reality. He considered many schemes for poisoning Mrs. Dawes, always, I should suspect, enjoying the fantasy rather than proceeding in a deliberate and practical spirit. He came near enough to putting his fantasy into practice at the party which Mr. Edgeworth gave at the beginning of the Easter holidays; he went so far as to put the necessary bottle, with a little poisoned sherry in it, into the garden on the day before the party. And then perhaps his nerve failed him, or perhaps the fact that Dawes was absent at the time seemed to mar the quality of his revenge; at any rate he did not poison Mrs. Dawes on this occasion and when he returned to collect his bottle from the garden he found that someone had taken it. The same thing may have happened at Rimmle's party and he may once again have lost his nerve at the last moment; perhaps this time he managed to collect his bottle after the party and get rid of it, but that we cannot expect to know. At Hickman's party he translated his long-continued fantasy into fact.

'When the murder had been committed a dreadful suspicion occurred to him; if Dawes had taken so lightly the death of his mistress, might he not be equally callous about the death of his wife? Might he not already have been unfaithful to her and already have another woman to whom he could fly for consolation? He heard that Dawes was going up to London and Dawes's trips to London were associated in Sinclair's mind with secret and shameful love-affairs. He followed Dawes up to London—when I met him in the train he told me that he had to take some children's pictures up to town and these, as I afterwards learnt, he could as easily have sent by post. He followed Dawes to the British Museum and no doubt waited outside while I was within, observing Dawes's meeting with Isobel Walker in the print-room.'

'You never told me anything about that,' Julian said.

'I was just going to tell you,' I hastily answered, 'when you found out about Isobel Walker from another source. But Sinclair, as I was saying, must have waited outside the Museum and he must have seen Dawes come out with Miss Walker. I expect he knew her, and made inquiries, or perhaps he followed them and saw enough to inflame his already aroused suspicions. At any rate, as he saw it, Dawes was going to be happy again and it was obvious that he could not incessantly murder each woman to whom Dawes might apply, one after the other, to the end of Dawes's life.

'He devised the expedient of sending an anonymous letter to Isobel Walker, warning her that if Dawes had murdered his wife, she herself might be murdered when he was tired of her. This had much the effect that Sinclair intended; it frightened Miss Walker away from Dawes, at any rate for the time being, though what she will do now I cannot hope to predict. But the flavour had gone out of Sinclair's revenge; he saw that Dawes's character kept him immune from the extremes of grief. I expect that at this time he began to consider even more seriously than before the possibility of suicide; there was nothing much left for him to live for now that the fantasies of revenge which had kept him alive were dissolved by the complicated and dreary reality.

'He was continually afraid that his plot might be discovered, for to be tried and hanged would be dreadful even for a man contemplating suicide. He heard a good deal of talk about my investigation and he feared that I might have discovered some essential clue. He probably did not like what he had heard of my conversation with Rimmle about the time that it would take for powdered atropine to dissolve in water. He had a letter ready for the police and was making up his mind to kill himself; I arrived and asked him some vague but, to a guilty conscience, too pertinent questions, and this decided him. His letter ensured that no one else would be suspected of his crime.'

'I'm not so sure,' Colonel Redder said. 'We might easily have thought that Sinclair had gone off his head. Suicide while of unsound mind... and a confession of murder made in that state of mind was not much good to us.'

'What did the letter actually say?' I asked.

Julian took a copy of the letter from his pocket-book and referred to it.

'He just says that he killed Mrs. Dawes, but gives no details,' Julian said. 'And then he adds "I suppose I ought to have killed Dawes himself, and if you like to think it was all a mistake you will not be so very far wrong." It's all very vague.'

'Perhaps I ought to have told you,' I said, 'that in my last conversation with Sinclair he said, when I rather foolishly asked him what he really thought about Susan Dawes, that he was not interested in her. There seemed at the time to be a strong undercurrent of meaning in his words. And just before he drowned himself he complained of Dawes's poems.'

'You must have guessed that he was going to make away with himself,' Julian said.

'I might have guessed,' I answered, 'but I couldn't know.'

'I really don't know what to say,' Colonel Redder said. 'It's not satisfactory, not from our point of view. If you'd told us more at the time, I expect this wouldn't have happened.'

'Oh, but Sinclair would certainly have killed himself,' I protested, 'the moment you began to ask him any searching questions, and you could hardly have arrested him at once on what I could tell you.'

'We could have found out more,' Julian said.

'But you didn't,' I answered.

'Oh well,' Colonel Redder said. 'It's no good crying over spilt milk. The law's a lot of rot, anyway. Waste of time and money having a trial when you already know a man's committed a murder.'

I did not make any attempt to combat these atrocious but at the moment extremely convenient sentiments.

I stayed on at the Dower House for another two days before I returned to London. Julian busied himself in tidying up some loose ends; he discovered, for example, that the anonymous letter to Isobel Walker, though written in capital letters, was almost certainly in Sinclair's handwriting—this is apparently the sort of thing that handwriting experts can manage, though I should never have thought it. Edgeworth was very busy devising some method of soothing the troubled nerves of boys who might be passing through the gangster stage of adolescence; he thought that there might be quite a number in the school, though none so troublesome as Crossley. It appeared that Crossley had been induced to confess to his part in the fires by, of all people, Miss Symonds, the matron; he had had a bad cold and spent a few days in the sanatorium where Miss Symonds, suspecting that he was worrying about something, had so worked upon him with her vague but persistent uplift that he eventually owned up. According to her, Crossley was very, very sorry for what he had done, and Edgeworth was angry with Miss Symonds because he feared she had increased the boy's sense of guilt. Crossley and Miss Symonds must have indulged in a most curious orgy of remorse and expiation. Edgeworth was beginning to wonder whether he could not have a separate part of the school, a kind of little Chicago, which Crossley and his like might be allowed to organize by themselves. But it was, as he admitted, a very difficult problem.

Mrs. Eakins thanked me most ceremonially for what I had done and as a reward—over and above the cheque which I was given for what Edgeworth called my services as a consultant psychologist to the school—she presented me with a copy of one of George Moore's novels, in a limited edition, and with an inscription from the author to herself. Perhaps she thought that it might make a pleasant occupation for me in my spare time to detect under what name and in what disguise she herself appeared in the novel.

Caroline did not return to London with me but took lodgings in the neighbourhood and stayed on at Scrope House. Three weeks later I learned that she was going to marry John Dupuy. This was distressing, of course, and I am not going to pretend that the grapes were not reasonably palatable, but I have always maintained that detectives should not have love affairs. On the other hand, if I had not been attracted by Caroline I should never have become a detective; it is very difficult to apply any general rule to so controversial a question.